Asmodel

Keri Kruspe

I0630209

Table of Contents

Preview

Can an optimistic librarian and a cynical alien hybrid be the galaxy's only hope?

Asmodel, a powerful psychic born in the distant past, finds himself thrust into the complexities of the modern world. After thwarting an invasion that threatened Earth, he is given a new quest: Find Izzy, a compassionate and brave librarian from Earth who has been kidnapped from the galactic exchange program. Fearing she is the target of a sinister plot by the mysterious crystal beings known as the Krystalii, Asmodel embarks on a perilous journey across the galaxy.

Isabella "Izzy" Torres always dreamed of becoming an astronaut, exploring the stars, and finding love like the heroes in her favorite romance novels. When she's offered the chance to go into space and meet an alien soulmate, she jumps at it, leaving everything behind. But her dreams take a dark turn when she is abducted and crash-lands on the alien jungle planet, CeluriaVO. Here, she finds herself amidst a civil war decimating intelligent panther-like humanoids, the Scikvak, who are on the brink of genocide. The leading faction of Scikvak are in league with the inter-dimensional Krystalii, who demand Izzy be handed over for their own nefarious purposes.

As Asmodel races against time to save Izzy, he is forced to confront his own trust issues, which clash with Izzy's unyielding optimism and kindness. Their journey is fraught with danger and unexpected revelations, testing their resolve and drawing them closer together in ways neither expected.

Which leaves two profoundly different souls a choice. Can they conquer their inner demons and dare to trust not only each other, but themselves as well?

"Asmodel" is the second installment of the Alien Legacy Brotherhood series. If you like a gripping tale of survival combined with a sensual love story that teems with raw emotions, you'll love this sci-fi romance.

Copyright

StarChance Productions

so, the facts and events in the story may not be accurate except in the universe where the book takes place.

Just so you know... I've used several editing programs, which include Prowritingaid and ChatGPT. These tools were used to support brainstorming, refine ideas, and enhance the writing process.

Cover art by Jacqueline Sweet
Edited by ELF

Chapter One

The Akurn science/mining operation in South Africa, circa 5000 BCE

An earth-shattering boom erupted, causing the very ground beneath Asmodel's feet to convulse violently. He pinwheeled his arms, then put his back against the wall to hang on. Even with his knees bent, the turbulence made it hard to stand upright. Debris from the adobe room rained down from the ceiling onto him as the stench of seared metal mixed with smoky ozone that burned his nose. Wide-eyed, he glanced at his three brothers, who were also scrambling to stay upright in the violent earthquake.

Arakiba was flung face-first onto the dirt floor, his blond hair flying loose from its tight queue.

Azazel floated above the ground from the cross-legged position he'd been in on the floor.

As for Abalim, their dark-skinned brother stood tall with his arms crossed, glaring out the tiny prison window as he rode out the next wave of blasts with his knees bent and a frown creasing his full lips.

"What the *fruk* is that?" Arakiba pushed up from the floor.

An earsplitting whine pierced the air, followed by a blast of heat as the ground viciously rumbled.

1

Asmodel raised an arm to protect his eyes from the dust and chunks of the roof that continued to fall around them.

Cracks in the dusty ground ripped apart, creating a vast chasm in the middle of the room.

"Goddessdamn it! That *zihui* Prince Murduk must be attacking!" Abalim's voice rose against the noise. "We've got to get to the *Zikia* right now!"

"But that ship isn't ready..." Asmodel didn't finish his sentence. Caught and yanked into a teleportation stream, he hurtled until he landed outside the lab compound where he and his brothers had lived as prisoners.

The ground outside wasn't any better than the inside. A massive earthquake ramped up between laser blasts from the Akurn ship swooping through the air and aiming its massive weapons at the surrounding buildings, disintegrating them into a cloud of silt and fine dust.

Under Asmodel's feet, the ground tore apart, and he leaped to the other side. Out of the corner of his eye, he noticed his older brother, Adapa, running to the ship's hangar with a tight grip on his lover, Inanna's, hand. The man sprinted so fast, the poor woman had to run double-time.

"There!" Asmodel raised a finger at their retreating brother on the far side of the compound as he and Inanna entered the open hangar door where the spaceship *Zikia* waited for them.

"We'll never make it in time!" Arakiba shouted.

"We've got to try." Abalim turned to run, but Azazel grabbed his brother's forearm before he moved.

"Wait." Azazel spoke in his normal soft tone, regardless of the mayhem surrounding them. "Adapa must've already started the ship by now."

A massive, thunderous noise rumbled and shook the ground harder.

Asmodel and his three brothers fell to the ground as a savage earthquake shook them. A mind-numbing roar became louder and more chaotic, like a continuous thundercloud touching Earth.

"By Tiamat's titties, what was that?" Arakiba wobbled as he swayed when the ground beneath his feet rumbled.

"We're out of time," Azazel's voice quivered. His normally calm demeanor was long gone. "Quick, everyone in a circle now."

No one said a word as they formed a small circle. In unison, they tilted their heads back and closed their eyes, with their hands at their sides, palms facing forward.

Asmodel sensed the psychic heat gathering in the middle of the circle as their psionic energy merged in power. Even without Adapa's commanding presence, their combined forces should be enough.

"Envision the interior cargo bay of the *Zikia* and I'll teleport us there. Hurry, my brothers, our future depends on it." Azazel's soft tone rose in inflection as the background noise boomed closer.

Asmodel took a sharp breath as the teleportation started by Azazel tore him apart. His consciousness remained intact while the rest of him splintered into an infinite number of molecules before getting slammed into his cohesive form once again. He opened his eyes, his head still tilted back so all he saw was the metal roof of the *Zikia's* cargo hold. He released the breath he held.

"Thank the goddess we made it." Arakiba whooshed out a breath, planting his palms on his upper thighs.

"See, Adapa? I told you to stop nagging. We were just outside." Abalim crossed his arms and widened his stance as he glared at their elder brother.

Adapa sat on the floor in the middle of their circle next to Princess Inanna.

"Abalim?"

Adapa's wide-eyed expression made Asmodel frown. It was then he noticed what his brother was wearing. It was the strangest thing he'd ever seen. Instead of the normal light linen pants and shirt the Akurns made them wear, he had on some type of heavy black material with pockets down the legs. His simple dark-blue shirt was short-sleeved but made of something Asmodel'd never seen before. Like it contained unnatural materials.

"Why in the hell are you lying on the floor?" Abalim asked him. He reached down and pulled Adapa up to stand. Beside him, Princess Inanna moaned. "Highness! Are you all right?" He squatted next to her and took her hand and elbow to help her sit up.

"Abalim?" Adapa squinted as he repeated the question. He looked at Abalim as if he hadn't seen him before.

"By Gilgamesh's balls, what's wrong with you?" Arakiba fisted his hands on his hips as he glared at Adapa.

"Arakiba?"

It was then Asmodel noticed they weren't alone. A strange group of people were in a circle behind them.

"Adapa, who are all these people?" Now he became the focus of Adapa's unusual behavior. If he didn't know any better, he'd swear his brother was drunk. Being surrounded by a group of strange people made him nervous. He doubted any of them were Akurn scientists. None had their pale coloring except Princess Inanna. "Are they part of Rummeh's group?"

Rummeh was the Akurn captain of the ship Inanna took when she came to Earth to escape her sadistic father and brother.

"Asmodel?"

Asmodel's eyebrows rose when he watched tears gather in Adapa's eyes. *Oh, for the love of a motherless goat.* What was going on?

"Brothers." Azazel's soft voice made Asmodel frown. He stilled as the world tilted. His brother never used that tone unless something bad was about to happen. It felt like everything was about to change in a way he'd never could have imagined.

Azazel stood with his hands clasped behind his back. "I'm afraid it is us who are confused, not Adapa. I believe we are not where we think we are."

Asmodel sucked in a breath as fat tears rolled down Adapa's flushed cheeks. He'd never seen his stoic older brother cry before. "Azazel?"

Azazel slowly approached Adapa and covered his heart with his hand. "My brother, how you have suffered." He clasped Adapa's hands in his. "Now that we are together, you no longer have to endure the deterioration I sense within you. You will enjoy full rejuvenation." He let their brothers' hands go and scratched his chin, giving Adapa a sheepish grin. "I must have overshot teleporting us to the ship."

Asmodel's vision narrowed and he became light-headed. Overshot? What did that mean?

Adapa grabbed Azazel in a tight hug. They stood that way for a few moments until they stepped apart. Azazel, their empathic brother, wiped Adapa's tears away with his thumbs and murmured comforting words in a low voice.

Asmodel glanced at the strangers in the room surrounding them. While he sensed nothing but awe and confusion between them, he stood ready to protect himself and his brothers if necessary.

New York Public Library, Early Evening, Present Day

In the labyrinth of towering shelves, the musty aroma of ancient tomes mingled with the hushed reverie of a room filled with knowledge seekers.

Here, Izzy went about her day with quiet contentment. Each book she placed with care on the cart whispered of adventures in other worlds and exciting lifetimes. At her fingertips was the wide universe of words and unbelievable wonders. As she navigated through the cozy aisles of the library, she glimpsed the tattered spine bearing the title of "Cosmology's Century" upside down. She chuckled at the absurdity of such a serious book put in that comical position. After pulling it out to straighten it, she turned to the cover page and rubbed her hands over its canvas feel, worn by the touch of many curious hands.

As her eyes unfocused, the weight of the novel stirred a dormant yearning inside her, one she thought she'd long forgotten. But the dream of a life spent unraveling the mysteries of the cosmos as a revered scientist was now far beyond her grasp. As she stood immersed in her memories, everything around her faded away as her gaze lingered on the faded gold lettering. Her mouth curved into a soft, wistful smile.

"Ack, look at that. She's off in the clouds again."

Izzy jerked at the nasal tone of her middle-aged co-worker, Evelyn. The woman's lilting Irish accent was still thick, even after living in New York for the last thirty years.

"Well, what do you expect? After tonight, she's quitting and running away."

This from her other co-worker.

Young African-American Marcus stood there with his casual chinos paired with a button-down shirt covered with a dark blazer, his lips furrowed into an indulgent smirk. Today he matched his expensive smart-watch band with a stunning set of multi-colored socks. The modest diamond stud in his left earlobe twinkled.

Izzy flashed them a wide smile. "Oh, you guys. I'm really going to miss you." She glanced around the comforting atmosphere of the library that had been her home for the last fifteen years. Leaving was hard, but her decision to do so excited her beyond belief.

"I can't believe you've landed a scholarship in India to study cosmology, of all things." Evelyn sniffed. "I'd wager you won't feel like you belong there." She shuddered.

"What?" Marcus glared at the other woman. He scratched the side of the well-groomed cropped beard he'd started a couple of months ago, claiming it gave him an air of maturity. "You have a problem with people from India?"

Evelyn snorted. "Ach, don' be such an eejit! I weren't talking about their race. I meant it'd be easy to get lost in a country with over a billion people." She bumped her shoulder against him. "You know I'm green with envy of anyone who doesn't have to go about looking like a translucent blob like meself."

Izzy bit her bottom lip to stop from blurting the truth. She wasn't going anywhere near India, or anywhere on Earth, for that matter. Her face flushed as she squirmed. It didn't sit well with her to lie to anyone, especially her two friends.

"Izzy?"

Thank God the croaky voice of ancient Herbert from Queens interrupted. He was a regular who spent a good amount of his time in the library and was always respectful to the workers. She was grateful for him now more than ever. His interruption stopped her from blurting out her confession to Marcus and Evelyn. Even if she had, they'd never have believed her, anyway.

"Yes, Mr. Herbert. How can I help you?" Izzy leaned closer to the short, shrunken man.

Although bent with age, his sharp gaze remained intense. "I hear's it's yer last day, an' I wanta gives you dis." He held up a single, perfect stem of magenta-colored, funnel-shaped gladiolus flowers.

Izzy gasped and reached for the sweet and slightly spicy blossoms. "Oh, Mr. Herbert." Her eyes filled with tears. "You didn't have to." The old man was on a strict financial budget, and the money he spent on the precious gift made her throat squeeze.

"I's had ta," he replied. "You's need dis just like them Roman gladiators running into battle, as a symbol of courage and strength." His shrunken cheeks turned a soft pink as he blushed. His dark eyes lowered. "No ones has ever been as nice to an old man like me as you's is."

Izzy didn't think twice. She grasped the old man in a warm hug. "I will miss you, Mr. Herbert." She stepped back and wiped a tear from her eye. She held on to his upper arms and gave him a narrow-eyed warning. "You take care of yourself. Be sure to eat more and take those walks like you're supposed to." She nodded to Evelyn, who stood with her arms crossed and an exasperated expression. Really, the woman needed to learn patience. "Or you'll have to answer to Ms. Harper. Okay?"

Mr. Herbert returned Evelyn's glare. "She don' scare me none." He turned back to Izzy. "But's fer you, I'll do it."

"Good man." Izzy patted his thin shoulder. "Now, I've saved the newest Joanna Penn thriller for you. Go sit in your favorite chair, and I'll bring it over." With an indulgent smile, she watched Mr. Herbert amble with his cane to an old leather recliner that had to be as old as he was.

"I swear, Izzy, I don't know where you find yer patience." Evelyn huffed. "If it was up to you, you'd mind every miscreant in New York."

Marcus's eyebrows rose, almost taking over his hairline. "Miscreant? Damn, what century are you living in?" He shook his head and waggled his forefinger at her. "Don't tell me you've put in a claim for social security already." He snapped his fingers. "But, wait! If both of you leave, I'll have the best chance of becoming head librarian!"

"In your dreams, zygote." Evelyn huffed. "Get a move on, then. Them stack o' books over yonder won't shelve themselves."

"Yeah, okay." Marcus gave Izzy a brief hug. He moved away and thumbed over his shoulder at Evelyn. "The old party pooper and I are having lunch brought in. It's our small way of saying we'll miss you. Okay?"

Again, Izzy's throat tightened. She'd sure miss them. They were the only bright spot in her mundane, lonely life.

"Miss Izzy, ma'am?" A small child's voice matched the tugging on her linen pants. "Can you reads us this story?"

Izzy squatted, bringing her eye level to the small four-year-old, Anna. She glanced at the popular children's book the small girl wanted read to her every time she came into the library.

"You bet, Anna." Izzy nodded to the section of the room dedicated for book readings to a small audience. "I'll meet you there." She stood and smiled at the girl's mother, who gave her a grateful grin.

The woman took the child's hand and whispered to her as they walked away.

Yeah, no doubt about it. There were a lot of things she'd miss.

Izzy turned the key in the lock to let herself out. The familiar click of the library's grand doors echoed a poignant farewell through the cavernous halls of knowledge she had tended for years. Glancing over her shoulder, she took one last look. The dimming lights cast long shadows across the rows of books, each a silent witness to the dreams and aspirations she'd nurtured within these walls. She breathed in the comforting scent of old pages and unspoken adventures, a tangible reminder of the life she was leaving behind.

She clutched her coat a little closer, shivering as the weight of her decision settled in her heart. For once, she was on the brink of the unknown, about to embark on a journey beyond the confines of Earth. Added to that was the opportunity to explore the possibility of true love, as mysterious as the cosmos itself. This was no ordinary night for her. She was on the threshold of a new beginning, ready to take a chance she never dreamed would come her way.

The grand clock at the end of the room chimed, signaling the end of not only her day but an era. Time to go. Everything was ready. Throwing her head back, she walked through the entryway and locked it behind her. This was a strange symbol of her closing one chapter of her life and stepping into a new one. Shoulders back, she focused on the New York skyline, a mesmerizing sight of millions of shimmering lights twinkling merrily. What a satisfying backdrop for her future.

Her small one-room apartment was just a block away. The compact overnight bag she'd packed yesterday waited for her on her neat bed. The memory of how she'd gotten to this point in her life made her smile.

Was it only a few days ago that her life had changed so much? And it all started when she woke in a cramped room no bigger than her *abuela's* bathroom back in the day. The starkness was an afterthought, the suffocating white prison having no windows or doors.

She gasped when the wall unfolded and expanded into a colorful geometric square, swirling in high definition. It was enough to make a girl dizzy. At least it was pretty. Terrifying, but pretty.

"Welcome, Isabella." The voice sounded male, but it had a definite computerized twang to it. "Please do not be alarmed. You are in no danger." As it spoke, the geometric pattern expanded and spiked with each word.

"Um, hello." Izzy put a hand over her chest, as if that'd calm her racing heart. "You know who I am?" Amazingly, she wasn't the least bit scared, just excited. Despite not being a hardened woman after living alone in New York, she rarely jumped to conclusions. If whoever brought her here had intended to hurt her, they surely would have done so by now.

"Yes, we are quite aware of who you are." The voice continued. "You grew up as an only child after your parents passed when you were young. Your maternal grandmother, your *abuela*, raised you, instilling within you a love for books and literature. While you excelled in the public school system, you did not have the funds available for college. To pursue your higher education in library sciences, you worked within the system. After several years, because of your dedication, organizational skills, and innovative ideas for community engagement, at thirty-two, you are now one of the youngest head librarians in the New York system."

Izzy was about to make a comment when the voice continued.

"You have a small but close-knit group of friends with whom you share your interest in literature, arts, and cultural events around the city. You've secretly yearned to be a part of the space program, but have never found the courage to pursue it. Would you agree we have a realistic grasp on who Isabella Pilar Ramirez Torres is?"

Izzy's mouth opened and closed, then opened and closed again. The hand over her thundering heart turned into a fist. Well, wasn't that humiliating? Her whole life summed up in two small paragraphs. Hard to say if that was scary or impressive. She let the silence linger until she found the answer. "Yes?"

"Excellent. We have a proposition for you. Are you amiable to discuss your future?"

Izzy glanced around the small room. "I guess so?" Always eager for information, she saw this as a perfect opportunity to gather as much as possible.

"Excellent. However, if you wish to be returned to your domicile, we will send you back right away."

Izzy sucked on the side of her bottom lip.

"For now, we would like to present to you a proposition in order for you to make an informed decision."

The geometric pattern shifted until a blank screen took its place. Various covers of the sci-fi romances she'd downloaded and read on her electronic reader floated on the screen. "Do you not have these in your possession and read them?"

She cleared her throat and nodded.

"Excellent."

Guess she didn't have to speak to answer their questions.

"Tell us, how would you feel if you found yourself in a position to have one of these alien males fall in love with you? Would you be interested in exploring the possibility?"

She frowned. "What? I don't understand." Of all the things these unseen people could say, this was the last thing she expected.

"In addition, we can make your dreams of exploring space come true."

The voice seemed to become warmer, more human than mechanical.

"Isn't that one of your desires? To go into the space program? What if you had the chance to not only live the life you've craved but also have a handsome soul mate join you?"

The random pictures changed. Now the scene showed the heavenly male models from the book covers she'd read, seductively flaunting their buff bodies in various poses, exposing the hills and valleys of their impressive naked chests.

Izzy gasped as the pictures of some of her favorite models lingered.

"Well, Isabela Pilar Ramírez Torres, shall we continue with our proposal?"

She dropped her hands to her sides and wrinkled her nose. "Okay?" It wouldn't hurt to hear them out, right?

"Excellent!" The warmth in the voice continued. "We propose to you a reality you assumed was a fantasy."

The video shifted, and the images transformed into 3-D holograms, displaying various alien males in what she assumed were their natural habitats. It was easy enough to recognize the different species and planets from the novels she consumed.

Now the holographic images walked around her as if they were in the same room as her. Large, primal, sexy males she'd always dreamed about.

"The various cultures and their circumstances described in every story you've read on your electronic reading device are based on reality. There are thousands of humanoid cultures looking for respective mates. And the females of Earth are more than compatible with most of these species who face extinction."

Her face heated as the males walked around her, eying her as if they were there in the room. One of them, a hunky male with deep-purple skin and black, curling horns like a ram's on the sides of his head, caught her eye. His deep-magenta eyes with the horizontal pupils were both scary and sexy.

"Thus, the galactic government called the Federation Consortium created an exchange program. Its goal is to aid those worlds that desperately need females. And there are millions of human women on Earth who are willing to join this exchange program to find a true mate of their own."

"How's that possible?" Izzy whispered. "Aren't we all different species?" She bit back a moan when the images disappeared.

The colorful geometric symbol was back, accompanied by a metallic sigh that sounded sincere. "Human women are unique since your DNA adapts to a good portion of the humanoid males within the galaxy. Once you mate, your human genome usually gives way to allow the nonhuman species to survive." A warm chuckle. "That is why various races across the Milky Way have sought human females."

Izzy rubbed her forefinger along her jawline. "I'm not sure I understand. You're asking me if I'm willing to leave Earth, attend this exchange program to find an alien husband, then live on his planet and have his children?"

"Yes! That is correct. We are giving you the opportunity to find the family you have always yearned for among the deserving males of the known galaxy. And you will do so in a safe environment. Imagine, one male just for you. One who will cherish you as the valuable female you are. One who would never forsake you for another. Say yes, and you will never have to worry about being alone again. All your dreams will come true." The last word came out in a solemn whisper.

Oh, phooey. Now the silly voice just had to spout, "All your dreams will come true.". Even a dingbat knew if something sounded too good to be true, it usually was.

"We know how unbelievable this seems. But would you be amenable to let us prove our sincerity?"

It only took a moment to decide. "Yes, I would. If you can prove to me what you say is true, I'll consider joining this exchange."

After all, what did she have to lose except everything?

"Come then, Isabella."

The metallic voice continued with a warm and gentle inflection. There had to be a person behind that voice and not some kind of computer simulation.

"If you are amiable, we will show you a small portion of our ship, the *StarChance,* to convince you of our sincerity. Please do not be alarmed when one of our liaisons greets you and shows you around."

Izzy's heart raced. Was this really real? Was she about to meet an honest-to-goodness alien on a spaceship? With fresh eyes, she glanced around. She took a deep breath, and it dawned on her the faint stench of the New York's atmosphere was missing.

The wall to her right disappeared. There, in the doorway, stood one of the most stunning women she'd ever seen in her life. Oh, wait. That wasn't a woman, that was some kind of alien female. One way taller than her. Over six feet, at least. With long, dark, wine-red hair bound in several braided dreadlocks that reached the back of her thighs. Izzy couldn't imagine how long it took to wrestle her hair into those creative braids.

With the female's hair pulled back so tight, her pointed elf ears were on prominent display. Multicolored crystal earrings dangled in a single rope that started at the tips and ended an inch from each lobe. But it was her eyes that were most captivating. They were almond-shaped, the irises a darker shade of yellowish green surrounded by a light shade of khaki. Her long lashes matched her brows, the same deep burgundy of her hair.

The alien woman's outfit was something she'd expect from a typical science-fiction movie. Formfitting in a lustrous cream color that offset the slight iridescent sheen of her skin. *Oh, goose feathers*. Izzy shivered. What she wouldn't give to have a figure like that.

"Welcome to the *StarChance*, Ms. Isabella Pilar Ramirez Torres."

Izzy froze.

As the female spoke, a hint of tiny fangs peeked out.

But it was the sharp bite in the woman's tone that warred with the slight smile that gave Izzy pause. The alien said one thing, but her body language was the complete opposite. Izzy mentally slapped herself upside her head. Now, Izzy, you've got to remember you're dealing with an alien. It was ridiculous to compare her to how a human would react.

"You may call me Aja." The woman extended her hand. "If you decide to join us for the exchange, I will serve as your liaison."

Izzy hesitated before clasping Aja's hand. The alien's skin was warmer than hers. "Please call me Izzy." She released the other female's hand and waved hers between them. "Is this one of your traditions when you meet someone? A handshake?"

"No. However, I am trained in several Earth customs to make your transition as easy as possible for you." Aja cocked her head, indicating the corridor behind her. "Follow me, and I will show you a small portion of our ship." She turned and walked away.

Izzy expected to hear the hard metallic footsteps, but the shiny golden floor mysteriously muffled the female's movements. Shrugging, she followed.

"I am only bringing you this far in order to show you this." Aja stood in front of an expansive window and waved her left hand.

For the first time, Izzy noticed that the woman had one thumb and three fingers of equal length. "Oh wow," she murmured. Not wanting to offend by pointing out the differences in their hands, she turned to where Aja indicated.

Her breath caught and her eyes widened. In all its glory, there was Earth, floating like a vibrant jewel against the velvet backdrop of space. The blues of the oceans were deeper than any she'd seen before, even in simulated vids. Swirling clouds of white and gray floated gracefully across the surface in stark contrast. Continents lay sprawled below, their outlines familiar yet surreal from this vantage point. As the ship orbited, day transformed into night in a mesmerizing display. The glittering lights of the cities pierced the darkness, creeping across the globe, like countless stars mirrored on the planet's surface.

From this high vantage point in the vastness of space, Izzy felt the quiet hum of the alien vessel more than she heard it. Time stood still as she experienced a profound connection to the tiny, fragile world below—her home, seen as never before. It reminded her of the famous astronaut, Buzz Aldrin, describing Earth as a "brilliant jewel in the black velvet sky."

The word *awe* was a lousy way to describe her feelings at this moment.

But, to be honest, it was what lay beyond Earth that called to her. The vastness of space, dotted with distant stars and the occasional passing satellite, seemed to urge her to join them. To become a part of something bigger than she could ever imagine.

Such a simple decision. With a wide smile, she turned to Aja.

"Where do I sign up?"

Chapter Two

A *t the hidden moon city of Azadi, present day*
Asmodel sat at the round conference table, tapping his finger on the surface. He half-listened to the intense conversation bouncing around him, losing interest the moment he sat down.

He was too busy trying to remember the dream he'd had the previous night. The image of a pretty, dark-haired woman was vague, but her sense of warmth and welcoming presence made it hard for him to forget her. What was frustrating was no matter how hard he tried, he couldn't get a clear picture of what she looked like. Even so, deep inside he knew she was real and somehow important to him.

When the chancellor claimed everything was in order, Asmodel blinked and tried to recall what was said that could have involved him.

He glanced at his brothers' smug expressions as they all nodded to each other with satisfied smirks. *Oh, for the love of a motherless goat.* No telling what they'd volunteered him for.

The chancellor of the Federation Consortium, an alien Zerin named D'zia E'etu, was in holographic form. The fellow was actually at his palace on a space station orbiting his home planet.

Asmodel straightened and narrowed his eyes, taking in the expressions of everyone in the room. Good. At least it didn't look like anyone noticed he'd tuned them out.

"It's settled, then." The chancellor's hologram pounded his fist on the table where he was. "The four of you will go to FiPan and see what you can find out about those missing women. If you need any other assistance from us, don't hesitate to ask." The alien's blond hair lifted and settled over his shoulders as if it was a separate limb moving out of the way when he sat back in his seat. With a slight wave, he and the other holograms from Zerin disappeared.

His older brother Adapa, the undisputed leader of their merry little band of runaway slaves from Akurn, was staring at his next-to-the-eldest brother, Abalim.

When nobody spoke, Asmodel brought up the one thing that bothered him since he heard about the missing human women. "Why weren't the women in the exchange program safe? I thought the Zerins were an advanced civilization."

Adapa and Inanna looked at each other before his brother shrugged. "They assured us they had everything under control in their exchange program when they first approached us."

Asmodel shared a snort with Abalim.

And another thing...

"Doesn't anyone else find it strange only four women are missing?" Asmodel smirked. "And there are four of us with nothing better to do?"

That last part galled him. Because of the alien attack by their creators, the Akurns, forced Azazel to pull him and his three brothers seven thousand years into the future, he'd been at loose ends. The monumental task of preventing eight billion humans from realizing they'd just survived an alien invasion left the four of them with little to contribute. Despite their powerful psionic abilities, the modern world confused them. Finding where they fit in turned into an insurmountable task.

Not that any of them would admit it to each other. Or even to themselves.

"Well—" Queen Inanna, his sister-in-law, touched her fingertips together and leaned back. "—we don't know for sure that's all who's missing. We must wait for the Zerins to check their records and account for every human who boarded the ship for the exchange."

Asmodel grunted.

"Damned careless, if you ask me," Adapa muttered under his breath before clearing his throat and continuing in a louder voice. "I agree when they first came to us about asking human women to join the exchange, we shouldn't have assumed they had everything under control."

"I'm sure they had every reason to believe they weren't putting human women in danger." His brother Azazel spoke in a soft, firm tone. "But no matter how diligent one believes they are, those who seek to benefit themselves, even at the expense of others, are everywhere. No matter how carefully you strive to ensure those working with you are trustworthy, betrayal can still occur. I'm certain they were unaware of the deception."

Asmodel nodded, putting his elbow on the armrest, and supporting his chin on his fist.

Inanna laced her fingers together and nodded. "So true. I believe Prince Qay did not know this was happening on his ship. Or he would have taken immediate action."

"There's no doubt the deceased Chancellor U'unk took advantage of the prince's exile to install his covert operatives. It gave him an opportunity to not only steal these needed females, but the fallout, if discovered, would have disrupted Qay's bid to get back into his father's good graces. Which would have left Zerin ripe for a revolt." Abalim interjected his analysis. "That's how bad guys work. Even today, assholes like that are everywhere." His tone was bitter.

Asmodel nodded, his jaw tightening. The Akurn scientists had violated their own protocols to create him and his brothers, to use as slaves for their own selfish purposes despite it being illegal. That was a perfect example of people committing harmful acts, regardless of the cost to those suffering under their thoughtless whims.

"While that's true, that's not what's bothering you. What's going on, Abalim?"

Adapa's sharp tone made Asmodel catch his breath. He agreed with Adapa. It was subtle, but there was a psychic block from Abalim that wasn't normally there. Their even-keeled brother had previously held nothing back from them. Now that he thought about it, Abalim'd been standoffish since his return from the desert planetoid Hiigar. There had to be something going on with him. Something he didn't want to share.

"Yeah, Brother. Just make it easy for yourself and confess. No need to get your panties twisted in a knot," Arakiba piped up.

"I don't know what you're talking about," Abalim groused in a rumbling voice. He glared at Adapa across from him.

I need to speak to you alone.

Asmodel snorted. He couldn't believe the idiot didn't know their supposed private path wasn't so private.

Oh please. Like we'd let you get away with that stupid idea.

Asmodel swung his gaze to Asmodel when he spoke psychically on the same path.

You only thought we couldn't hear you. Dumbass. Arakiba added.

What he said. Both he and Azazel said that at the same time with a nod. No doubt their smirks matched.

Well, fruk. Abalim tugged on his earlobe with a sheepish grin.

After some teasing and complaining back and forth, Abalim agreed to tell them what bothered him. "While I was on Hiigar searching for Althea MacGregor, I came across this." He shrugged his right shoulder where a small silver-and-green spider-shaped robot named JR15 sat.

Asmodel admired the small AI given to Abalim when he went to that small planetoid to find the human woman. He'd love to have a companion like that.

"Go ahead, show them." Abalim encouraged his bot in a soft voice.

The tiny bot shivered before wagging his bulbous butt. In the center of his forehead, a round lens opened, and a video displayed on the center of the table.

Watching the interaction between Abalim and the blue crystal creature was mind-numbing. The threat the creature presented made the invasion from the Akurns look like child's play.

When the scene ended, Abalim's tiny companion scuttled back under his dreadlocks.

"Damn. *Fruk* me sideways."

As usual, his elder brother Adapa summed it up best.

"Come on, you *mulla xuls*." Adapa announced. "I've a surprise for you."

"I've got your evil devil right here." Arakiba hopped away from his seat and cupped himself with a lopsided grin.

Adapa ignored Arakiba and stood.

His mate, Queen Inanna, put her arm through his elbow and headed out the door with him.

The rest of them followed.

Asmodel gripped his hand into a fist to stop from slapping Arakiba upside his head. What a thing to say in front of the queen.

"Where in the world did you learn to act like that?" He hissed in a quiet tone to his unrepentant brother. His face heated when Inanna looked over her shoulder at them with her eyes narrowed and her nose wrinkled.

As usual, Arakiba was oblivious.

"You know all those movies we watched?"

At Asmodel's nod, he continued. "You can learn a lot about modern culture in those American and British television shows. It's a great way for me to hear the colorful language used today." His grin turned into a laugh. "I can't think of a better way to learn about modern life." He shrugged. "Except maybe social media."

Inanna smiled at them before she turned to whisper something to Adapa, making him throw his head back and laugh.

Asmodel relaxed. Thank the goddess, the queen wasn't offended. "I doubt they reflect real life, Arakiba."

"Of course they do!" His blond brother exclaimed. "Especially things posted on the internet. No one would dare put lies there. They'd be kicked off like that." He snapped his fingers.

Asmodel opened his mouth to argue when Azazel patted his shoulder.

"Remember, never argue with delusional people. They'll drag you down to their level and then beat you with experience."

Asmodel raised his left eyebrow and glanced at his shorter brother. "Did you just make that up?"

Their quiet brother chuckled with a soft smile and shook his head. "No. Unlike the rest of you, I've immersed myself in human literature. That's a portion of a quote from the great American writer Mark Twain."

Asmodel chuckled. "Well, Arakiba is far from stupid, but he has a lot to learn about the modern world. I guess I'll follow your lead about the so-called entertainment business. I find sitting around watching all that boring." He eyed the back of Arakiba. "But it has given me some ideas on how to teach that fool a lesson."

"If you needed any help with that, just ask." The twinkle in Azazel's eyes matched his slight smile. "You know I'd love to help."

"Thanks for the offer, but I can handle Arakiba."

"I know you can," Azazel agreed. "That's what worries me."

"Over here." Adapa and Inanna led them into a small family room.

Asmodel stepped into a room both unfamiliar and inviting.

The warm glow of the recessed ceiling lights and strategically placed orbs compensated for the absence of natural light and created soft shadows across the room. The harmonious balance between the modern comforts and the rustic, earthy ambiance of the alien subterranean haven was homey and inviting.

A soothing vid depicting the natural landscape of the planet Akurn adorned the far wall. The raw beauty of exposed stone or brickwork left visible on the other walls lent an authentic, cavernous vibe to the space.

As Asmodel walked by, he ran his fingers over the textured surface and marveled at the blend of nature and craftsmanship. Facing the room, he was drawn to the center, where a plush navy-blue sofa beckoned. Lying on those soft cushions would help take his cares away. A place to unwind among various pillows scattered in different colors and sizes.

A heavy wooden coffee table, worn yet elegant, stood as a centerpiece in front of it. Across the room were well-stocked bookshelves filled with scrolls, hardbound books, and ePads waiting to be used. The artwork and digital photographs around the room added personal touches to the place.

It was the type of room he'd dreamed about enjoying when he was a slave. Somewhere inviting to set his own creative nature free.

"Are they here?" With his hands on his hips, Abalim looked around. "Where are they, JR15?"

The little spider-shaped robot wiggled on Abalim's shoulder and pointed a sharp foreleg to the top of the coffee table. "They are right there, Mister Abalim, Sir."

Asmodel peered at the top of the table.

There, next to a bowl filled with dried floral petals, stood three small bots in the same shape as JR15, but in different colors and sizes. Next to them were two other bots. One was bigger than the rest, with a solid silver body complete with twelve legs. Next to it stood a smaller spider-droid in a contrasting violet with eight black legs and two large multifaceted eyes in a rainbow of colors.

Asmodel and his brothers surrounded the table and glanced at the little AI bots. His heart raced. Could he be getting his own JR unit? He eyed them, captivated by the seamless blend of the black-and-silver bot that had a mirror-like sheen. The silver parts glistened, while the black segments absorbed the light, giving it depth and a hint of mystery. What a study of contrasts. The silver exuded a sense of high-tech sophistication, while the black hinted at something more enigmatic and stealthier.

The spybots' forms were loosely based on Earth spiders, but were far from living creatures. They had different numbers of legs that demonstrated a precision of advanced technology. Their movements had a hypnotic fluidity that was almost hypnotic. Each leg ended in delicate, almost needle-like points, suggesting intricate manipulation capabilities or perhaps even potential defensive measures.

Asmodel became mesmerized by the silver-and-black bot's eyes, that were tiny and glowing. They were alive with intelligence that was clearly beyond ordinary machinery. They flickered with a soft luminescence as the bot scanned his surroundings. For a moment, the bot's eyes met Asmodel's gaze, giving him an unsettling sense of awareness.

"These, my brothers, are for you." Adapa claimed with a wave of his hand.

"Hey, now!" The larger silver bot jumped in front of the little ones. The violet-and-black one stood at his side as if joining in defending the others. "My children aren't something to be handed out like candy, you big oaf."

Asmodel's eyebrows rose. Children?

"My mistake." Adapa gave a slight bow with his hand over his heart. "Please forgive the insensitive way I started the introduction, JR10." He looked at the violet bot. "JR11, I never intended to disrespect you. Please forgive me."

Ah, here was the famous, or should he say infamous, JR10. Asmodel smiled and crossed his arms. If he understood the situation right, JR10 created JR11, and then she, in turn, created four little bots—Abalim's JR15 included.

JR10 gave a good impression of a human snort. "Well, okay then." He lifted one of his pointy front legs and jabbed it in Adapa's direction. "And don't you ever forget it, bub."

"Should we introduce them?" The soft feminine voice of JR11 interjected. "Let them get to know one another so they can see if they're compatible?"

"Come, my brothers." Adapa waved his hand at Asmodel and his two other brothers. "Say hello to the bots."

Abalim smiled at the small green-and-silver bot on his shoulder. "You'll love your JR. I can't imagine a better companion. That right, JR15?"

"Oh yes, Mister Abalim, sir!" The bot wiggled a little dance. "I love traveling with you."

If Asmodel wasn't mistaken, Abalim's companion had lost some of the mechanical mannerisms it had before his brother left for Hiigar. Now it acted and talked more "human". Maybe spending time with Abalim caused the AI bot to become less stilted and more natural.

Azazel squatted close to the table until he was eye level with the red-and-gold spider bot.

Arakiba had the small gold-and-silver one on his palm and had brought it to speak face-to-face.

That left the smallest droid on the table. The black-and-silver bot that caught his attention earlier,

To get comfortable, he sat cross-legged on the floor to speak eye-to-eye with the small thing.

"Hello," he addressed the bot.

JR10 and JR11 backed away but kept a sharp eye on him. No doubt they'd spring into action if he somehow hurt the little guy. "My name is Asmodel. What may I call you?"

The bot's rounded head tilted. "I am called JR13." It scuttled closer to him. Its multifaceted eyes had a rainbow sheen as he studied him with an up-and-down glance. "You aren't human, are you?"

"JR13!" JR11 scurried to the little bot.

It was then Asmodel noticed the similarities in their design, compact while elegant.

"That came out rude! You must filter what you say before you say it."

Damn. He never thought he'd witness one robot berate another like that. Like a... mother. Since he had never had a mother, it wasn't something he was familiar with.

"That's okay, I'm not offended," he assured JR11. Far from it. He liked clear speech. It made translating another's intention easier. Especially since he couldn't psychically connect with the droid. "You're right, JR13. I'm not human." He shrugged. "I'm a mix of unknown alien and human DNA."

"Fascinating," the bot stated. "You resemble a Native American human, but my database doesn't include your specific alien genome." JR13 tilted its head the other way and trotted close to him. "I must analyze you."

JR10 intercepted the small bot by standing in front of his "son". "You will not!" He crossed his thin front forelegs as any father would when chastising his child.

JR13 lifted a spindly foreleg in Asmodel's direction. "But I must examine this male on a higher level to determine if this organic creature and I are compatible. And there is only one way for me to do that properly."

Asmodel grinned. "And what is the proper way to do that?"

"I assure you, it's barely invasive for someone as massively built as you." The bot turned to JR10. "Father, if you will allow me..."

Wanting to defuse the situation, Asmodel nodded to JR10. "I don't mind. Let him do whatever he wants." *And then I'll give you something your inquisitive circuits couldn't dream up to mull over.*

"Okay, it's your dog-and-pony show." JR10 scuttled back to JR11.

Hard to tell if JR10 was talking to him or to JR13.

JR13 approached until he was so close, Asmodel's eyes crossed.

Asmodel's right cheek stung before he could respond. He cupped the soft pain on his face. Damn bot took his blood.

"Thank you, organic man. I am now analyzing." JR13 shuffled back. "Done." Then, its multifaceted eyes widened. "Fascinating. You are correct in saying your human genome is a minute part of your makeup." The bot tilted his head as if confused. "But I believe your appearance can be deceptive. Why do you choose to look like that?"

"Oh?" Asmodel straightened and stood. "Would you rather I look like this?" With minimal effort, he changed his appearance to look like a Zerin—complete with iridescent dark skin, dual-colored green irises, and three fingers on each hand. He even changed his clothes to match that of a typical member of the spaceship *StarChance* in a one-piece, formfitting suit.

"How about this?" Now he resembled an Akurn noble. Pale, alabaster skin, blinding-white shoulder-length hair, and flowing robes of cream and gold. He changed his eyes to a dazzling turquoise.

Not waiting for an answer, he changed once again. "I kinda like this one."

Now he stood as a citizen of the destroyed planet of Peinuewei. Complete with dark-eggplant-color skin, curling black horns that resembled a ram's, and skintight, thigh-length speedos in a blinding neon orange. He widened his blood-red eyes with their horizontal black pupils. Just so they weren't missed.

"Like any of these better?" Asmodel smirked. He swore he stunned the little guy as he turned back to himself.

JR13 nodded, eager as if presented with something he couldn't wait to get close to. "Yes, I mean, no. Your current appearance is the most tolerable. I agree to be your companion."

Asmodel held out his hand on the table to allow the small robot to climb on. "Well, come on, then." He grinned. "I'll do my best not to disappoint you."

Izzy couldn't believe how her life had turned into a cliché. Getting kidnapped by aliens and all.

It all started when she and the other humans aboard the *StarChance* were about to enjoy what was called a "repose interval".

Which was alien-speak for a day off.

And after four weeks of grueling training about the different alien cultures, having some time off was more than welcome. So, the day before the exchange, the Zerins promised all of them a fun-filled vacation in their holodeck.

Izzy was as eager as anyone for a little fun. Besides the stress of the twelve- or thirteen-hour days in extensive classes, she also spent many a late night sitting in her comfortable, small quarters devouring whatever she found on her personal tablet that the Zerins provided.

It captivated her when she found out most of the aliens she'd read about in her science-fiction-romance novels were based on reality. And just like in those novels, they were looking for human women to share their lives and help repopulate their dwindling species.

At the same time, she delved into Earth's history and became obsessed with the Akurns, an alien race. The Akurns had played a significant role in creating most humans thousands of years ago, using them as gold-mining slaves on Earth. They crafted human genomes not only from the existing humanoids on Earth but also from a mixture of several alien species. This explained why human women could have children with many of the humanoid species in the galaxy.

Sleep had been an afterthought.

So, when the promised "repose interval" was announced, relief spread throughout the ship. Everyone looked forward to enjoying a day filled with fun and games before their lives changed forever.

It was finally here. The promised day off.

Izzy rushed to the dining hall to meet up with a large group of human women waiting to enter. Instead of being open, the massive doorway was closed, making the group mill around in the crowded hallway.

"What do you think aliens consider is a day off?"

This question came from a tall brunette with curly hair.

Izzy sighed. She'd always wanted to have more volume to her straight, baby-fine hair.

"Come on, Althea. You know how they have fun."

This from a pleasantly plump blond with shocking exotic-gray eyes.

Althea crossed her arms and gave the blond a playful, narrow gaze. "Oh yeah, Lora? What's that?"

"You know, instead of Mai Tais and piña coladas, they'll make us sit all day in an auditorium and listen to one lecture after another." Lora laughed. "Without the human custom of lunch or breaks."

"That ain't happening." An African-American woman next to Lora waved her expressive hand. "If they think I'm going to be doing that crap, I'm outta here!"

"Like where would you go, Chloe?" Lora snorted. "Back to your room?"

Chloe nodded. "You bet your ass. I've got a comfy bed just callin' me."

Izzy agreed with that. Although she was excited about the upcoming vacation day, she wouldn't mind getting some more sleep. That way she'd be in top form to meet her love at tomorrow's exchange.

"I wonder what's taking so long." A woman next to Lora placed a hand on her arm and stood on her tiptoes. Her head bobbed back and forth like a curious pigeon's.

Izzy, just as short, didn't even bother trying—she knew she'd see nothing but backs.

"Do you see anything?" Lora grabbed the other woman's elbow.

The woman shook her head and dropped back to the soles of her feet.

All at once, people moved and shoved Izzy until the tight group halted. She wiggled between two solid bodies of the taller women around her and muttered, trying to get their attention. "Excuse me. Please excuse me. I can't breathe."

Instead of anyone responding, someone elbowed her out of the group.

Izzy stumbled into the solid golden side wall. The sea of women flowed past her, leaving her just outside the doorway. She put her head down with her hands on her thighs and tried to calm her racing heart and catch her breath.

"Ah, perfect."

When the familiar female voice spoke, Izzy jerked her head up. "Oh, Aja! You scared me." She put her hand over her heart as her eyes widened. What in the world was the liaison wearing? She'd traded her normal one-piece cream suit for something quite different.

It reminded Izzy of a character from a steampunk novel she'd read.

Aja wore a silver chest plate adorned with intricate swirling patterns that matched the designs on her silver wrist bands. Her black leather boots reached over her knees, and the steel over the toes matched the pattern on her chest plate. The formfitting outfit shimmered whenever she moved.

"Oh, are you in a play?" Izzy asked. The large doors of the auditorium banged shut with a resounding thud, making her jump. She glanced around the now-empty room, the place eerily vacant. Everyone was gone, no one around but the two of them.

"No." Aja's sigh was as sincere as a politician's promise. "I'm happy to say my days of playing the disgusting part of a human liaison are over." She grabbed Izzy's elbow and tugged. "Come on, human." The word *human* came out heavy with derision. "Time to exchange your destiny for something a bit different."

"What? But I... wait, the exchange isn't until tomorrow, and the party's over there!" Izzy pointed to the entryway behind her, now getting smaller as Aja dragged her farther down the corridor.

"Now, you don't need to worry your pretty little head about that."

The mean smirk crossing Aja's lips made Izzy twitch. She'd never seen an expression like that before. On anyone. Human or alien.

"Where you're headed, parties will be nothing but a distant memory." Aja hissed, leaning closer and tightening her hold.

Her hot breath sent a shiver down Izzy's spine, raising goose bumps all over.

"I promise you're going to hate every moment."

A sudden, searing pinch on Izzy's neck drove Aja's last word home. "Ow!" She slapped her neck over the pain. "What was..."

Her only answer was a thick blanket of nothingness.

Izzy's eyes fluttered open. She gasped when a woman's face hovered just inches from hers. The bright pair of green eyes speckled with golden flecks captured her with their burning, untamed, fiery spirit.

"You okay?" The woman's voice was mixed with a clear, confident resonance layered with the bare touch of a smooth, southern accent. Her chestnut brows furrowed, matching the smooth caramel of her skin as her full lips pursed. A voluminous cascade of curls fell over her shoulders and framed her high cheekbones, straight nose, and a firm jawline that lent a no-nonsense air.

"Who are you?" Izzy whispered and put her hand on the side of her head. "And where the heck am I?" Ugh. Her mouth and eyes were as dry as a crisp autumn leaf.

The woman moved back and looked her over.

Izzy realized she was lying flat on a hard, unforgiving surface. Doggone it, her upper back and bottom were killing her. No telling how long she'd been lying like this.

"I'm Morgan Jackson. And this place—" The woman waved an expressive hand and sat back on her heels. "—is Chez de Captivus. The glory hole in this stupid gangster planet called FiPan."

Izzy frowned. "Huh? Chez de what?" She leaned up on her elbows and glanced around. She didn't recognize the small, dirty-white room that was no bigger than the cramped lunchroom at the library. "I'm not on the *StarChance*?"

Morgan laughed and stood. "Yeah, uh, no." Her lips pressed into a tight line. "You, my friend, can now rightfully claim you're a living stereotype." She put her fists on her trim hips. "You've been kidnapped by aliens."

Izzy must've heard her wrong. "No, I went with the Zerins willingly. I wanted to go into space." She rolled with a grunt into a sitting position. "I'm part of an exchange program to meet an alien soulmate."

A zing of pain shot through her temple. She rubbed it. "I think Aja was taking me... um, somewhere?"

Morgan smirked. "Aja. That's the name of the Zerin who brought you here?"

Izzy nodded and stumbled as she tried to stand. She swung her arms as her legs wobbled like they'd forgotten what they were supposed to do. Thank goodness Morgan was there to help her get steady.

"Hang on there," the other woman cautioned. "Give yourself a chance to come back online."

"Thank you." Izzy took a deep breath when her body stayed upright. She eyed Morgan. "Online? You some kind of coder?"

Morgan's face went blank. She shrugged. "Something like that."

When she didn't elaborate, Izzy took another look around. "My goodness. There isn't much here, is there?" That was an understatement. Three small cots along the side walls and a small bowl in a corner. Nothing else.

"Where did you say we were?" Her nose wrinkled when a shimmering light caught her eye. "Oh, what is that?"

She approached the open arched doorway with her fingers extended. A rainbow of colors flowed like a waterfall, except up-and-down instead of just down.

"Don't touch that!" Morgan jumped and grabbed Izzy's hand before it got close. "You'll burn your fingers!"

Izzy clenched her fingers and took a step back. "What?" She peered at the reflective surface. "Is it some kind of force field?"

"Yeah. Something like that." Morgan tugged her to a small cot. "Come on. Sit down. Tell me your name and where you're from. Then I'll tell you what I know."

Izzy's face heated. Darn it! Her *abuela* would scold her for her lack of manners. "Oh gosh, I'm so sorry." She stuck her hand out. "My name is Isabella Pilar Ramirez Torres."

Morgan accepted the clasp and shook her hand before letting go.

"Please call me Izzy. I am, er, I was, one of the head librarians at the New York Library." Her face heated as she chuckled. Sometimes it was easy to forget she wasn't that anymore.

Morgan nodded and sat on one of the small cots. "Come, sit, and I'll tell you what I know."

"Oh, I'd appreciate that. Thanks." Izzy plopped onto the thin mattress next to Morgan and sat cross-legged with her hands on her lap.

The hours flew by as Morgan went into a fantastical narrative about being abducted by a female Zerin she'd never seen before who gave her to some kind of "gray alien", like those from Earth's UFO lore. Complete with a large, bulbous head and massive black oval eyes with spindly fingers on their hands. They put a wide leather collar around her neck that immobilized her. Then she was injected with something that made her pass out. Next thing she knew, she'd woken up here.

When Morgan mentioned the collar, Izzy grasped the similar one around her neck and gasped. "What is this? Will it hurt?" Even a hint of pain turned her into a total wuss.

"One of the sexbots told me it was called a *nutesh* snare."

Izzy watched Morgan's knuckles turn white when she gripped the black collar around her neck. "Sexbots?" What in the world...

"Oh yeah. Wait till you see one of those." Morgan's firm lips softened into a tight smile. "One of them should be bringing us something to eat any time now."

On cue, Izzy's stomach growled. She hadn't eaten anything that morning because she was looking forward to all the goodies promised at the "day off" celebration.

A light clanking sound outside the room caught her attention.

"Oh good. Here's one now." Morgan put an arm in front of Izzy as if to protect her. "Stay here. Don't move from this cot," she admonished. "They don't like it when you get too close. When I first got here, I tried to grab one. Bitch knocked me out by using something in this collar. I was out for hours. And believe me, the headache lasted for days."

"Days?" Izzy put a comforting hand on Morgan's arm. "How long have you been here?"

Morgan squinted. "Not sure. How far was the *StarChance* from Zerin?"

"We were just arriving." She winced. "The Zerins planned a party for us the day before we went to the exchange. And that's when my liaison injected me with something. Next thing I knew, I woke up here."

"Hmm." Morgan put her forefinger on her bottom lip. "They nabbed me the third week in." She put her hand on her lap and shrugged. "I guess I've been here a little more than a week."

The enharmonic sound of metallic footsteps came closer.

"Wonder which one it is today."

Before Izzy asked what she meant, a shiny figure strode toward them holding a tray on an open palm with several square blocks resting on it.

Izzy hissed. "Oh my goodness. Is that a robot?"

"I am Delight 9D33."

Izzy winced at the shrill tone coming out of the robot's blinding-orange lips.

"You will stay on that bedding while I disconnect the field and place your substance on the floor," the robot commanded.

Izzy couldn't move even if she wanted to. The collar had her in a tight grip. With wide eyes, she watched the neon-orange robot turn off the iridescent, hazy force field, giving her a clear view of the machine.

The darn thing could have stepped out of a Barbie-doll box—complete with a slender figure, long legs, and a disproportionately small waist. The face was delicate and symmetrical, with two large, wide-set, bright-orange eyes, a small nose, and full lips. Instead of having hair, this robot was bald. Her metallic-orange head shone in the low corridor light.

The strangest thing was the four breasts tipped with pumpkin-colored nipples. It reminded Izzy of a female dog after having a litter of puppies.

Izzy's eyes widened at the five-inch stiletto heels it had instead of feet. They were a startling neon green that matched the see-through sarong wrapped around its waist that hid little.

"Oh my stars, Will Robinson." Izzy whispered with her hand over her heart. For the first time since leaving home, it hit her. "I'm really lost in space!"

Chapter Three

Asmodel never expected cheering crowds or bands playing the first time he stepped on an alien planet. But for the *love of a motherless goat*, he'd have given anything to avoid this hellhole. The smell alone was enough to make him want to run back into the spaceship and head straight to Earth. Taking a shallow breath, he narrowed his eyes and studied his surroundings.

"Holy shit, what a dump." Arakiba scowled with his fists on his hips. "I bet this place didn't look any better before it fell apart."

"Agreed." Asmodel humphed.

"This is not an appropriate place to remain," JR13 whispered into Asmodel's ear from his perch between the man's neck and shoulder. "It may cause irreparable harm to your inferior organic systems the longer we remain."

Blunt, but true. The air was thick with the acrid stench of burning synthetic materials and the putrid tang of decay that seeped into his very pores.

The closer he and his brothers got to the sprawling ghetto of a village, the more it reminded him of a festering wound clinging desperately to life. As they journeyed into the village, the collage of mismatched buildings became clearer. Their state of dilapidation might have once gleamed with the promise of a utopia, but now stood in ruins. Their facades crumbled, as if weeping for lost glory.

Narrow alleys snaked between these husks, choked with refuse and the desperate forms of its inhabitants. Those souls moved like shadows, their eyes hollow with defeat and their bodies draped in tatters, embodying the despair that hung over the place like a shroud.

Asmodel's heart clenched at the sight, his psionic senses heavy with the unspoken stories of struggle and loss that emanated from the very buildings around him. It was a place abandoned by hope, where survival was a daily battle and the specter of despair an ever-present companion.

"Let's hope we're not here long." Asmodel spoke low to JR13. "Let me know if you sense any threats coming our way."

"Affirmative." JR13 agreed.

"Do you think that's where we should go?" Azazel pointed at a wide building with a massive doorway, its broken doors hanging lopsidedly on the edges.

"Yes," JR13 told him. "I sense this was the key hub of this provincial community."

Asmodel grunted and followed his brothers. Once he passed the threshold, the shadowed light made him pause to give himself a chance to get used to the dimness.

"By Tiamat's titties! I wonder what these babies did when they were awake." Arakiba chuckled, staring at a shocking-pink robot in obvious female form lying on the ground.

Various robots in obnoxious neon colors lined the path to the building's entrance. They stood or lay on the ground, even inside, unmoving, as if someone switched them off.

"JR15 tells me they are called sexbots, from a dead gangster named Dread Pirate Maynwaring, who ran this disreputable planet with strict, oppressive control," JR13 supplied. "He programmed these droids to give sexual pleasure to several humanoid species." The tiny creature huffed. "Why advanced units like these androids would willingly provide organics with sexual pleasure is beyond me."

Asmodel watched Abalim chastise Arakiba into leaving the prone sex-droid alone. "Who knows?" He wasn't interested in getting into a lengthy discussion with his bot about the need for most organic beings to procreate. Now, or ever, if he was honest.

"Are you sure this is the place that the human Althea said they held her prisoner?" Azazel asked Abalim. He glanced around. "I can't imagine them surviving in this sea of disarray."

Asmodel had to agree. The room was bare except for smashed furniture and broken robots.

He eyed an open hallway to the right, then spied another on the left. "Which way?"

"You two go that way." Abalim pointed to the right. "Azazel and I'll go this way." He thumbed over his left shoulder. "If you find anything, have your JR bots tell ours."

Why would Abalim have the bots do that instead of using their shared psychic link? Oh well, maybe he just wanted to make the little guys feel useful.

Arakiba smiled at Asmodel. "Come on, bro. Let's see what we can find."

He frowned at Arakiba's mischievous smile and glowered at his brother. "No funny stuff, *bro*." He'd better keep an eye on his easily distracted brother to make sure he stayed focused on what they were there for. It's not like they'd find anything useful. Looked like everything worth taking was already gone.

"You sense anyone here?" While his psionic abilities were strong enough to detect any living creature within these walls, he asked Arakiba, whose strength in other areas might pick up something different.

"Nah, just us and the two oldsters goin' the other way." Arakiba whistled and put one of his hands into the back pocket of the black jeans he wore. He sauntered ahead as if he didn't have a care in the world.

Asmodel glanced around the dark corridor and created a ball of light on his palm for illumination.

Arakiba chucked. "Sucka! How can we sneak around in the dark when you brightened everything up?"

Asmodel ignored his brother's banter. "How about you, JR13?" He nodded to his companion on his right shoulder. "You picking up anything online?"

"I am not," came the bot's terse reply. "I assure you, I will inform you if that changes."

The steady light shone on the empty cages made of clear walls. Several of the neon sexbots were motionless, either standing or stiffly sitting on the ground with their backs to the walls. He stepped over a badly scratched green one with its eyes plucked out.

All too soon, they came across Abalim and Azazel. Asmodel closed his palm to extinguish the light.

"How did you get here so fast?" Azazel raised an eyebrow at them.

Arakiba grinned with his arms crossed. "Place is just a round hallway with a lot of little rooms like this one. All are empty, just a few droids scattered around like that one." He pointed at a red sexbot on the floor with its hand extended.

With a chuckle, Arakiba stepped into the room and froze.

Asmodel almost ran into him. With a scowl, he sidestepped around his brother and glanced back, then noticed the man's frozen expression. Damn. A vision must have caught him. A deep one from the looks of it. "What do you suppose he's looking..."

He never finished his sentence as a vision captured him as well. He found himself swept into the psychic plane along with his brothers. They were still in the cell on FiPan, but sometime in the past. The force field was up, and five women were crammed into the small room.

"Where do you think we are?" Well, that was stupid. Why ask? He knew perfectly well they'd picked up a psychic thread leftover from the women.

"Where do you think we are, dumbass..." Arakiba stopped in mid-sentence when his focus narrowed in on one woman.

Asmodel frowned as Arakiba's eyes lost all color. That told him his brother was lost on a deeper plane of consciousness. Caught up in another type of vision that only

Arakiba could see. He blinked, then he too was swept into a different vision.

He drew in a sharp breath at the sight of the alluring woman before him, her lush body enveloped in a wispy fog. Her umber-brown hair blended with the warm, smooth olive tone of her skin. Wide, intelligent cognac-brown eyes gazed at him, filled with longing. Her expression was beseeching, arms outstretched, silently begging him to come to her.

"Who are you?" he croaked before clearing his throat. Her apparition yanked at his heart as if his soul recognized hers.

"Where are you?" He clenched his jaw as the urgent need to find her overwhelmed him. Everything narrowed to one instinct—to find her now, before it was too late.

"I'm... sure... but I'm... planet... CeluriaVO." Each word came out broken, like a cell phone with a poor reception. She dropped her arms and glanced behind her. "Hurry... Krystalii... coming!"

Her misty figure faded.

"Wait!" he yelled, stretching out his arm to grab her. But the only thing he caught was air as his hand passed through her misty form.

"I... am... Izzy...! Please... find me!"

She disappeared.

The haunting image of the terror on her face would torment him for the rest of his life.

"Hey, organic man!"

The metallic voice of JR13 jerked Asmodel to awareness.

"What is wrong with you?" the droid demanded.

Asmodel shuddered and blinked himself back to reality. While the vision felt genuine enough, it wasn't something that happened in the past. It was more of a premonition. Gulping a deep breath, he glanced at the spider-bot on his shoulder. "I'm fine." He straightened his shoulders. "Got caught up in a vision, that's all."

"Oh?" The voice of the bot rose an octave. "Is that something you normally suffer from?"

Asmodel inhaled through his nose before blowing out through his mouth. He wasn't used to being questioned about every little thing he did since he escaped Akurn slavery. He had to remind himself that as a newly made bot, JR13 would have a tendency to ask a lot of questions. "Not as much as some of my brothers. But when it involves me directly, I do."

"Fascinating." JR13 scuttled to the end of his shoulder.

The bot's tiny, pointed feet tickled.

"Did you ascertain anything interesting?" JR13 cocked his head, his bulbous eyes roaming over Asmodel as if examining him under a microscope.

Ignoring the question, Asmodel closed his eyes and opened his senses to see if there was anything lurking on the esoteric plane. An image of a dilapidated pub on FiPan came to mind. He sensed he had to go there to find the transportation he needed.

Shit. Just great. Looked like he wasn't going to leave this goddess-forsaken planet any time soon. "Yeah, I did. We've got to go somewhere else in the village."

"That should be interesting." the bot replied. "I hope you know what you're doing."

Asmodel snorted and glanced at his brothers.

Azazel stood with his hands behind his back, a serene expression on his face. His gentle eyes softened as he gave a slight nod.

One thing Asmodel admired about Azazel was how hard it was to get him riled up. The man was as unflappable as a statue in a windstorm, no matter how hard Arakiba tried to get under his skin.

Speaking of Arakiba, the man was rapidly blinking as if coming out of his own vision.

Asmodel went to him and wrapped his hand around his brother's upper arm just in case he had a hard time coming back to reality. "You okay?" Despite Arakiba's laid-back, carefree attitude that often drove him nuts, he couldn't help but worry about the guy.

Arakiba shuddered, his gray eyes still unfocused. He blinked and patted Asmodel's hand on his arm. "Yeah, I'm okay, bro." He smirked and gave him a wink. "It's all good."

Asmodel dropped his hold. He hated being called bro.

"Were you able to get a link on any of the women?" Azazel asked in his serene tone with his hands behind his back.

"Yeah, shot right to one of 'em." Arakiba's hand whooshed upward. "I know just how to get to a gal named Morgan. You guys?" He crossed his arms with a smile.

"I did." Asmodel nodded. "I even think I know how to get to the woman named Izzy."

"The woman who called to me is named Tony." Azazel nodded. "Since we've all had visions of different women, I believe it'd be best if we split up to search for them."

He glanced at Abalim's still form. "I wonder why he's still in a trance."

Arakiba frowned. "Think he's okay?"

Abalim groaned and shuddered.

Ah, looked like the man was coming out of his trance. Asmodel crossed his arms with a frown. It wasn't like Abalim to get lost on the psychic plane. What if one of those crystal aliens from another dimension somehow grabbed him?

"What? Why are you looking at me like that?" Abalim narrowed his eyes and growled at them.

"What took you so long?"

Asmodel couldn't help the harshness of his words. The habit of worrying about all his brothers was hard to break. It was a deeply ingrained result of being raised as slaves by those sadistic Akurn scientists.

"Our visions weren't nearly as long." Asmodel waved between himself and his other two brothers. "We don't have all day to wait for you, you know."

The indulgent expression on Abalim's face made his own heat. He lowered his arms.

"The three of us have locked onto the psychic trails of the other women who were here. We need to separate and find them before the trail grows cold."

Asmodel didn't like it when Azazel and Arakiba teleported out of the cell on their own. The entire situation was nerve-wracking. The only reason he didn't stop them was he'd kept a small thread of their psychic connection embedded in the back of his mind. Without another word, he followed Abalim out of the FiPan prison.

Once outside, he maintained a vigilant eye on their surroundings. Despite not displaying any weapons, he and Abalim still caused the natives to keep a wide berth. The most threatening thing they came across was a pack of canid-looking animals. Their fur, matted and patchy, bore the signs of the village's pervasive filth. With eerie synchronization, they prowled in silence, following the two of them. With a gentle psychic push, he sent the leader a wave of calm, giving him a suggestion they hunt elsewhere.

The alpha narrowed his white eyes with a snort. With a threatening growl showcasing dull fangs, he gave a brief nod before running away, his pack close behind.

Maybe when all this was over, he'd come back to help the abused and neglected animals on this planet.

"I believe there is an establishment ahead that might aid you in finding the transportation you seek," JR13 offered.

"If not, at least we can ask someone." Asmodel mumbled.

As they approached the only lighted building on the street, Asmodel paused. "With any luck, this is the place."

The harsh environment had weathered and worn the exterior, which blended seamlessly with the surrounding decay. Graffiti adorned the walls over paint faded under the relentless sun.

Makeshift lights, cobbled together from scavenged parts, hung above the entrance sign, casting a weak glow onto the uneven, cracked pavement below.

Patched metal and remnants of other building materials reinforced the main door. A series of mismatched windows, some clear, others opaque with age, allowed brief glimpses of the lively camaraderie inside. The muffled sounds of laughter and music could be heard, while spirited debates echoed into the dark street.

At the entrance stood a massive humanoid guard who gave them a steady glare. When they approached, he didn't say a word, just kept his steely three-eyed gaze fixated on them as they crossed the threshold.

Inside, the pub was a stark contrast to the biting despair outside. The air was thick with the aroma of spiced meats and hearty stews simmering in the kitchen, layered with the sweet undertones of fermented brews. The vapor from oil lamps and the occasional whiff of some type of recreational smoke added an earthy depth that gave the place rustic comfort. An occasional draft from the patched-up windows and door caused a decided chill that the small fire pits dotted around the room couldn't warm.

Laughter and conversations of clandestine agreements permeated around them. Dark figures lurked in the shadows as grizzled space mercenaries made deals with enigmatic beings cloaked in hoods. A band of multi-limbed musicians on an elevated stage occupied one corner. The sounds were disorienting instead of soothing.

Asmodel wasn't fooled. No one missed the moment he and his brother entered. Even without using his psionic perception, he sensed keen eyes fixated on them. Violence might not be tolerated here, but that wouldn't protect them once they left.

He glanced around the busy room. Yeah, this felt right. The person who was supposed to help him was here.

Asmodel stayed vigilant, his eyes scanning the room full of aliens. He focused on those with a dangerous vibe, sensing the greed and anticipation swirling around him like a palpable force. "Arakiba would love this place," he told Abalim.

"No doubt." His brother agreed and headed to an open space at the bar.

"How is Abalim going to converse with that alien being?" JR13 asked from his perch on Asmodel's shoulder.

"We were injected with a universal translator by the Zerin before we left." Asmodel stood behind his brother and watched the room with his arms crossed. No need to invite someone to sneak up on Abalim and try to steal from him. Or stab him in the back for fun.

"Yes, patron? How may I assist?"

Asmodel couldn't watch the bartender when he spoke, but winced at the lyrical tone the large being had. The pitch was just high enough to give him a headache.

"I'm looking for Captain Saphira. Would you know if she's here?"

Asmodel jerked and glanced at the back of Abalim's head. Who in the hell was Captain Saphira?

A small alien with a billowing cloak approached, heading straight for Abalim. The short, wiry creature was around three feet tall with a hoodie over its head, leaving a good portion of his face hidden in the depths. Visible was the creature's mottled facial skin in a putrid shade of green with scaly patches. Large bug eyes with irises in a strange mixture of orange and red gleamed with intelligence.

Since Asmodel didn't sense any hostilities from it, he moved to the side and let the creature stand at Abalim's back. Served the ass right for not filling him in on whoever this captain was.

"What do yer want 'er for?"

When Abalim jumped in surprise, Asmodel snorted.

He got a glare from his brother.

I think Arakiba is rubbing off on you. Abalim's tone had a slight warning to it.

Asmodel shrugged. *Not my fault your JR is falling down on the job.* Hey, he wasn't the only one who was supposed to protect Abalim.

After giving Asmodel a dry glare, Abalim turned to the little alien. "Rerqel from Qorath sent me here to obtain passage to their planet from her."

"Fer the both o' ya?" The alien glanced at Asmodel before turning back to Abalim.

A strong negative psychic wave hit Asmodel before the alien spoke his last word. His head jerked up as he took in his surroundings. Something tugged him in the opposite direction. "No. My path lies elsewhere," he murmured.

This time a separate force from the front door told him time was running out.

"As a matter of fact, my destiny just arrived."

Without looking back, instinct led him to the far corner of the room, away from the front.

You going to be okay? Abalim asked on their private telepathic connection.

Yes, don't worry. Everything is fine. The sense he was going in the right direction became stronger. *I expected things to turn out this way. I'll keep our pathway open.*

Focusing on what was ahead, Asmodel left his brother behind.

Izzy struggled to wake up. Good grief. Her head pounded like Evelyn was stomping through the halls of the library in one of her fits of fury. Groggily, she peeled her eyes open, and her vision swam, trying to focus. She moaned as shots of pain all over her body clamored for attention. Her right hip screamed at the abuse it suffered from lying on something sharp. Her arm under her agreed as her elbow throbbed in agony. She rolled onto her back. A little better. She could even pry her eyes open now.

At first, it was hard to understand the fuzzy kaleidoscope of unfamiliar hues weaving in and out of her vision. Putting her arm over her eyes to stop them from tearing, she noticed something else. The ground she lay on was not the cold metal of the suffocating stasis pod that a strange but cute little creature put her in when he stole her from her cell on FiPan.

Flinging her arm away, she blinked at the disorientation and sighed as her vision cleared. Sucking in a breath, her eyes widened at the sky above her. It was a work of art that reminded her of the famous paintings of Jason Pollock or Cy Twombly. Instead of one color, several unusual swaths of various hues blended into the canopy high above her.

Izzy pushed herself to sit, her heart pounding. Okay, good. That worked. The consuming, blinding pain turned into a dull throb. Taking in a deep breath, she tasted the clear but unfamiliar scents coating the back of her tongue. Around her was a chorus of eerie sounds from foreign animals and insects, creating a symphony in the distance all around her.

A sizzling sound popped and made her jump. Oh dear. It looked like the small ship she had been in was a goner. Broken in half, the front was smashed beyond repair. Plumes of smoke rose as sparks flared on and off, landing on the lush flora around her. Glancing around, she didn't see the short fuzzy guy who kidnapped her anywhere. Her throat closed as tears gathered. Poor little thing. He must've gotten trapped in the ship and died inside.

The ship rumbled and the pungent scent of fuel made her scramble to her feet. Not taking any chances, she raced to hide behind the nearest tree. She made it before that part of the small ship exploded. Keeping herself flush against the protective surface of the rough bark, she winced when metallic debris flew past her and embedded in other trees and the ground. Gulping in deep breaths, it took a moment before Izzy realized the tree protecting her was unlike any other she'd seen before.

Pushing away from the bark, she looked up and gasped. Instead of a linear trunk reaching for the sky, this one had a spiraling pattern, its branches and trunk twisting skyward in helical shapes. It didn't have leaves. This plant bore thin, flexible... feathers? All different colors and textures. Where her fingers braced against the wide trunk, the smooth surface had a warm, rubbery feel, and the color changed from stark eggplant purple to a light violet. She yanked her hands back, which left an outline of her palms behind. Her eyes widened when the image faded away, leaving the original color behind. She stepped back, and her heel snagged on a raised limb. She pinwheeled wildly before regaining her footing. Whew. She put a hand over her heart. That was close. Last thing she needed was to break something since she was stuck here all alone.

Oh, lordy. Alone. She was all alone.

Sniffling back unwelcome tears, Izzy straightened her shoulders. This wasn't the time to feel sorry for herself. With determination, she studied everything around her with a more critical eye. First things first. Was she hurt anywhere? Closing her eyes, she rubbed her arms as she paid attention to her body. Nothing but a few scratches and bruises. She opened her eyes. Good. As the old saying went, if you had your health, you had everything.

She glanced around with a rueful smile. Well, not everything. She must be on an alien planet with no food, no shelter, and no friends. No telling if there were any intelligent beings around or if only dangerous animals roamed about. She shivered. First things first, she'd better find some kind of shelter. Taking a chance, she peeked around the wide trunk of the tree. The smoldering ruins of the craft left little hope anything survived. The surrounding foliage was ablaze, making any attempt to approach it ridiculous.

"What are you?"

The raspy, masculine voice behind her made her jump. She spun around and slapped a hand over her thudding heart. The sounds in the jungle faded into the background.

Standing at the edge of a clearing stood something she couldn't have imagined in her wildest fantasies. There stood a humanoid creature on two legs with a sleek muscular form clad in hunting attire that melded into the shadows and light of the alien wilderness. But having two legs and arms was where any resemblance to a human ended. The face of the masculine creature displayed striking features of his feline ancestry with the concentrated expression of humanoid intelligence. Covering his body was a canvas of soft, short fur of a dark midnight blue marked with subtle orange stripes, like a tiger but sleeker. High cheekbones, accentuated by a snout complete with light-orange whiskers, gave his face a noble, almost regal appearance. His lustrous, streamlined look reminded her of a panther.

The creature's eyes were large and expressive, rimmed with a hint of exotic emerald-green irises and vertical pupils, reminiscent of a predatory heritage. His pointed ears were mobile, swiveling around as if to catch the various sounds around them.

There was deliberate patience in this creature's stance, a careful assessment in his gaze that spoke of curiosity rather than hostility. The subtle tilt of his head, the slight relaxation of his posture as he observed her, made her think he wasn't going to harm her. At least not yet. But she didn't doubt for one minute that if he thought she was dangerous, he'd have no trouble using that large bow-like weapon slung in a harness across his back.

Keeping a wary eye on him, Izzy concluded this was someone who was as much a part of this world as the trees and the sky. If she was lucky, he might be some type of guardian, like a forest ranger of sorts.

My goodness. Did he say something she understood? Oh, that's right. The Zerins injected her with some kind of translation serum when she agreed to join the Exchange. "I beg your pardon?" She laced her fingers over her throat.

"I said—" The creature crossed his muscular arms and slightly narrowed his eyes. The slight smirk on his thin, black lips told her he wasn't threatening her. "—what are you?"

She ran a hand down her worn-and-tattered clothes. At least most of her outfit survived. Flipping her hair behind her, she threw her shoulders back and gave him a little wave with a tremulous smile. "Hi! My name is Izzy, and I'm a human from Earth." Lordy, she never thought she'd ever introduce herself as a human.

The creature's brows rose. "Earth? Are you talking about the forbidden planet at the edge of the galaxy?"

"Yes!" she squealed. "You know about Earth?"

He snorted, his wide nostrils quivering. "Of course." He put his hands on his trim hips.

For the first time, she noticed he had extended short claws.

"As part of the Federation Consortium, we scikvak are well aware of any planets under a protective order." He tilted his head. "So, how did a human from Earth end up here?"

Izzy nodded. "I... I'm not sure." She glanced around and rubbed her upper arms. "Last thing I knew, I was being kidnapped from FiPan by some fuzzy little alien. Where am I?"

"Welcome to the planet CeluriaVO, my lady." He gave a short bow with his fist over his chest. "I am Jaltaar of the house of Zarvix from the city of Panterion Prime at your service."

A psychic tug pulled Asmodel in a specific direction, toward a dark, hidden corner at the other side of the tavern. He left his brother behind and tromped through the crowd of aliens, weaving through a cacophony of dialects that mingled with the pungent aroma of exotic scents. When he squeezed through a compact group, he tripped into an open space the other patrons had given a wide berth.

Once he oriented himself, his eyes widened at what lounged in a corner booth, half hidden in the shadows. There sat something, or rather someone, he never imagined he'd ever see this far from Earth.

A human.

A human male. There were many humanoids in the galaxy that looked like humans, and with his psionic sense, Asmodel had no trouble telling the difference. But this guy, this guy was one hundred percent human from Earth.

Sitting in a disreputable tavern surrounded by aliens of all shapes and sizes.

Asmodel stood at the edge of the man's table with a wide stance and crossed arms.

The man appeared to be in his prime with a rugged air that spoke volumes of his survival and resilience. His attire, a mix of practicality and style, included a weathered leather jacket that had seen better days, over a dark, form-fitting shirt. Hard to tell what else he wore since he sat behind a thick, round wooden scruffy table that hid the rest of him. His psychic sense picked up an unknown type of weapon under there, aimed in Asmodel's direction with a steady hand.

"Tell me, what's a human from Earth doing here?" Asmodel narrowed his eyes at the rugged figure. He examined the man's aura, trying to absorb as much about him as he could through silent inquiry. He did the same to the small group of aliens behind him. What he got was they wanted nothing to do with the notorious figure sitting by himself. Not sure why. The guy didn't seem all that dangerous sitting there all by himself.

The man eyed Asmodel with a smirk, lounging with his free arm across the back of the booth as if he didn't have a care in the world.

"What's it to ya?" The man's gravelly drawl was a sharp contrast to the boisterous hum of the muffled conversations around them.

"I am interested in hiring you to take me to CeluriaVO." Asmodel laced his tone with firm confidence and an underlying layer of urgency. He stepped closer to the booth to get a better sense of the man. What he picked up was a bit of a surprise. A tinge of panic from the guy belied his nonchalant attitude.

"What?" The man cocked his head. "I look like a cab to you?"

Asmodel studied the throbbing vein at the side of the guy's flushed neck. How interesting. Fear oozed from his pores.

"Organic man," JR13 whispered. "I believe there are several hostiles headed to this establishment. I overheard them saying they were eager to claim a bounty on this human. You'd better advance the negotiations."

Negotiations? He hadn't even gotten this guy's name yet. Asmodel pushed out his psychic tendrils to grab a brief glimpse of the emotions coming from the outside of the tavern. *Hmmm*, JR13 was right. A blast of antagonistic intent headed their way. "Mind if I sit?" Asmodel waved to one side of the booth.

The guy shrugged. "Makes no never mind to me."

Not sure what that meant. Keeping his attention on the man, he plopped onto the outer edge of the booth and settled onto the lumpy seat. Holding out his hand in the manner of the modern humans, he introduced himself. "I am Asmodel from Earth. And I believe we can help each other."

The man hesitated, eying Asmodel's outstretched hand. After a moment, he raised his brown eyes to hold Asmodel in a firm gaze. "I am Raxx Jorlen." With a firm grasp, he shook with the hand he'd had across the back of the booth before letting go. He leaned back with a nonchalant air. His hidden weapon under the table didn't move. "So, what gives you the idea I need help?"

Asmodel leaned on the table and laced his fingers together. Lowering his voice, he answered. "Less than five minutes away, there's a group headed to this pub intent on either tearing you apart or selling you to the highest bidder." He shrugged. "Could go either way at this point."

Raxx jerked his head back, then narrowed his eyes. "What makes you think..."

Asmodel sliced a hand through the air. "We don't have time for this." He glanced at the bot perched on his shoulder. "JR13, how much time do we have?"

"Three point five minutes." The bot replied loud enough for Raxx to hear.

Raxx glanced at Asmodel's shoulder before his lips thinned. "What do you have in mind?"

Asmodel sat back. "If you agree to take me where I want to go, I guarantee I can get you safely out of here."

Raxx tapped his forefinger on the faded wooden tabletop marred by scratches, stains, and cracks, his head tilted with a slight frown.

Time to convince the guy. Asmodel trusted his instincts, and they screamed he and this guy needed to get out of here. Like right now. "You're outnumbered and outgunned." His smile wasn't warm. "I can more than even the odds."

The man secured his hidden weapon in a holster at his hip and placed his fist on the surface of the table. Any attempt to look cavalier vanished. "Oh, how so?"

Asmodel scooted out of the booth and stood. With little effort, he changed his appearance to mirror the man sitting in front of him. Down to the shirt and jacket he wore.

"I can act as a decoy and draw the *idimmus* to me so you can make your escape." All he had to do was freeze the aliens before they got close to him. Not that he'd confess that part of the plan. No need to share all his secrets just yet.

Raxx didn't so much as twitch at the change of Asmodel's appearance. Never taking his eyes off him, he slid out of the booth. He stood next to Asmodel, his gaze roaming over him before staring into his eyes. "It could get rough," he warned. "There are certain, ah, individuals pretty ticked off at me."

"Really?" Asmodel smirked. "I never would have guessed." He crossed his arms. "But don't worry, that's nothing I can't handle."

Raxx shrugged. "Well, if you're sure, you've got a deal. I'll take you anywhere you want to go." He glanced at the loud exclamations rising in volume at the entrance to the tavern. He nodded to the other side of the room that had to be the back exit. "I'll meet you the next block over in front of a red shack with an image of a sexbot on it." He tensed as the noise at the entrance grew louder.

"How do I know you won't just leave me here and escape by yourself?" Asmodel grasped the man's upper arm.

"Wait." Raxx unclasped a compact, egg-shaped contraption from his belt. The thing flickered a soft, pulsing light. "This is Echo. Without her, I can't navigate my ship." He nodded to JR13. "Trust me, I wouldn't be alive today without her." He put the device to his face and whispered to it. "Echo, you stay with this man until we meet up. Okay?"

The light on Echo's surfaced throbbed with each word Raxx spoke.

Asmodel's eyebrows rose. That was interesting.

Tilting his head to JR13, he whispered, "Analyze that. Is it what he says it is?"

"Analyzation complete. What the human described to you is true. It is a sentient AI, similar to me, who is an integral part of his ship's navigation. Instead of verbally communicating, she has access to him by an implant in his head." The bot's voice was low.

"Can you understand her?" Asmodel asked. While he could read the man's mind if he wanted, he couldn't infiltrate an implant.

"Somewhat. I will continue to work on opening communications with Echo."

Raxx handed him the oval device and thumbed over his shoulder. "I'll go out this way and meet up with you." His eyes narrowed. "Are you sure you want to fight the Vargrux? They're stupid but deadly."

Angry yells headed toward them.

Raxx took a step back.

"Don't worry about me." Asmodel put Echo into an inside pocket of his leather jacket. "We'll be just fine." He nodded to the exit. "Go! I'll take care of this."

With one last glance at Asmodel, Raxx spun around and hurried through the small doorway.

Asmodel picked up the indecision that warred with the man's inclination to stay and fight.

At a boisterous yell, the crowd behind him parted. A strange assortment of ugly and just-as-ugly aliens surrounded him. All growling and spitting with raised weapons in his direction.

Asmodel smiled. This was going to be fun.

Chapter Four

"Um, thank you?" Izzy rubbed her arms, keeping them crossed. She studied the creature, Jaltaar. So far, he seemed nice enough. But she had to remind herself not everyone was. Her tendency to take everyone at face value made things hard for her more than once.

But he hadn't attacked her or anything. That had to count for something. Right?

He stood with his elbow clasped in one paw while he petted his whiskers with the tip of an extended claw of the other. He tilted his chin at the smoldering spaceship behind Izzy. "Were you in that?" His large, bright-emerald eyes with their black vertical pupils narrowed. "Are you hurt?"

"Yes, I was, but no, I'm not hurt." She glanced at the smoking ship behind her. "At least I don't think so." She shivered as hot adrenaline rushed through her, making her shiver. Biting the side of her bottom lip, she studied the alien. "Do you know what happened?"

Jaltaar frowned and stepped closer. "No. My crew and I were sent here to investigate that ship after it entered our atmosphere. What can you tell me about it?"

Izzy gave him a wan smile and looked around. Where was his crew? Not that it mattered at this point.

"Believe it or not, I can't tell you much. Like I said, a small alien kidnapped me and put me into stasis on that ship before we left." She rubbed her arms again. "I don't know how I ended up here." The stench of the burning ship made her cough.

He tilted his head, and his whiskers fanned up. "Sit here while I check out the wreck as much as I can before the flames become too much." He placed a paw on her shoulder and guided her to the root of one of the large trees.

She sat with a grateful grunt.

"You'll be okay here, but don't move." Jaltaar removed the bow from the harness at his back. "This area is an undeveloped sanctuary for wild animals. You're lucky the crash kept most of them away. Before we head out, I've got to contact the rest of my team."

He turned to the side and touched a claw to the front of the black leather collar around his thick neck, growling and hissing.

The words translated in her mind.

"Yes, I'm on site and I haven't found anything yet." His ears twitched. "No." He chuckled. "Stop nagging, I'm not in any danger. Of course I'll let you know after I finish sorting through this wreck. I suspect it's an Ozevroc ship." He snorted. "Yeah, incompetent as always." He gave Izzy a quick glance. "Don't worry, I'll let you know if I find anything."

Ozevroc? Oh, that must be the name of those furry little aliens who forced her into the small spaceship. Wait, didn't he just say he hadn't found anything? Izzy glanced around at the thick foliage. Why would he say that?

"Okay, I'll meet you then." Jaltaar poked the collar again, and she became the focus of his attention. "Stay here and don't move. I promise I'm not going far, but if anything approaches you, shout." He pulled an arrow from the quiver strapped to his back and placed it on the bow with a solid grip of his claws to ready it to use.

Izzy nodded and leaned back against the solid bark. "No worries." Taking a deep breath, she chuckled. "I'm not going anywhere."

All at once, the last few moments caught up with her. It wasn't every day a person survived an alien kidnapping, was held in prison with four other women, got kidnapped again and then woke up on an alien planet getting rescued by a formidable cat-man. She shivered, pulled her knees up and wrapped her arms around them, rested her chin there, and stared at nothing.

The world was silent except for a soft breeze rustling the feather-leafed trees, causing them to sing an exotic song.

Izzy didn't pay attention to the muffled sound of Jaltaar's footsteps walking away. She closed her eyes as tears gathered and rested her forehead on her hard knees, trying to grapple her careening emotions.

The back of her neck prickled. She lifted her head and looked around. She searched through the small bushes covered with strange colorful flowers and fruits that mingled with the earthy musk of the moss-covered ground. With a tilt of her head, she strained to hear anything that might be coming close. Glancing left and right, she noticed nothing different. Except... there. In the thick bushes on her left she swore there was a pair of large, midnight-blue eyes sprinkled with lighter blue and silver spots surrounding a vertical black pupil that held the universe in their depths. They peeked at her between the foliage.

"Um, Jaltaar person..." Izzy's voice came out a rough whisper. She cleared her throat and sat straight. Keeping her gaze locked on those mesmerizing eyes, she didn't dare blink. Pushing up with her hands behind her, she stood on shaking legs.

The round eyes now were at her level and moved closer. Holy cow, she was being stalked.

"Jaltaar?" Look at her, talking like a normal person. The wobbly terror in her tone was hardly noticeable. Not like someone who was about to be eaten by some vicious alien monster. The darn thing crept closer, making it easier to see pointed ears, slightly larger than a human's, twitching as they moved. Between those ears was a fur-covered forehead, a lush velvety texture in a deep, rich shade of midnight blue, a perfect canvas for the array of orange strips lining long fur in harmony.

Too stunned to move, Izzy's mouth dropped open as a wondrous figure emerged from the thick bushes. It was a cat-woman. No, not a cat, but a sleek, graceful panther standing on two legs wearing a form-fitting outfit that enhanced her curvy, human-like figure. A string of coils covered her neck and had to be made of some kind of brass or gold, etched with exotic symbols and figurines. On the outside bottom of her wide, pyramid-shaped ears were metallic bars that glinted against her thick head of dark midnight-blue hair that flowed down her back. Izzy got the impression that instead of decorations, they were some type of communication devices.

And in a tight grip, the cat-woman held a long pole lodged in the ground, the tip of a spiked ball pointed up at the same height as the female's head.

This was one lady Izzy didn't want to mess with.

"Talira!"

Jaltaar's masculine roar made Izzy jump.

In a blur, his form raced toward them, his short dark-blue fur gleaming with black-and-deep-green highlights as he raced toward the female.

"Jaltaar!"

The female ran in his direction, sprinting with strong, muscular legs that made the distance between them evaporate. With a joyful cry, she leaped at him, landed with her legs wrapped around his trim waist, and gripped her arms around his thick neck.

Izzy's eyes widened when she noticed neither one of them had dropped their weapons in their eagerness to be together.

Dual purrs filled the air as the two felines nuzzled and scraped the sides of their muzzles together. A few light licks here and there as they rubbed their faces together and entwined their tails around each other.

The beauty of their obvious heartfelt love brought tears to Izzy's eyes. That's all she'd wanted when she left Earth. To find a deep and abiding love like that. Too bad that dream more than likely wouldn't happen now.

Izzy did her best not to make a sound and interrupt the lovers' reunion, but her deep sigh escaped as she watched the joyful reunion between Jaltaar and the female he called Talira. Even though the sound was barely a whisper, they must have heard her because they broke apart and glanced at her.

"Golly." She put a hand over her heart. "I didn't mean to interrupt."

The two lovers looked at each other with a smile. A brief nuzzle at the side of their snouts blended their whiskers together.

Talira dropped her legs from Jaltaar's waist and gripped his upper arms. With one hand she petted between his ears.

His purr rolled louder.

"Is this the human you told me about?" Her voice came out as a sensual rumble.

He preened into her caress with eyes half shut. "Yes, and unfortunately, we don't have much time." He took her paw and brought her middle claw to his lips for a light lick. "My team will soon be here, and there's something I need to show you—" He nodded in Izzy's direction. "—and her. It's imperative you both know what's at stake."

He pulled a rectangular steel box from one of the side pockets in his pants.

It was a marvel of alien engineering that seamlessly blended art and technology. Sleek and elegantly crafted, its surface shimmered with a subtle luminescence that captured and played in the dappled light filtering through the forest canopy.

"Oh, is that a new Lumiview Prism?" Talira exclaimed as she retracted her claws and fisted her palm over her chest. "I heard it not only responds to your commands, but can analyze your intentions and provide you with information you never thought to ask." She tilted her head back with a twinkle in her eye. "I don't suppose you brought me one?"

Jaltaar's sheepish grin made Izzy chuckle. The boy was busted.

"I promise to work on getting you one, my *tsuki*." He caressed the whiskers on the side of her face, his expression filled with tenderness.

"I'll hold you to that." Talia's tone lowered as she nuzzled his paw before giving Izzy her full attention. She stepped away from Jaltaar but kept a grip on his paw and put her other one over her heart. "I am Talia of the House of Cyndor from the village Nekojin."

For the first time, the tension pinching Izzy's shoulders loosened. "Hi!" She gave a little wave. "I'm Isabella Pilar Ramirez Torres. But please call me Izzy."

Talira gave a brief nod. "I am honored." Her whiskers fanned out. "Are you really a human from Earth?"

"Yep," Izzy rocked on her heels with her hands behind her back. "That's me. A good old-fashioned human from Earth."

Talira eyed her up-and-down. "You are a strange, but graceful-looking creature."

Izzy stopped fidgeting and scratched the side of her jaw. "Thank you. I think."

"Were you harmed by the crash?" Talira nodded at the smoldering wreck behind her. "You don't look like you're hurt." Her vertical pupils widened, making the midnight blue of her eyes all but disappear. "How is that possible?"

Izzy shrugged as Jaltaar answered.

"As I said, I have something to show you." He held out his Lumiview device. "I recorded the meeting I had with the Dominion Collective led by the Supreme Alpha Regent Korvax himself."

The long fur on Talira's tail waved in the air as she thumped it hard on the forest floor. "You met with Alpha Regent Korvax?"

Izzy stilled. Wow. Sounded like Talira wasn't a fan of that person.

Jaltaar nodded with downcast eyes. "Yes."

The hurt tone in his voice made Izzy raise her eyebrows.

"He didn't have a choice since I'm the commander of the largest squad in the palace guards." He looked up as a shadow crossed his face, his whiskers drooping.

Talira gasped. "I can't remember the last time you told me he talked to you." The fur under the coils covering her neck expanded, several strands peeking out. "It must have been really important."

"Watch."

Jaltaar's claw poked at the device's face. It hummed as an image projected in the air with astonishing clarity. The scene unfolded in an elaborate, spacious chamber. Cold, blinding-white marble covered the room, with gold, silver, and bronze etchings outlining the moldings on the ceiling and floor.

On a throne made of dark wood and platinum sat a male scikvak. He had the same orange stripes Jaltaar had, except his navy-blue fur was more prominent than the stripes. He leaned forward with his paws gripping the armrests while his tail, complete with a ball of midnight fur with orange stripes, wagged back and forth in sharp bursts. His fire-orange eyes narrowed on the strangest thing Izzy had ever seen.

It looked like a woman made of living crystal. She appeared sculpted from a translucent, crystal-based material that captured and amplified the soft light of the room. It was easy to see her in all her glory since the creature didn't have a stitch of clothing on. All over her was a mesmerizing array of sharp, geometric crystal shapes, each facet meticulously carved to reflect and refract a spectrum of fiery hues, from the softest amber to the deepest orange, mimicking the warm glow of a setting sun.

Instead of hair, the creature had a crown of crystal spikes emanating from her head. Each one glowed and cast a halo of light around her, illuminating her surroundings with a warm, golden light. The spikes varied in length and shape.

Izzy shivered at her untamed appearance.

But it was her alien face that held a mesmerizing masterpiece of exotic elegance. High, sweeping cheekbones created a slender, elongated silhouette. Her large, pupilless eyes commanded attention, intense with a fiery light that flickered and danced like flames.

Izzy sensed a sharp, fanatical gleam in the crystal person's gaze.

"You dare threaten *me*?" The rumbling question came from the scikvak sitting on the massive throne in front of the crystal woman.

The surrounding guards kept still as they focused on the alien.

"Good Supreme Alpha Regent of Pantherion Prime." The crystal woman gave a respectful bow, but the gleam in her eyes screamed insolence. "I am offering you an unheard-of opportunity for you and your people." She straightened and gestured to the crowd behind her. "Not only will Lord Baelon allow all zaltrixan to exist, but he is offering you the chance to rid yourselves of the inferior pardalions, leaving you sole control of CeluriaVO."

The Alpha Regent glared at the female and tapped an extended claw on the ornate armrest with one hand while he rested his chin on a closed fist. "So, what you're saying is you want us to retrieve a human female in our protected wilderness that you caused to crash here on CeluriaVO. How do we know she even survived?"

The yellow crystal alien curled her full lips. "As I explained to you before, being a strong telekinetic, I pulled her out of the craft before I lost control of my ship and ended up on the outskirts of your city instead of in the jungle." She crossed her arms, her bright pupilless eyes narrowed. "Unfortunately, I utilized most of my internal power to remove the human from the ship without causing harm to her. In doing so, I cannot recharge in time to retrieve her on my own." Her bald head tilted, causing the protruding crystals to glimmer. "I fear if left alone, the creature won't live long enough in your wilderness for me to obtain her."

The Alpha Regent sat back. A slow, satisfied smirk creased his thin, black lips around his snout, exposing the tips of his upper fangs. "So, Prisma-Solara." He waved a negligent hand at the crystal woman. "If we bring this human to you, you will help us eliminate the disgusting pardalions?" His clear pumpkin-orange eyes filled with fanatical joy.

"No, Alpha Regent." Prisma-Solara took a step closer to the elaborate throne. "I will not *help* you." Her satisfied smile was hard. "I will eliminate them *for* you."

In low light of the raucous confines of the Grub & Grog, the clueless patrons ignored the oncoming confrontation between Asmodel—now in the form of Raxx—and the newcomers.

The group of aliens facing him scowled and snarled over the sounds of boisterous conversations and clinking glasses with the bass-thumping music in the background. Asmodel nonchalantly grabbed a drink from a table and surveyed the group. The anticipation of the impending aggression made his muscles tense as he studied his new challengers with a smirk.

"You secure back there, JR13?" He side-mouthed the question to his bot companion.

"Affirmative, organic man. Don't spend useless energy if you can help it."

The answer came with a sharp pinch at the back of his neck, letting him know the droid had a steady grip. "No promises," Asmodel grinned.

The leader, a towering brute with a jagged scar running across his face, locked eyes with "Raxx" and growled, "There you are, Jorlen. Thought you'd hide in this cesspool?"

Asmodel studied his new foes, noting their rugged appearance.

They stood around seven feet tall, with thick necks and rough, rust-red or drab-gray skin. Their broad shoulders and trunk-like, muscular limbs made them formidable opponents. Their faces were sharp and angular, with deep-set, narrow eyes filled with calculating coldness. Short, spiky ridges covered their bald heads that matched their prominent lower jaws and jutting sharp bottom teeth.

They wore dull utilitarian battle-suits devoid of any decorations except for scratch marks and various dents. They looked as uncomfortable as hell.

Asmodel took a sip of the drink before replying with feigned surprise at the Vargrux. "Oh, was I hiding? Here I thought I was just having some drinks here with my friends." He waved his glass to the now-quiet crowd, the green liquid inside splashing over the lip. "So glad you're here to tell me what I was really doing." He gave a loud, insincere sigh with his hand over his heart. "You know how it is—everyone wants me, and there just isn't enough of me to go around."

In unison, the smelly group of Vargrux blinked, as if surprised their prey talked back to them.

"Funny." The leader growled. "Let's see if you're still joking when we pull your spine out of your ass."

Behind the group, the tavern patrons edged away as the Vargrux surrounded Asmodel. The idiot in front, probably eager to prove himself, lunged forward, only to slip on a spilled drink of unknown origin—courtesy of Asmodel *accidentally* spilling it with his telekinesis.

Asmodel jumped away as the mercenary crashed into the next table, sending glasses and customers scattering. "Oops," he chirped, "Careful, my friends. This place is really dangerous. You'd think they'd at least put up a 'caution, wet floor' sign."

Not to be outdone, another Vargrux charged with head down and an energy blade in hand.

Asmodel ducked, resulting in the unfortunate alien head-butting the bar. "Now, now," he tutted. "Violence isn't always the answer. Especially when you're so bad at it."

With a roar, another one charged, only to be hit by a round container filled with liquid from behind the bar that Asmodel swung at him with his mind, knocking the Vargrux off his feet.

The bin exploded and soaked the unconscious alien.

The skirmish burst into action.

Asmodel danced around the attackers, his moves almost comical in exaggerated grace. With psychic ease, he turned their own momentum against them, causing more than one to collide with their comrades, turning the fight into a farce.

The leader, with bulging eyes and fangs exposed, made a final, desperate attempt by lowering his head and charging.

Quick as a flash, Asmodel placed his hand on the mercenary's head and used his psychic push to slide the Vargrux face-first across the bar, wiping out an array of drinks before his head crashed into the wall.

Untouched, Asmodel wiped his hands together with a dramatic flourish. "I'd say your approach needs a bit more finesse. But hey, who am I to judge?" He crossed his arms with a wide stance, then he smiled. This was fun. The laughter in the tavern agreed with him.

The defeated Vargrux leader pulled himself off the bar, his gray suit colorful from the various drinks and food he'd crashed into. With a glare, he kept his puke-colored eyes of yellow on Asmodel and pulled out a sharp triangle of glass from his cheek. Deep-, almost black-, red blood gushed out.

In a voice that carried a deadly calm, he hissed, "Enjoy your laugh, Raxx. This isn't over. We'll find you in the shadows where you hide, and there won't be anyone there to watch you die. The next time we meet, it'll be your end."

"Yeah, yeah, yeah. Scare me a new one, asshole."

With a flick of his fat fingers, the leader sent the large piece of glass in Asmodel's direction, which he easily swatted away.

With a last glare, lips curled in a snarl, the Vargrux turned, his armored figure disappearing into the neon haze of the night outside the bar. Behind him, his troop followed, their unconscious liquor-soaked companion carried out by two of his companions. They left behind a lingering sense of foreboding, putting a wedge in the previous camaraderie of the Grub & Grog.

Asmodel watched the mercenary aliens leave with a thoughtful frown. If those aliens found the real Raxx, he doubted the human would escape as easily as he did. Maybe when everything was all said and done, he'd find a way to help the guy.

But for now, time to leave with a lasting impression. He hefted the wrist unit he 'borrowed' from the leader. Tossing it to the bewildered bartender, he quipped, "Use this to buy a round for everyone." He glanced at the mess. Broken tables and chairs littered with splintered glass among a river of mixed drinks. "And maybe something for the cleaning crew."

The Grub & Grog erupted into cheers and laughter. Everyone returned to their previous revelries. Looked like the night's entertainment faded as the brawl turned into distant memory.

Asmodel, with a satisfied grin, blended into the crowd and morphed back to himself, leaving no trace of Raxx Jorlen behind.

Izzy frowned when Jaltaar poked the Lumiview device with an extended claw and the image faded. "I don't understand." Her face flushed. What choice did she have but to admit her ignorance. "Who or what is that, uh, unusual-looking woman... lady? And why does she want me?" The thought of that mean-looking alien wanting her for whatever reason made her shiver. "And why does she agree to eliminate pardalions, whatever those are?"

"That, my human friend—" Jaltaar put the now-silent device back into the side pocket of his pants. "—is a Krystalii by the name of Prisma-Solara, who hails from another dimension. Their primary goal is to take over our galaxy by raping our planets of their resources for their own use." He turned his bright-emerald eyes her way. "And their leader, a fellow by the name of Lord Baelon, believes they can use human women to speed up their ability to create more of their crystal citizens. Apparently, it takes thousands of years for one of them to grow into a sentient being. And he's looking for a way to cut that timeline in half."

Izzy wrinkled her nose. "That doesn't sound right." She clasped her hands behind her. "I may not be a biologist, but I don't see how we're compatible with something like them. And are you telling me she's the one who caused that ship—" She thumbed to the billowing smoke from the crash behind her that now coated the air with noxious fumes. "—to crash and then somehow pulled me out before I got hurt?"

Jaltaar shrugged. "Apparently. She comes from a race with a high degree of various psychic abilities. Which somehow got depleted when she pulled you out of that ship." He glanced at Talira. "We should keep that in mind. Knowing what makes her weak might be something we could use against her later."

Talira's pink tongue peeked out and wiped across her downturned thin black lips surrounding her snout. "Do you think she has the power to eliminate all of us pardalions?" Her concern came through loud and clear, even in a whisper.

"What do you mean, eliminate you pardalions? Why would the Alpha Regent want to kill his own people?" Izzy swore if the furrow on her forehead got any deeper, it'd get stuck like that.

"The Alpha Regent doesn't want to kill all scikvak." Talira's long tail swished in hard strokes behind her. "Just the pardalions."

Well, goose feathers. Now the frown lines around her mouth were going to get stuck, too. "A pardalion? What's that?"

Talira pointed an extended claw from her paw at her chest. "I am. I'm a pardalion." She gestured to Jaltaar. "And he's a zaltrixan."

"Huh?" Okay, call her confused. She glanced between the two feline scikvak. "Is that the name of the country where you come from?"

Jaltaar shook his head. "I don't know what the word *country* means, but on CeluriaVO, the ruling class are my people, the zaltrixan. Talira is part of the lower class called the pardalions."

Izzy's eyebrows rose. "Why? What's the difference? You're both the same species, aren't you?"

Jaltaar's whiskers twitched. "Yes, but the differences between us is unsurmountable for a great majority of our population."

Her brow tightened, giving her a headache. Not sure how to avoid offense by her observation, she did her best to be as careful about her wording as much as possible. She nodded at Talira. "Is it because she's a female?"

Jaltaar's incredulous expression made Izzy giggle.

"Female?" Talira snorted and crossed her slender, muscular arms. "What would that have to do with anything?"

"Because you have dark-blue eyes and his are a pretty green?"

Jaltaar rumbled.

Okay, that was a definite no. Looked like color and gender weren't the issues. Must be something else. "Is it because Jaltaar has a bow and arrow and you carry a stick for a weapon?" She was grasping at straws here.

"Are you being deliberately obtuse?" Talira's whiskers, in their pale-orange color, fanned out. Her pointed ears twitched back and forth. "Can you not tell the obvious difference between our races?" She waved a paw between her and Jaltaar.

Izzy tapped her forefinger on her bottom lip. Okay, this was serious. She narrowed her eyes and studied the couple in front of her. They both had pretty midnight-blue fur covered in orange stripes.

There stood Jaltaar, proud and erect, the epitome of feline masculinity. Strong jawline, high, chiseled cheekbones framed a slight snout over a slit of a mouth outlined in black. The only thing on his face with any hint of softness were his beautiful eyes, a swirling blend of iridescent emerald green.

The midnight-blue fur on his visible chest had wide, dramatic orange stripes that reminded her of a Bengal tiger. Even his thick tail swishing behind him coiled with dark-orange stripes. Not an ounce of extra skin or fat marred his muscular form.

Izzy turned her attention to Talira. Her face was soft and streamlined, as graceful as a ballet dancer's. Lush black lashes outlined with striking black tracks framed her midnight-blue eyes, speckled with silver star-like streaks.

Luscious, long, dark fur, a touch lighter than Jaltaar's, covered Talia's graceful, lovely feline form. Her form-fitting garment was a light tan that showcased her toned arms in short sleeves and ended at her mid-thighs. Her slender tail had freedom of movement, now agitated in bold swipes behind her. The entire ensemble allowed a full display of her willowy and lightweight feminine form in its hourglass, human-like figure.

Looking at them both, the only thing Izzy saw were two sentient beings of the same race who looked like the large cats on Earth, but walked on two legs instead of four. They were both wildly pretty while imposing at the same time.

Izzy shrugged. "No offense, but I can't see anything different between you—" She gestured at them. "—except for what I said before."

Jaltaar's chin jutted and his lips pulled back, exposing his upper fangs. "I cannot believe you don't see the major difference between us."

Talira crossed her arms and nodded to the male beside her. "Look closely at our fur."

Squinting, Izzy stepped closer. Both had thick, glossy coats she'd love to pet under other circumstances. "You're both absolutely beautiful." She fisted her hands to stop herself from reaching out to stroke either of them. It's not like they'd appreciate being treated like pets or anything.

"No!" Jaltaar barked with a strangled laugh. "Look at us! Closer."

Closer? Well, okay. Izzy shrugged and walked around them. Both had to be excellent examples of their race. Tall, lean, and muscular, with the most interesting tails imaginable. Her mischievous side poked up. How great would it be to have something like a tail to create a playful puppet on the ends to entertain the children on reading day at the library? Ooh, maybe they could hold things with those strong-looking appendages. Think how easy it'd be to shelve books! Like having three hands instead of two.

Izzy cocked her head and watched Jaltaar's tail. It had a ball of fur like a dandelion at the end. "Is it because you have fur at the end of your tail and she doesn't?"

Said tail thumped as Jaltaar spun around.

Talira laughed. "Oh, I think she and I are going to get along just fine." She smiled, exposing her upper and lower fangs. "Izzy, can't you see I have gloriously long fur and he goes around practically naked with his minuscule excuse for a pelt?"

"Hey!" Jaltaar's tail wrapped around Talira's waist and brought her close to nuzzle her snout. "You stroke my minuscule excuse for a pelt every chance you get."

Talira purred and twined her tail with his. "Yes, I agree with the human. You are quite beautiful."

Izzy frowned. "The Alpha Regent wants to kill you because your fur is longer than his?"

How crazy was that?

Chapter Five

A block away from the Grub & Grog, Asmodel spotted the building Raxx had described. It was slightly larger than a shack, and its color was a deep, thick brick-red, reminiscent of congealing blood. But the neon image of an outlined three breasted sexbot was hard to miss. Especially since it throbbed on and off with mind-numbing consistency.

There. Raxx leaned against the dilapidated wall with one leg bent, his foot planted on the planks, staring off as if lost in thought.

The whispering sounds of the citizens moving about in the shadows were nonthreatening as they gave the strangers a wide berth.

Even though Asmodel didn't make a sound, Raxx jerked and looked their way. He shook his head as his lips curled in mirth. With a brief nod, he headed toward them with a swagger, as if he didn't have a care in the world. He approached Asmodel with a confident tilt of his head.

"Damn. Glad to see you've made out it of there in one piece." A hint of amusement laced Raxx's voice. "I gotta tell ya, I'm really impressed with you getting out of there." He narrowed his dark eyes and gave him an up-and-down look. "And nary a scratch, too." He held his hand out, his eyes glued to the side of Asmodel's chest where Echo lay. "You got my baby in there? She okay?"

Asmodel reached into his pocket and placed the oval device in Raxx's outstretched hand.

He brought Echo close and whispered soothing, soft words, stroking the top of the AI's metallic body. "You bodacious love o' mine. Come to Daddy."

Asmodel's eyebrows rose. The slang the man used wasn't like anything he'd heard since being brought into the future. He narrowed his eyes. There had to be more to this guy than he previously thought. "JR13?" He whispered to his bot as Raxx continued to speak to Echo in a soothing, singsong tone.

"Yeah, organic man?" JR13 sat in his favorite place on Asmodel's left shoulder. The bot lifted his chin.

"See if you have anything in your database about Raxx Jorlen, would you?"

The spider-shaped droid snorted. "I already did that." He lifted his right foreleg and waved it around. "In the general database, he's a blank slate. But I've asked Dad to look further into him."

It took a moment before Asmodel remembered JR13 called JR10 his father. He grunted. No doubt the older bot had vast resources, between Earth and Akurn at his disposal. Not to mention the resources from the Federation Consortium he had access to.

"Good. Let me know what he finds out."

JR13's only reply was another dismissive snort.

"How'd you get away unharmed?" Raxx clasped Echo back to the harness on his belt. "Everybody knows they are ruthless, bloodthirsty mercenaries who'll take any job as long as the price is right. One person against a group of them doesn't normally stand a chance."

Asmodel offered a wry smile and a shrug. No need to divulge his secrets. "Oh, they weren't all that bad. We just had a little fun keeping the locals entertained." He put his hand over his heart. "I have to tell you, your friends gave a captivating performance."

Raxx snorted, his eyes scanning the empty street. "Well, let's not stick around for an encore. I think you said you've got someplace to go?" He gestured to an innocuous bracelet on his wrist.

Ah, must be some type of sophisticated remote.

After a subtle click from Raxx's device, a sleek, dark shape descended from the night sky.

"There she is, my other baby, the *Shadow Drifter*. I activated her advanced-cloaking technology and kept her on standby until I was ready for her," Raxx explained. "And she's ready to rip."

As the ship landed, its ramp descended with a hiss, revealing a utilitarian interior.

Raxx led the way, his steps confident and assured.

Asmodel followed, impressed by the seamless operation.

Inside, Raxx headed straight for the cockpit, his hands dancing over the controls with practiced ease. "Buckle up." He didn't look back as he started the lift-off sequence. "Next stop, CeluriaVO."

Asmodel secured himself, and his mind raced with the possibilities of their impending journey. "Hey, just out of curiosity…how often do you make hasty retreats from angry alien mercenaries?"

Raxx laughed. The sound echoed in the confined space of the cockpit. "Ah, let's just say I like to keep life interesting."

The ship's engines roared to life, propelling them into the inky blackness of space, away from the depressing landscape of FiPan.

With a quick mental update to his brother Abalim, Asmodel sat back and let the strange human man take him to the tantalizing promise of the dark-haired beauty he'd seen in his vision.

The zinging cosmos outside the *Shadow Drifter's* cockpit was a vast tapestry of darkness and light, stars streaking past like fleeting thoughts.

Asmodel sat in contemplative silence, his gaze lost in the infinite expanse. Now that the fun tangling with the Vargrux was over, the weight of their recent narrow escape hung heavy on his mind. It might have been the most fun he'd had in a long time, but he had to admit it could have turned out different in a heartbeat.

A rambling sigh from Raxx shattered the silence. "I guess you're curious about the whole Vargrux debacle." He stared at the navigating console in front of him.

Asmodel turned from the window, the light reflecting off JR13 on his shoulder.

The silver-and-black spider body rested with his legs folded under him.

"The thought crossed my mind," Asmodel responded. Not really. But it was a good conversation starter. He laced his voice with calm curiosity.

Raxx chuckled dryly, a sound devoid of genuine humor. "Well, let's just say I possess something they desperately want back." He paused, and the corners of his mouth twitched in a slight grin. "And not just them. If anyone in the galaxy knew what I had, we'd have more to worry about than just those assholes." He leaned back and rotated his chair to face Asmodel. "Ever heard of the Quantum Lattice Resonator? The QLR?"

Asmodel's interest piqued, and his analytical mind latched onto the term. "Space-folding technology," he mused aloud. "I believe it's theoretical." He glanced at Raxx's smug expression. "Until now, I assume?"

Raxx nodded, a hint of pride breaking through his rugged demeanor. "Not so theoretical anymore. This ship"—he patted the console like a favorite pet— "is equipped with one, thanks to yours truly. Makes jumping vast distances more than just a fantasy. That's why we can shoot off to CeluriaVO without growing old on the way."

JR13 jumped up on all six legs. "Can I scan it?"

The breathless tone from the bot made Asmodel's eyebrows raise. The little guy's butt was quivering like a dog offered a juicy bone.

"Eh, no. I'm afraid Echo won't let you." Raxx laughed. "Yeah, she's a bit possessive about her QLR. Wants it all for herself."

Okay, change of subject. "So tell me, how are the Vargrux involved in all this?" Asmodel pressed.

Raxx's dark eyes reflected a mixture of pride and resolve. "Can't imagine why. All I did was 'borrow' their little toy they stole from god-knows-who," he admitted, his voice tinged with lighthearted defiance. "I gotta tell ya, after being stranded and left to rot in a forgotten corner of space more than once, you learn to take chances so it doesn't happen to you again. No matter how stupid it seems."

The mention of being stranded sparked a new layer of understanding in Asmodel. "Stranded?"

Raxx crossed his ankle over his thigh and linked his fingers together on his lap. "Back in good 'ol 1984 Earth, I was kidnapped by aliens when I was around twelve or so." He put up a hand to stop Asmodel from commenting. "I know, I know. Cliché, ain't' it?" He got a faraway look in his eyes. "A different life, a different world." He looked away with a wan smile. "I don't remember much about being taken from my friends' backyard." He rubbed his chin. "And I don't know if I was the only one taken or if my friends were as well. Hell, I never got a glimpse of the aliens who grabbed me." He straightened. "Hey, Echo, send me and my friend that special beer, would ya?"

He was silent for a moment.

Must be talking to his ship.

"Yeah, I get it. Okay, just one, Mom." Raxx's smile widened. "She bitches and nags better than my mom did on a bad day."

Two dark-cobalt bottles appeared on the console between them. The tops were open and teal-green bubbles fizzed over the lip and rolled lazily down the side of the bottles.

"Ah, my favorite!" Raxx grabbed the one closest to him and raised it in Asmodel's direction. "Glarthian Hopsar Ale." He winked before taking a deep draw. When he pulled the bottle back, he closed his eyes and smacked his lips with a deep sigh, followed by a loud belch. "Yeah, that's what I'm talkin' about."

Raxx opened his eyes and focused on Asmodel. "Well, go for it." He tsked, waving the bottom of his bottle in Asmodel's direction. "Trust me, you'll want nothin' else once you let this baby go down your gullet." He took another swig. "Damn, that's good."

The guy had almost finished his bottle, and Asmodel hadn't taken a taste yet. He took a cautious sip, and his senses were assaulted by a complex blend of flavors. Coating his mouth and tongue was a vivid fusion of sweet and bitter notes, reminiscent of dark cherries mixed with a tangy zest of an unknown alien grain. Underlying these were subtler hints of spice and something floral, creating a sensory experience unlike anything he'd encountered before. The aftertaste left a cooling, almost minty sensation, an underlying contrast to the initial robust flavors. He pulled the bottle back to examine it. Not sure if he liked it or not. He braved another taste. This time, the concoction went down smoothly with a bare hint of a bite. Its subtle bitterness lingered on his tongue. He wanted more. This time, he took a generous gulp before pulling the bottle away. He grinned, then belched. Loud enough to match Raxx's.

"Dude." Raxx put the end of his bottle out.

Not sure what the guy wanted, Asmodel glanced at him.

Raxx nodded and clicked the end of his now-empty bottle against Asmodel's nearly empty one. "Yeah, freakin' A."

Asmodel relaxed, his body warm and his thoughts light with a bare hint of fuzziness. Not enough to incapacitate him, just enough to release the tense pain pinching the back of his neck. He slouched back. "So—" He took the last gulp of the ale and put the empty bottle on the console next to Raxx. "—finish your story."

"Oh yeah. Where was I?" Raxx laced his hands over his flat stomach. "I guess I was in some type of stasis for what felt like centuries. Then, about twenty years ago, I was found on a shithole of a planet by some farmers plowing their field." He shrugged. "I was lucky they took me in and raised me. There was no sign of anyone else on that crashed ship but me."

Asmodel absorbed the tale, the pieces of the guy's life falling into place. "You've had quite the journey, Raxx."

Raxx looked at his hands. "Because Earth is in a protected status, I wasn't allowed to go back." He lifted his head, a mischievous smirk on his face. "But since you're from Earth, maybe I can talk you into smuggling me there."

Asmodel laughed. "I won't have to sneak you in. I bet if we offer Earth your QLR technology, we'll just waltz in like we own the place."

"Yeah, that might work." Raxx rubbed the side of his chin with his finger and thumb with a faraway look before shaking his head and glancing at Asmodel. "So, dude. What's your story?"

"Like you, I'm a man ripped out of his own time."

Asmodel told the other man about traveling seven thousand years into the future to help stop the Akurn aliens' invasion. And how he and his brothers were now tasked with finding some missing human women.

He omitted telling Raxx the more intimate details about himself, especially how he was a mix of human and alien DNA that created a powerful man with psychic abilities. Raised by the cruel and maniacal Akurns, he and his brothers struggled to trust anyone.

When he finished his short tale, they both fell silent. Asmodel couldn't help but think how two beings from vastly different worlds could be kindred lonely souls. While he had his brothers, the man next to him had no one except a bossy AI.

After a few comfortable moments, Raxx waved a hand over a light on the console in front of him. "Well, sit back and take a chill. It'll take me a momento to get the QRL ready. Then we'll book it to CeluriaVO and rescue the babe, eh?"

Asmodel nodded and studied the view through the cockpit window as the *Shadow Drifter* coursed through the silent void. For the first time in a long time, a sense of renewal gave him purpose. With the tentative bonds between him and Raxx becoming stronger, it wouldn't be a surprise if he and this man ended up more than just mistrusting strangers.

Maybe, for the first time in his life, he could call someone friend.

Asmodel settled in the seat beside Raxx aboard the *Shadow Drifter's* cockpit, the weight of anticipation pressing down on him with each passing moment.

Raxx faced him with a mischievous grin. "You ready, dude?" He put his right hand over a blinking yellow light on the panel next to him. "Once I punch this, it's all or nothin'."

Asmodel's eyebrows furrowed together. "What do you mean 'all or nothing'?"

"Well, ya know, there's no guarantee in life, my man. It's just I haven't had a chance to test this prototype yet." Raxx tilted his head and tugged on his earlobe with a grin. "Too busy runnin' from the Vargrux and all." He chuckled. "Hell, for all I know, it'll fold us into space and squish us into pancakes."

"I believe the human is misleading you." JR13's tone was matter-of-fact. "He and Echo have run thousands of simulations, and each one was successful."

Raxx wiggled his dark eyebrows up-and-down. "So, whaddya say, buddy? Ready to live dangerously?" He bobbed his hand over the yellow button, blinking in a lazy rhythm.

"I suppose..."

"Bitchin'! Let's do it!" Raxx slapped his palm on the light.

The Quantum Lattice Resonator roared to life.

The air in the cockpit thickened, charged with an unseen energy that made Asmodel's skin tingle at the unusual sensation. It didn't hurt, but it was nothing he'd ever experienced before. It was as if the very fabric of his being hummed in tune with the ship's escalating vibrations.

Outside the cockpit vid window, reality warped in ways that defied understanding. Stars elongated, stretching into brilliant streaks of light that painted the cosmos in surreal, shifting patterns. The constellations, once static and unchanging, now swirled as if stirred by an invisible hand. The universe itself turned into a fluid, malleable expanse, bending around the *Shadow Drifter* as it prepared to leap through the vastness of space.

A brief wave of vertigo hit Asmodel as the QLR engaged. The sensation vanished almost as quickly as it came, leaving him with a profound sense of detachment before he could even process what happened. Time and space were irrelevant as he struggled to describe the indescribable.

On the outside vid, the spectacle calmed. The stars realigned, snapping back into unfamiliar positions with an abruptness that was startling in its normalcy. If he understood the mechanics correctly, the *Shadow Drifter* had just crossed an unimaginable distance in the blink of an eye. An outstanding feat that left Asmodel breathless with the sheer impossibility of it all.

Beside him, Raxx let out a loud whoop with a wide grin. "That was hellacious!" His eyes never looked away from the controls. "Echo, analyze the results and confirm where we are."

A small ping rang in the cockpit.

Asmodel shook his head in wonder. How strange that the universe, vast and mysterious, just shrank a little more. The Quantum Lattice Resonator wasn't just a tool; it was a key to untold adventures, a door to the unknown. And he was one of the first to step through that door.

"Great!" Raxx announced. "Echo has confirmed we are minimal parsecs from the planet CeluriaVO." He blinked, then chuckled. "Yeah, hail them."

"Wait." Asmodel reached over and grasped Raxx's arm. A hard sensation of caution cloaked him. "Let's look around first."

Raxx's dark eyes stared at him before he shrugged. "Okay, dude. Whateva. It's your call." He glanced at the star-studded view screen. "We're just outside their communication scans. Should I cloak the *Drifter*?"

"Yes. I'd rather we did some investigating before we announce ourselves." Asmodel leaned back and rubbed the side of his prickly jaw. It helped him think. "While I'm pretty sure Isabella Torres is on this planet—" His psychic sense hadn't been wrong before. "—I'd like your ship to scan the surface and see if there's a human there." Hate for this to be the first time his senses were wrong. No telling what he'd do if that happened.

"Echo insists you call her by her name and not just *ship*." Raxx chuckled and shook his head. "My beauty is stubborn." He leaned back in his command chair and linked his fingers behind his head. "Go ahead, babe. You know you're just jonesing for a chance to learn as much as you can about the place." He glanced at Asmodel with a wink. "You know you can't resist learning about a new culture."

"While Echo is using her own sensors, I will do the same." JR13 wasn't asking for permission.

For the first time, Asmodel understood the urge to roll his eyes. "Of course. Thanks."

"Ah, great." Raxx sat forward, dropping his hands to the counsel. "Echo has confirmed there is a human female on CeluriaVO. Would you like her to bring up the woman's image?"

"You can do that?" Asmodel's heart raced. Partly from relief that he was right and partly from hoping to get a clear picture of the woman he'd only gotten a brief glimpse of in a quick vision.

Raxx's sniff was pure scorn. "Dude."

Without another word, a holographic image of a woman appeared on the console.

Asmodel sucked in a hard breath, staring in awe. There she was, the woman with a captivating, natural beauty. Her warm, olive-toned complexion radiated a healthy glow, and her large, expressive coffee-colored eyes sparkled with curiosity and kindness. Dark, luscious tresses framed her face, falling around her shoulders in a silky curtain and framing her stunning features. Her subtle, inviting smile revealed aligned, pearly-white teeth, outlined by plush, kiss-worthy lips.

Holding his breath, Asmodel let his gaze roam down her figure. While her clothes might have seen better days, the overall impression was someone with a gentle nature. Her downy pastel-colored sweater hugged her full breasts, and its soft hues highlighted the warm glow of her radiant complexion. Her loose-fitting pants were in a delicate pattern. To complete her ensemble were comfortable-looking shoes made of some kind of canvas with a rubber sole in a light pink that graced her feet.

He clenched his hands to stop from reaching out, as if he had the right to touch her. How could this hologram shake him to his core? She was just one woman out of millions—no, wait—billions on Earth. Once he tasted freedom in the modern world, he and his brothers indulged in the mind-numbing choice of females around them, willing to partake in a variety of sexual pursuits.

Never, not once, had he reacted to anyone like he was with this mere image. A sense of possessiveness overwhelmed him. *She was his.* The thought took him aback, leaving a sour taste in his mouth. Just his luck—the way he was acting, he'd probably turn into a total ass when he met her face-to-face. Swallowing hard, he chastised himself for lusting after Isabella, but he still couldn't tear his eyes away from her captivating image.

Watching Talira and Jaltaar nuzzle and lick each other's snouts as they said their goodbyes gave Izzy the warm fuzzies. She sighed. Too bad the constraints of their society kept them apart. Kind of like Romeo and Juliet with fur. Izzy crossed her arms with a huff. Prejudices about how someone looked always irritated her, especially when directed at her. As a proud Latina, she'd had her share of uncompromising bigots who'd take one look at her brown skin and think she was stupid or only good for menial labor.

Or worse. Make a living on her back or as a drug mule for the bullies in her neighborhood. But, as her *abuela* drilled into her, "You are more than your appearance."

She took that advice to heart and worked her way through high school and college to get her library science degree. Even though her grandmother died during Izzy's first year of college, she never looked back and pursued her goal with single-minded determination.

"*Tsuki*, please be careful," Jaltaar rumbled the request at Talira, holding the back of her head in his large paw, placing his forehead against hers.

The striking difference in their fur textures made Izzy sigh again. They were so beautiful together.

"I hate being apart like this," he continued. "But I promise it won't be much longer. Once we deal with this Krystalii problem, we'll go before your council and petition about us living there together."

Talira smoothed her snout against his before stepping back. "I've been working on changing their minds about you for months now. I think if we can keep this human away from your Alpha Regent, together we can dispose of that crystal creature."

"Yes." Jaltaar nodded. "In the meantime, contact the Federation Consortium and tell them what's happening here. Let them know they'd better send someone to get Izzy and keep the Krystalii from getting their hands on her." His large body shivered. "No telling what those bastards would do to her when they try to make her species computable to theirs."

Yeah, Izzy wasn't on board with letting that happen either. Suddenly, a flashback hit her. The image of a painfully handsome man with dark, silky, brown hair framing a face too perfect to be real. She imagined she'd pleaded with him to find her. Telling him she was on CeluriaVO. He yelled, "Wait!" with an outstretched hand, an intense expression on his face, before he disappeared.

Izzy sighed. *Geeze Louise.* She'd give anything for someone like that in real life coming for her.

"Come on, Izzy. We'd better go before Jaltaar's troops find us."

Izzy jumped at the sound of Talira's voice. Putting a hand over her racing heart, she gave the pretty cat-woman a small smile. "Okay, I'm with you." She followed behind the lithe grace of the female trotting ahead of her.

Talira glanced behind them.

Which, of course, made Izzy do the same.

There stood Jaltaar with his striking colorful eyes glued to their retreating forms.

Izzy gave him a small departing wave before looking in front of her to watch where she was going. The last thing she needed to do was to fall flat on her face, tripping over a rock or something.

She shortened the distance between her and Talira in the dense foliage of the CeluriaVO jungle. Large fronds and feather-leaves brushed against her arms and face with each step. The air was thick with humidity and carried a symphony of scents—fragrant blooms with a sweet, heady perfume that mingled with the earthy musk of moist soil and the tangy aroma of strange fruits dangling from the twisted branches.

The forest floor was spongy under her feet, a carpet of mosses and unknown foliage that cushioned each step, so her stumbling progress was silent except when she occasionally stepped on a twig or swatted a biting bug. Overhead, the canopy formed a living mosaic of colors as sunlight filtered through, the beams dancing with a mix of floating spores and tiny, luminescent insects. Together, they added to the ethereal beauty all around her.

All at once, Izzy's nose twitched as a rancid stench burned. "What's that smell?"

"A skalderbeast is hunting us," Talira whispered. "Stay close and we'll be out of his territory soon." Her striped tail flicked in silent agitation. Despite the warning, her voice was calm, a stark contrast to the chaotic chorus of alien wildlife around them.

No telling what a skalderbeast was, but from its smell, it couldn't be good. Izzy jumped when exotic creatures skittered and slithered around her. Small winged insects danced above her like living embers. In the distant were roars of unseen predators. Good golly, that said it all. She was nowhere near home. A group of strange creatures resembling frogs caught her eye. They had translucent skin that revealed their luminescent innards, and were perched on feathery branches, eying them with four eyes that rotated as they passed.

A thundering growl pierced the air in the seemingly never-ending jungle.

Talira didn't change her stride, moving with purpose as she guided them through hidden trails and secret paths. "Don't worry, we're almost there."

The underbrush became less dense, the air cooler, and the sounds of the jungle fainter. Ahead, the forest opened, revealing a towering cliff face. The mouth of a vast cave yawned like a portal into another world.

Talira approached a seemingly random section of the rocky wall and pressed her palm against it.

The stone shimmered and then dissolved into thin air, revealing the entrance to a hidden village.

Izzy's eyes widened as she followed Talira inside.

The cave was alive with activity, illuminated by glowing crystals hanging from the ceiling like stars in a subterranean night sky. Structures of stone and natural materials adorned the carved cave walls.

The harmonious blend of nature and scikvak craftsmanship took Izzy's breath away.

The sound of bubbling water flowing from various natural springs created a serene scene, the soft melody echoing.

"Welcome to Nekojin." Talira's eyes gleamed. "This is where the pardalions thrive, away from zaltrixan tyranny."

The villagers, in their long midnight-blue fur with their distinctive tiger stripes, stopped and stared at Izzy.

She didn't get a sense of hostility, just expressions with a non-threatening mix of curiosity and caution. Children peeked from behind adults, their eyes wide and filled with wonder as their tails swished behind them.

Relief washed over Izzy. Here, in this hidden sanctuary, the weight of what she'd been through melted away. Her journey might be far from over, but in the heart of the pardalion hidden village, she experienced a flicker of hope. Maybe, just maybe, she could catch her breath and figure out what to do next.

Chapter Six

"Well, how in the hell are we going to get over there?"

Asmodel winced at Raxx's question. After the man landed the *Shadow Drifter* in a small clearing, he and his new companion slipped through a small sliver of a dense jungle until they reached the edge of a cliff. Squatting on one knee, he stared at the panorama before them.

Across the gorge was the capital city of CeluriaVO, Panterion Prime. Instead of a conglomerate of buildings settling on flat land, the alien city was built along the sheer walls of the cliff. Its structures were seamlessly integrated into the rock, with buildings clinging to the vertical surface like natural extensions of the stone.

The vast metropolis spread out for miles, a prime example of an advanced technological civilization that made the alien planet Akurn look like a primitive village of cave dwellers. Rushes of gentle waterfalls created clouds of moisture-laden fog that swirled up from the dark canyon bottom below and surrounded the natural foliage between the dwellings.

"How do you suppose we..." Raxx began.

"I think someone..." JR13 said at the same time.

"Stand up and turn around." A growling, hissing voice interrupted them. "Slowly, where I can see your paws."

Asmodel closed his eyes and groaned. How the hell did he get caught like this? Clenching his fingers, he slowly stood. He was such an idiot. How could he forget to keep his psychic senses open? *By the love of a motherless goat.* If Arakiba ever found out...

It was a male scikvak. Some kind of guard, if he wasn't mistaken. Easy enough to tell with the guy pointing a long, hollow pole made of a dull, silver metal in their direction. Asmodel doubted the guy was going to whack them over the head with the thing. Had to be armed with a laser of some kind.

"JR13—" He tilted his head and whispered to his AI bot, never taking his eyes off the scikvak as he raised his hands. "—when he gets close enough, can you render him unconscious?"

The spider-bot snorted. "Of course, organic man."

"Stop talking." The guy stepped closer and poked Asmodel in his chest with the end of the pole.

"Now listen, friend," Raxx smiled wide, his hands high in the air. "We're just visitin'..."

"You will be quiet!"

The guard shoved Raxx with the pole on his shoulder so hard he stumbled.

"Now, JR13!" Asmodel stressed in a low voice.

The black plates on JR13's back fanned open, revealing soft, iridescent wings. Without a word, he jumped from Asmodel's shoulder and headed straight for the shoulder of the scikvak, whose back was to him. He landed by the short fur between the male's shoulder and neck and drove his spindly foreleg into the skin.

The male dropped to the unforgiving ground.

"Duude!" Raxx's dark eyes widened. "Did you just give him a Vulcan neck pinch?"

Asmodel frowned. A what?

"Affirmative," JR13 answered him. He flew back to rest on Asmodel's shoulder and sniffed as if exasperated.

Raxx whooped with laughter. Asshole didn't bother to put his hands down yet.

"Can we focus, here?" Asmodel gestured to the prone guard. "I'm sure he's not the only one around."

"He's not." JR13 interjected. "I can hear the communication he has in his ear. Someone is trying to get hold of him. I'll put it on audio," he volunteered.

"Cool beans, Spider-man." Raxx put his hands down. He squatted next to the unconscious feline and turned him over.

"Talonar! Do you have them? Talonar, report!" The command came through loud and clear.

Asmodel made a split decision. He turned to JR13. "Can you respond for us?"

"Of course." The small droid snorted. "I can even sound like this guy." His multifaceted eyes studied the unmoving male. "What do you want me to say?"

"Respond by saying one of them got away, but he'll bring in the other one." He snapped his fingers. "Oh, wait. Find out where they want him to meet them." He looked around the dense jungle behind them and glanced at the futuristic city across the gorge. "Hopefully on this side of the canyon."

"What are ya gonna do?" One of Raxx's black eyebrows raised. "Turn into one of them?" He grinned.

"Yeah." Asmodel grinned back. "Unless you got any other ideas?"

Raxx shook his head. "Nope. Not really."

"Okay, then." Asmodel pulled his shirt off. "Strip the guy so I can wear his clothes."

Both Raxx's brows rose. "Even his underwear? That'd be heinous, man."

JR13 snickered.

"Yeah, ah, unnecessary."

He drew the line at wearing something another guy had against his dangly bits.

"Yo, here's hoping you aren't allergic to cats."

Damn, he never thought of that. But it was too late to back out now. He pulled his pants off, leaving him in his tight briefs. "I guess we'll find out."

Asmodel transformed into the prone guard and finished putting on the creature's battle-suit clothing. Once everything was in place, he used his telekinetic ability and transferred the unconscious guard to the nearby thick underbrush. With a brush of his mind, he covered the cat-man with leaves and loose branches. The poor guy would wake up in a couple of hours confused, but otherwise healthy.

Hopefully, they'd be on board the *Shadow Drifter* with Izzy long before then.

"Here they come." Holding his hands out, Raxx faced Asmodel. "Hurry, put me in those cuffs you found on our friend."

To conserve his psychic strength, he unhooked a set of binders from the belt he'd "borrowed" and clicked them around Raxx's wrists, over the sleeves of the leather jacket he wore. That way, the metallic cuffs wouldn't eat into his skin.

"That okay?" Asmodel asked.

Raxx tried to pull his arms apart, but they stayed in place. "It'll do for now." A sheepish grin creased his lips. "Just keep the key handy, will ya?"

Asmodel gave him a lopsided grin before glancing at JR13 on his shoulder. "Better get yourself out of sight."

"No, really?" JR13 snarky reply came as he scuttled and hid in a side pocket on the battle-suit vest. "All set, organic man." The muffled announcement was reassuring.

With the thick, wiry midnight blue-fur of his Scikvak form, Asmodel didn't feel the small bot's pointed legs brushing across him. He'd better keep extra vigilance on his companion since he couldn't rely on his sense of touch to do so.

"Talonar!" A male scikvak barked the name as he and several others burst through the brush. "Report!"

"Yes, sir!" Asmodel jerked to attention. Not sure if he was supposed to salute or something similar, he stood with his cat ears flattened sideways. Clutching the long pole weapon the scikvak threatened them with, he kept the end on the ground. One good thing about taking the shape of an existing organic creature, the body knew how to react even if he didn't. "I followed this creature from the crash site and captured him."

The leader walked around Raxx with the end of his thick tail pointed upwards. "I find it extremely odd that this human was on the same ship as the Ozevroc."

Asmodel had no idea what an Ozevroc was.

"That's the race of alien that took Isabella Torres." JR13's voice was low, but loud enough for Asmodel to hear. "That makes sense. He's suspicious since that kind of ship was a one-seater."

"I haven't questioned him yet, sir." Asmodel turned to Raxx. Hopefully, the guy came up with something.

The leader humphed. "You, human. Were you on that ship that crashed?" The cat-man looked him over. "You don't look the worse for wear."

"Name's Raxx Jorlen, friend." Raxx put his bound hands over his heart with a slight bow, never taking his eyes off the leader. "I was an unfortunate prisoner of the Ozevroc." He pointed a thumb behind him to the black smoke rising in the distance. "That rat bastard had more than one stasis pod on the ship, ya know?"

"Do you know if there were any other humans on that ship?"

Raxx shrugged. "Not that I know of."

"Commander Jaltaar." One soldier behind the leader approached him with dark ears back and flat against his head. "The Supreme Alpha Regent is insisting on an update."

The commander hissed.

Asmodel took a chance and touched his mind. The scikvak was not pleased about talking to whomever the regent was.

"All of you, monitor this human while I speak to the regent." The male walked a few steps away and touched a claw to the front of the black leather collar around his thick neck. Whatever he said was drowned out by the general rumblings of the group of soldiers around Asmodel.

"Hey, Talonar." One of the soldiers approached him with a hissing whisper. "You feeling alright? Your voice sounds funny and you're standing strange."

Damn observant scikvak. Before he responded, another guard piped in.

"I bet the kid got caught by surprise and won't admit it!"

This one was thicker in body and neck than the others and had a long scar sideswiping his face from the top of his right eye to the tip of his chin. His jowls jiggled as he hissed with laughter.

"Leave the kid alone, Varex." The first guard responded. "As I remember, you got that scar from a skalderbeast on your first assignment, didn't you?"

"Shut up, Sylas." The larger scikvak grumbled.

"Time to go." Commander Jaltaar rejoined the group. "We're to take this human back to the regent for questioning."

"Aren't we supposed to be looking for a human female?" Varex questioned, his tail swishing back and forth on the moist ground.

"They've sent the drone patrol out to look for any other heat signatures." Jaltaar responded. He glanced at the scarred guard with a brief nod. "Sylas, activate the bridge."

"Yes, sir!" Sylas snapped to attention before pulling out a handheld device that fit in his large paw. The alloy covering the device had intricate etchings that swirled and coalesced at a random pace. With a click of one claw, a holographic picture of a luminescent bridge appeared. With another quick touch, the same bridge solidified between the cliff where they stood and ended at a large building on the opposing cliff face.

"Alright, troop. Let's head home." Jaltaar led the way.

For the first time, Asmodel noticed the bow slung across his back and a gripper holding a quiver of arrows. With a grimace, he met Raxx's gaze before they followed the others across the rainbow-hued bridge.

"Talira." A young female pardalion rushed toward them, out of breath. She grasped Talira by her upper arm, licking her whiskers. The pretty orange stripes on the dark-blue fur between her eyes and down her snout were messy, as if she'd swiped her paw across it one too many times. Her golden eyes were wide and dilated as she panted.

Izzy stared at the youngster who had to be in her formative pubescent years.

"Calm down, Zolune." Talira stroked the smaller female on her snout and smoothed the ruffled fur. "Why are you so jumpy?"

"The elders have the chancellor of the Federation Consortium on the vid, and he's asking for *you*!" Her last word came out in an excited whisper.

Talira's thin black lips lifted across her delicate snout into an indulgent smile. She patted the young female on her shoulder. "That's good, Zolune. Nothing to worry about. It's going to save me time since I planned on talking to him, anyway."

"Really?" the youngling gushed. "Can I watch?"

Talira nodded. "Of course." She wagged a finger at her. "But you must observe only. No talking or you'll have to leave."

"Oh, I promise!" Zolune vowed with a lifted paw. "Thank you, Talira."

Talira glanced over her shoulder at Izzy before turning back to the young female. "This is Izzy, our guest. Would you make sure she doesn't get lost? I can't tell you how much that would be a big help."

Zolune's chest puffed with pride. "I'd be honored to!" Her golden eyes focused on Izzy. "I've never seen a human before." Her head tilted. "Oh, wow. You don't have any fur. Aren't you cold all the time?"

Izzy grinned. "I guess I am." She waved her hand over her torso. "That's why we wear clothes and don't run around naked." She pretended to shiver. "Every day we have to be plan what to wear so we don't find ourselves exposed to the harsh elements and get sick."

Zolune's snout scrunched as she glanced down at the one-piece jumper she had on. "I don't know what I'd do if I had to think about what I wore all the time. But don't you worry. Stick with me and I'll make sure you don't go someplace where you'd get hurt."

Izzy nodded. "I really appreciate it." She smiled and looked at Talira's retreating figure. "I guess we'd better catch up before she starts without us."

"Come on!" Zolune waved for Izzy to follow. "It's not far." She pointed one of her stubby paw forefingers at a large opening on the opposite end. "If we're lucky, they'll be serving something to eat!"

With any luck, Zolune was right that it wasn't far. If she had to keep this fast pace for long, she'd pass out. Didn't matter if it happened because of the lack of exercise or food. Face-planting in a strange place among aliens was never a good look.

Izzy trailed behind Talira, tired and hungry. With weary eyes, she watched Zolune skip beside her. The child pointed out places and people of interest, and the vibrant life pulsating within the cave village of Nekojin was impressive.

Looming ahead was a vast, illuminated cavern. The sheer width and breadth of it made it feel like she was about to step into the heart of CeluriaVO itself. Swirling bioluminescent fungi cast a soft glow and bathed the natural stone amphitheater in an ethereal light. The air was a mix of earthen musk and the sharp tang of electric machinery humming in the background. Even though she walked within a natural cave, the advanced technology around her was a stark reminder of the scikvak who created a harmonious blend of nature and advanced technology.

Around her, the cavern was alive with activity, buzzing with the indistinct murmurs of the scikvak as they moved about, their striped fur shifting like shadows under the luminous light.

At the far end, a group sat around a huge U-shaped table made of rock, their attention fixed on a large, crystal-clear HD screen. An image of a striking blond male flickered.

Her eyes widened. He had to be a Zerin, one of the aliens who invited her to join their exchange to find true love. Next to him was a pretty Zerin female, with dark-blonde hair and gray eyes. Wait, gray eyes? Every Zerin she'd ever seen or met had dual color eyes in some shade of green. Not a single color like this one had. Then she noticed the woman's ears. They had a rounded top, like a human's, not pointed like a Zerin's. How odd.

"Ah, here she is, Chancellor E'etu."

An imposing male scikvak stood, his silky long fur whirling around his exposed muscular arms that matched the glorious puff of hair covering his thick tail that lazily swished behind him.

The bright orange stripes on his face framed his eyes like eyeliner, giving him an almost feminine, exotic demeanor in a contrast to the low, deep masculine tone of his voice.

Talira waved Izzy to a chair next to her.

With a whoosh of gratitude, Izzy sat, thankful to be off her feet. She swallowed as a wave of exhaustion threatened to take over. She barely glanced at the other scikvak around the table. Her only impression was a mixture of male and female, young as well as old.

"Zolune, rush to the meal area and bring Izzy something to eat and drink." Talira told the young female. "Straight there and back, you understand?"

"Oh yes, Talira! You can count on me." Zolune rushed off, her thick thigh muscles undulating under her suit with each leap.

"Thank you, Praetor Vorlok."

The Zerin on the vid responded, his resplendent dual-color turquoise eyes zeroing in on Izzy. "I am the chancellor of the Federation Consortium, D'zia E'etu. Are you Isabella Pilar Ramierz Torres from New York City of Earth?"

Izzy nodded and interlaced her fingers on the top of the granite tabletop. "Yes, but please call me Izzy. I was on the *StarChance,* headed to the exchange, when I was forced to leave the ship before it reached orbit around the Zerin space station."

"Holy shamoka, sister. I know how you feel, since the same thing happened to me!" The woman next to the chancellor slapped her hand on the surface in front of her. Because she was transmitted in hologram form, the only sound was a muted thump when her hand hit the table. "How are you doing, doll?"

At first, Izzy had a hard time responding. The woman's declaration was so outlandish, it was hard to focus. Biting her bottom lip, she studied the vid image of the woman closer. Now the glaring differences she noticed at first were more prominent, but after the woman pounded the table, it was clear she had four fingers instead of three in equal lengths like a Zerin. Also, her Caucasian-colored skin had a slight iridescent sheen, even though the shine wasn't as deep as the male's next to her.

"I'm okay. Thanks for asking." Izzy tilted her head. "But, I hope you don't mind asking, were you were once a human?"

The woman laughed. "Yep, I was born Lora Callahan from Sioux Falls, South Dakota. Now I'm this one's Truebond." She lovingly glanced at her mate next to her, who placed his large hand over hers, as his return gaze softened his handsome face. Lora continued. "When that happened, I took on a lot of Zerin characteristics. Let me tell you, I couldn't be happier."

"Wow." Izzy sat back. "That's, ah, something."

"Which leads me to what we were first discussing." The chancellor returned his gaze to Praetor Vorlok, who'd retaken his seat. "Have you been able to verify the Krystalii is at Panterion Prime?"

Talira sat in a seat next to Izzy. She nodded. "Yes, my zaltrixan contact has confirmed a Krystalii is negotiating with Supreme Alpha Regent Korves."

An angry murmur sounded around the table.

Her midnight-blue eyes narrowed. "I'm afraid it's worse than we feared."

Immediate silence as all eyes focused on her.

"From what I was told, the Alpha Regent has agreed to turn over this female." She gestured to Izzy with a pointed claw. "And in exchange, the Krystalii will eliminate our people and our way of life."

Now the angry murmur turned into a riotous roar from the throats of the cat people.

Izzy sat there, stunned, as tears gathered. No... no. There's no way she wanted to be part of an entire race becoming extinct!

"We must get this human off CeluriaVO as soon as possible!" The cry came from an elderly female who pounded her fist on the table.

The voices lowered, but the anger hung heavy in the air.

"Yes, yes, Madam Fexa." Praetor Vorlok gestured to the Zerins on the vid. "We have requested assistance from the Federation, and they realize the severity of our situation. That's why we are speaking to the chancellor himself!"

"Quite right, Praetor Vorlok." Chancellor E'etu confirmed. "The Krystalii are not only threatening CeluriaVO, but all the organic life in the Milky Way. To aid in their domination, their leader is obsessed with obtaining a human female. He's sent out scouts to infiltrate our galaxy to grab human females and somehow combine their DNA with theirs. He's convinced once he does this, it'll give him the ability to speed up their birth cycle."

Izzy frowned as the chancellor gave a worried glance at Lora next to him. The woman's return gaze wasn't any more reassuring. It looked like they didn't have any idea how this strange Krystalii could use human women to intermingle with their non-organic species either.

"We've already sent an emissary to CeluriaVO to retrieve Ms. Torres. His name is Asmodel." A portrait of an impossibly handsome man replaced the chancellor's image. The 3-D picture rotated, giving everyone in the room a clear image.

Izzy gasped. The man's Native American features were symmetrical, making his masculine beauty almost impossible to believe. Her heart thundered, banishing all weariness, as his imposing, motionless figure captured her. If he looked half as good as his picture, what would he be like in reality? She shuddered to imagine.

"This man's sole purpose is to ensure the human woman's safe return." The chancellor's image returned, and his voice resonated throughout the cavern. He locked his gaze on Izzy through the screen as if to reassure her. "We have determined he has landed safely on CeluriaVO and is searching for you." His striking turquoise eyes looked away as if he was reading a report on another screen. "From our last communication, he is on his way to Panterion Prime to look for you there."

Talira gasped. "They'll arrest him!" She glanced at Izzy. "Or worse, execute him as an example of good faith to the Krystalii."

"Can you contact him to let him know she is here with us?" Madam Fexa asked.

The chancellor frowned. "Unfortunately, once he entered the city, all communication with him has been cut off. However, rest assured, we are looking into other options."

A hushed silence fell over the cavern.

Dread pressed on Izzy at the gravity of the situation. A hard knot formed in her stomach, a mix of fear and anticipation at the mention of Asmodel—a man who came all this way to save her and didn't know he was walking into a dangerous situation.

The gentle glow from the HD screen illuminated the concerned faces of the scikvak ruling body.

Their solemn commitment to not only her safety but saving their species was clear to see. Yet, despite the otherworldly beauty of the cavern and the sophisticated technology before her, Izzy couldn't shake the feeling she was a pawn in a much larger game—one that spanned galaxies with consequences far beyond her understanding. She didn't pay attention to the last few words discussed between the chancellor and the pardalions as they ended their communication.

Around the table, the meeting continued. Heated discussions ensued, getting louder with each argument about what their next steps should be.

It dawned on Izzy she wasn't part of the plans. She raised her hand. "Excuse me." Her voice was too low to overcome the lively discussions at raised volume. She cleared her throat and increased her volume. "Um... good people? Hello? Can I say something?"

"Yes." Praetor Vorlok nodded to her. He raised a paw at the male next to him, who continued to hiss in argument. Vorlok gave him a low growl that made the other guy shut up. "Now, human Izzy from Earth. You wish to say something?"

"Thank you, Praetor Vorlok." She stood with her hands clasped in front of her. Keeping her expression firm, she eyed each one to let them know she meant business. "Since I am the only human here, it's up to me to go to Panterion Prime and help rescue my fellow human, Asmodel." Just saying his name caused a memory of that handsome man telling her he'd find her. Well, that went both ways. He vowed to find her, and she refused to do anything less.

The male next to Praetor Vorlok snorted. "You look weak at best, and a burden at worst."

"Now, Caln. Let's not be judgmental." Praetor Vorlok admonished the male. "Let's hear what she has to say." He leaned forward with his elbows on the table. "Now tell me, my dear. Why should we allow you to put yourself in danger and join this rescue party? What skills do you bring?"

Izzy gave the obvious answer.

"Why, I'm a librarian!"

Chapter Seven

"Hey, organic man."

JR13's voice drifted up from Asmodel's vest pocket.

Asmodel looked around, following close behind Raxx. They'd finished crossing the bridge and now traveled through a wide and airy tunnel leading to a large building that might be a military headquarters.

Scikvak of all shapes, sizes, and sexes rushed about with stern expressions. The tense, no-nonsense atmosphere permeated the air, as if fear was an underlying theme of their lives.

"Yeah?" He made sure his voice was a mere whisper. No need to alert the others about his droid friend.

"You want the good news or the bad news first?"

Good thing the soldiers surrounding Raxx weren't paying attention to him since the bot wanted to play word games. Swallowing his impatience, the words came out between clenched teeth. "Let's start with the good news."

"My father just informed me they have located the human woman Isabella Torres here on CeluriaVO. She's safe with the minority faction called the pardalions."

Well, that *was* good news. Sounds like JR13 knew where she was in this large metropolis. Then it'd be easy enough to teleport the three of them to Raxx's ship. "Good. Tell me how to get to where she is."

JR13 snorted. "Well now, that's the bad news. She's at Nekojin, a cave village several kilometers away. It would take you a whole day to get there if you went by foot."

Oh, for the love of a motherless goat. It would've been helpful to know that before they entered the city. Asmodel looked around.

The guards all wore serious, stern expressions. The fur on their tails was puffed and their claws were wrapped around the weapons they carried.

Asmodel focused his attention on Commander Jaltaar. The overwhelming sense of fear coming off the male was a surprise. Probing deeper, he discovered his terror had nothing to do with him personally. It was a female scikvak he recently met in the jungle. With a sharp tendril of psychic energy, Asmodel entered the male's memories and discovered not only the illicit meeting he had with a female, but that he'd left Izzy with that female. Tal.... The female's name was Talira.

Asmodel pulled out. It was obvious Izzy was in excellent hands for now. But the village where Talira took her to lacked the advancements of Panterion Prime. If any zaltrixan found out where she was, it wouldn't be hard for them to capture her.

He took a chance to get into Raxx's mind without Echo blocking him.

Raxx. He whispered mentally. *It's Asmodel. Can you hear me?*

The man didn't so much as stumble. *Fuckin' A, dude. I should have known you were some type of freaky.* A mental sigh. *Okay, what now?*

JR13, just told me Izzy isn't here. She's in some type of village a day away from here.

Yeah, I know. Raxx shrugged his shoulder as if to settle a cramp. *Echo heard the message from his father to him.* He twisted his neck until it cracked.

Asmodel narrowed his eyes at the back of Raxx's neck. He didn't have time to bitch at Raxx for using Echo to listen in on JR13's transmissions. Letting his irritation go, he addressed what was more important. *We've got to get out of here and find her.*

Yeah? And just how are we supposed to do that? The tone in Raxx's answer was full of snark.

Once I put my hand on your shoulder, I can teleport us back to your ship.

Way cool, man! Wait, I think we're here.

Sure enough, the troop stopped before a huge double door with elaborate etchings of gold on the wooden surface. As the soldiers faced it, they stomped their booted feet in unison and snapped their fisted paws across their chest.

Their leader, Jaltaar, faced the two guards outside the door. "Announce us immediately."

"Yes, Commander!" The guard on the right snapped to attention and placed his paw on a panel on the wall behind him.

The doors had to be ten feet tall and slid open sideways, disappearing into the wall.

Hang on. Let's hold off for now. Raxx suggested. *If we just disappear, we won't know what they're planning. Besides, I'm dying to see what's on the other side of this door. Maybe when this is all over, there might be an opportunity for me to open some kind of trade with them.*

Asmodel grunted. He was right. And it couldn't hurt to see the dynamics on CeluriaVO. Maybe they'd end up as allies in the upcoming fight against the Krystalii.

Once they crossed the threshold, Asmodel stopped. There, sitting next to the obvious Supreme Alpha Regent Krovex, was a crystalline creature of bright yellow. She had to be the same species as the blue crystal man Abalim showed them on the video he brought back from the *Galaxy's Pub* on Hiigar. What took him aback was the alien was in a humanoid feminine form, dressed in a sheer, wispy luminescent gown that left nothing to the imagination.

"Who is this, Jaltaar?" The regent stood. The orange stripes bisecting his forehead went around his cheeks and down the sides of his throat. "I told you to bring back a human female." His thick claws slid out as he waved to Raxx. "I may not know anything about humans, but I know that is not a female."

"Too right, my man!" Raxx grinned and acted like he wasn't in a life-threatening situation. "Glad you recognize I'm one hundred percent macho man."

"Quiet, human." Jaltaar's voice had a bite of a hiss. "You will only speak if the regent or the Krystalii, Prisma-Solara, addresses you."

"Sure, sure." Raxx rocked back and forth with a grin. "Whateva you say, dude."

The crystal female gracefully rose from her seat and approached Raxx, her glowing eyes deepening in intensity. She gave him a brief up-and-down look before focusing on Asmodel in his scikvak disguise.

"What have we here?" She reached out and poked his forehead with a slim finger.

Asmodel didn't feel her touch as a wave of overpowering psychic energy hit him like a sledgehammer. He staggered as his body reformed without his control. When the sensation subsided, he slowly opened his eyes and stood in his full normal form. Thank the goddess, the scikvak clothing conformed to his bigger size.

The room filled with a collective gasp.

"Ah, another human." The female's voice was lyrical in its derision. "But yet not." Her shrug came across stilted and abnormal, as if she was trying to imitate something she didn't understand. "Tell me, abominable one, where is the female?" She moved in closer.

Asmodel's eyebrows rose at the warmth coming from her body as she stood mere inches from his chest. At first, he didn't understand the malicious glee crossing her face, until a small, worming sensation burrowed into his mind. With impenetrable firmness, Asmodel thwarted the crystal woman's attempt to enter his consciousness. But he couldn't prevent the grip she had on his body. "I don't know what you're talking about." His slight grin wasn't nice.

Her lips pinched, causing their deep-gold color to lighten.

Ah, frustration looked good on her.

"No matter. I don't need to enter your mind to know you're not suitable." Prisma-Solara gestured to Raxx. "However, here is a pure human." She narrowed her light-yellow eyes as she walked around Raxx's bound form. "Yes, he just might do. Who says I need a female?" She glanced at the Supreme Regent. "Since I have a human right here, why bother looking for another one?" She placed a hand on Raxx's chest and closed her eyes.

Raxx jerked out of her hold. "Hands off the goods, dudette. Or you'll be sorry."

Asmodel frowned at the man. *Don't antagonize her. She's a powerful psychic.* He warned Raxx mentally.

Oh, please. As if.

An evil leer crossed Prisma-Solara's clear lips. She reached out to touch him again.

Raxx's smile widened.

Once her hand settled on his chest, the crystal alien jumped back with a strangled cry, putting a hand on her forehead.

See. Raxx's mental voice was full of triumph. *Echo loves me. She'd let nothing or no one hurt me.*

Asmodel's eyes widened. *Good to know.* He nodded in solidarity. *I'll do my best to protect you as well.*

"Put this human in a holding cell!" The yellow crystal woman stomped back to face the regent. "I will take him with me once my rejuvenation cycle is complete."

"You mean after you've eliminated the pardalion infestation." Regent Korvex wasn't asking. He tapped an extended claw on his armrest with a scowl.

Her glance at the regent wasn't warm. "Yes, yes, of course. Before I leave, I'll take care of that insignificant problem for you."

Supreme Regent Korvex snorted. His triangular ears rotated backward. "Jaltaar, have some of your guards take the human to our strongest cell deep in the forbidden cave."

Jaltaar snapped to attention and motioned for the guards next to Raxx. "Make sure you keep an eye on him." The male frowned. "I don't trust him."

Ah, look. Raxx's mental brag made Asmodel smile. *One of them has little bitty smarts. Well, gotta go. I don't suppose you'll come and rescue me, will ya?* He batted his eyelashes like he was a damsel in distress.

No worries. He reassured his new friend. *You and I will be long gone before that crystal* idimmu *misses us.*

Cool beans, dude. I've asked Echo to sync with JR13 so we don't lose touch. Raxx winked at him as he walked by, two guards in front of him and two following. *Catch you later, gator.*

Asmodel chuckled under his breath. Sometimes Raxx's slang was harder to understand than the stuff Arakiba had picked up since they found themselves in the future.

"What about the other one, Prisma-Solara?" Regent Korvex shifted on his large throne. "Should we question..."

"No." Her decision sounded final. "Just get rid of him." She waved a negligent hand, and the stranglehold on his body was gone. "Throw him down the gorge for all I care. All I need from you is the place we discussed earlier to renew my energy." She snapped her fingers. "Hurry, now. I must return to Lord Baelon before the next lunar cycle."

"Jaltaar, have some of your guards deal with that." Regent Korvex indicated Asmodel. "You are to personally escort our guest to the royal gardens. Make sure she has everything she needs." The regent sat back, his tail flicking back and forth behind the throne. "When she's settled, come back here. There is much to discuss."

The pale-orange whiskers above Jaltaar's emerald eyes furrowed as the crease along his snout deepened before it smoothed. He gave a slight head bow, his expression blank. "As you command, Supreme Alpha Regent Malstyr Korvex."

When Jaltaar said the full name of the other scikvak, the elder's tail swished harder as he frowned.

Asmodel studied the two. How interesting. The hidden dynamic between them was personal. Not that he cared enough to use his psychic abilities to find out why.

Regent Korvex sat back and waved an impatient paw at the door. "Yes, well, we'll speak later."

The guard next to Asmodel bound his hands then shoved him on his shoulder. "Come on, alien. This way."

Asmodel took one last look over his shoulder at the enormous cavern as the guard led him away. His eye caught the cat-man on the throne and the unkind smile distorting his snout. He didn't need his psychic sense to know the ruler was narcissistic enough to gain power anyway he could.

Even if it meant he had to commit genocide on half the population.

"So, where are you taking me?"

The guards didn't answer.

Not that Asmodel thought they'd stop and chat. They silently marched him through the grand archway that led from the opulent throne room of Panterion Prime into the sprawling public plaza outside. The stark transition from the dim, hushed reverence of the royal court to the blinding light and cacophony of the plaza made him squint behind his raised hands. The suns of CeluriaVO hung low in the sky, casting elongated shadows, bathing everything in a golden hue that ignited the vibrant colors of the surrounding city.

Blinking to focus, he lowered his bound hands. Apparently, he was being paraded in the main plaza that was alive with activity as a bustling hub of scikvak society. Towering structures of sleek metal and gleaming crystals rose around him, their surfaces catching the natural lights that created dazzling patterns dancing across the ground. Foliage and plants intertwined with the architecture, adding a pulsating rhythm of color to the urban landscape. The air carried the mingled scents of exotic spices combined with the electric tang of advanced technology, the signature aroma he now associated with the scikvak civilization.

Asmodel shrugged at the weight of countless eyes studying him while he was led through the crowd. Whispers swirled around him, filled with exclamations and hisses of fear. Guess it didn't help he had to be the only human they'd ever seen, escorted by the royal guard. Despite their advanced nature, there was an undercurrent of primal fear bombarding his psychic senses. A hard, collective mistrust made sweat roll down his back.

The tight binding of the synthetic restraints on his wrists, along with the firm grip of the guards on his arms, were constant reminders of his captive status. Not that he'd let that weigh him down. Even when he'd been a slave in captivity, Asmodel had no trouble maintaining a dignified posture, his head held high, his stride purposeful. The cool breeze caressing his face contrasted with the warmth of the suns. It reminded him of the planet's duality—its capacity for both stunning beauty and harsh realities.

Speaking of realities. Asmodel had better protect his little bot for what he had in mind. With quick telekinetic manipulation, he fashioned a leather pouch and attached it to a long necktie.

"JR13"—he made sure his voice remained low—"hurry." He opened the pouch with his mind wide enough for the bot to enter. "Jump in here and hang on."

For once, the bot didn't argue. He leaped out of the pocket on Asmodel's vest and scurried to settle into the deep confines of the pouch.

Asmodel snapped it shut and transferred the string holding it around his neck and nestled the thing under his shirt. Now that he wasn't under the Krystalii's control, it was easy enough to do this without the guards noticing.

Shrugging and twisting his neck to stretch, he was ready.

As the guards led him across the plaza, the sound of the crowd ebbed and flowed in a symphony of alien languages, the hum of hover vehicles, and a melody of scikvak music in the distance. All around was harmonious chaos, a testament to the bustling life of Panterion Prime. It wouldn't surprise him if the city never slept.

Asmodel took it all in—the sights, sounds, and smells—a vivid tapestry of life on CeluriaVO that he wouldn't soon forget. Despite the circumstances, there was an undeniable allure to this world and its people—a complexity and depth he'd give anything to explore.

Without the threat of death, of course.

All too soon, they left civilization and walked through a large cave with a huge opening facing an opposing cliff with no buildings or signs of civilization. The roar of cascading waterfalls drowned out other sounds, and mist coated the air with the earthy scent of damp moss and wet rocks.

There were several civilian scikvak milling around the railing that kept them from the dangerous edge of the cliff.

With stern barks, the guards ordered them to leave.

Guess the guards didn't want any witnesses on what they planned to do to him.

"Go on. We don't have all day to deal with you, *human*." A derisive sneer from one guard. An elderly one by the looks of the silver lining of his black fur around his eyes and snout. He prodded Asmodel hard on the shoulder with his solid-steel pole weapon and directed him to an open area not protected by any railing. Just a path to open air. "Let's make this nice and easy for everyone. Go over there and keep going."

Asmodel raised his brows with a grin. When he got to the edge, he took a moment to peer down. Damn, the gorge was so deep he couldn't see where the raging river below. Just a plume of misty water bellowing upward. He glanced at the smirking guards behind him. He nodded to the wide chasm. "You sure you want me to jump in there?"

One of the younger guards laughed. "Well, you don't have to jump. All you gotta do is keep walking. Nice and easy like."

Asmodel turned his back on the yawning space and laughed, making the bonds on his wrists disappear. "Oh no. Why do something as boring as that?" With a flourish, he swept his arms wide and with a joyous cry, leaped off the cliff.

He watched as the guards ran to the edge of the cliff, their snouts and eyes wide as if they couldn't believe he jumped off the humongous precipice of his own free will. When he estimated he'd given himself enough room, he transformed. With a cavernous roar, he unfurled his wingspan that was almost as wide as the chasm itself.

Ever since he'd watched a popular cable series that mesmerized him a couple of months ago, Asmodel dreamed of transforming into one of those glorious, mythical creatures. With joy, he blew a fountain of fire at the guards. Not to kill them, just to scare the shit out of the bastards.

With an inhuman laugh, he watched them scramble like frightened children, running back into the perceived safety of the cave tunnel. The cries and screams they left behind created a satisfying echo.

With a contented snort, Asmodel made sure the pouch holding JR13 was secure around his neck. Shaking to settle into his copper-hued dragon form, he expanded his massive wingspan and raced to the brilliant sunset in the opposite direction of Panterion Prime.

Sensing now wasn't the best time to find the alluring woman of his visions, he'd rest for the night in this form before heading out to claim her come morning.

"A what?"

Izzy jumped at Calin's growl.

"Oh dear. That's right. So sorry." Izzy wasn't on Earth anymore, so no one here would know what a library was, much less a librarian. She threw her shoulders back. "What I mean is I was the keeper of one of the largest archives of vast knowledge and discovery on my planet. It was a place where people of all ages, races, religions, and backgrounds came together to solve various challenges we faced as a people."

At least that's what it was supposed to be. Some days, not so much.

Taking a deep breath, Izzy glanced around the small audience. "Also, as a human, if I'm with you, he'd know you are the good guys and won't hesitate to let us rescue him. I just know we'll need his help to stop the Krystalii from coming to kill you."

Fingers crossed, she hoped she wasn't stretching the truth. She didn't know his full capabilities, but if he traveled all this way to rescue her, he had to have some impressive skills.

Praetor Vorlok sat back and laid his paws on his wide chest, his claws retracted. "I see." He glanced around the room. "I believe she has a valid point."

"You can't be serious!" Calin slammed his paw on the table, his extended claws clicking on the hard surface. "Look at her!" He waved in her direction. "We can't afford to let the zaltrixan capture her, much less let her get in our way." He leaned forward on his elbows, his whiskers wide as his gold eyes narrowed. "We can't afford to anger the Federation's chancellor by allowing her to get hurt or killed."

"Valid points, young one." Madam Fexa nodded. "However, as a free citizen of this Federation, this human may choose her own path. I agree, she should go."

Calin snorted. "If that's the council's decision, then we'd better have our best warrior assigned to protect her." He grumbled, leaning back, his ears flicking back-and-forth to show his displeasure.

"I agree. Thank you for volunteering, Calin."

Calin frowned at Praetor Vorlok's derisive smile, but he didn't argue. Just gave a brief nod.

Izzy's mouth dried as the tension between her shoulders tightened. Oh dear. What had she'd gotten herself into? No matter. She'd never allow another human to suffer if she could do something about it. Squaring her shoulders, she murmured a quick thank you and sat.

"Now, we need to plan how we're going to Panterion Prime. Not only to get the human, but to capture that Krystalii. But first—" Praetor Vorlok glanced at Izzy. "—from what Talira has told me, this human has some personal needs to take care of. Is that so?"

Once he brought that to her attention, Izzy's stomach growled loud enough for everyone to hear. Putting her hand over her stomach, she blushed. With gritty eyes, she nodded. "Yes, but I want to help you plan."

"We appreciate that, Izzy. But your stomach argues with you," Talira admonished her. "I'm sorry Zolune didn't make it back with some food for you. Come with me." The feline stood and placed a soft paw on Izzy's shoulder. "And don't worry, I'll fill you in on whatever is decided. But for now, we'd better get you something to eat and a place to rest."

Izzy stood and gazed around the group as they studied her. Some expressions were open, others were blank or filled with mistrust. "Promise you won't leave without me?" She held her breath.

"Of course not, human female called Izzy." The praetor gave a regal nod. "I have said we would honor your decision, and I never go back on my word."

She pressed over her heart with a wide grin. "Oh, thank you. Thank you very much."

"Come on, Izzy. Your stomach is growling so loud, you'll scare all the skalderbeast away," Talira teased.

Now Izzy moved her hand to cover her rumbling stomach. She sighed. "I may not know what a skalderbeast is, but I'm so hungry I could eat one."

Talira laughed as she put her arm around Izzy's shoulder and led her out of the meeting room to another part of the cave. "They're actually pretty tasty. Let's see if we can get a piece of one for you."

As Izzy's tension eased, she gave Talira a small smile and followed her to a communal eating place in another part of the warm, luminescent cave. The food was presented in buffet style, showcasing roasted meats alongside an array of colorful vegetables and fruits. The pardalion took her to one of the large tables where other scikvak ate. Old, young, and the very young came and went. Some lingered after their meals, but most left with happy purrs.

"I'm afraid I have to leave you on your own for a bit," Talira told her, clasping her paws in front of her and nodding to an elderly female who approached them. "This is Tivessa, the presiding leader of those who prepare food."

Tivessa, her dark-blue downy fur laced with white, came over to where Izzy sat. She placed a large trencher in front of the hungry woman, laden with succulent meats and a smattering of fruits and vegetables.

"Eat," Tivessa urged. "You like." She turned and shuffled away.

Talira laughed, her eyes softening as the elder walked away. "She's always been a female of brief words." She turned to Izzy. "But she's reliable and will make sure you have everything you need. Once you're done eating, she'll take you to a comfortable place where you can sleep." She patted Izzy on the shoulder. "Don't worry, I'll come back in plenty of time before we leave for Panterion Prime in the morning. Then I'll fill you in on what we've planned." With a last look around the room, Talira left.

Izzy watched her go, but her stomach demanded attention with a loud growl. She studied the food resting on the plate in front of her. The slice of meat still sizzled from the fires, releasing a mouthwatering aroma that made her stomach growl. Next to it was an assortment of root vegetables slathered in a harmony of fresh herbs. A separate small bowl held ripe berries that looked like strawberries but were white with zigzagging black stripes.

Next to the plate was a set of utensils. A long two-tined fork rested beside a blade with a razor thin edge.

With a fortifying breath, Izzy grabbed the fork and knife and sliced the meat. From the first bite, she chewed in ecstasy and set about devouring the meal. Lordy, lordy. She couldn't remember the last time she'd eaten anything as fine. The meal was a journey through a myriad of flavors, each mouthful a discovery of the scikvak culinary mastery. Succulent roasted meat melted on her tongue, each fruit burst with sweetness, and the vegetables were cooked to a perfect tenderness. The meal settled in her unruly stomach, creating warmth that sent a deep sense of contentment throughout her.

When finished, Izzy patted her full belly. Unbidden, her lips smacked and she gave a soft belch. "Oh, gosh!" She covered her mouth and sat up straight, her back stiffening. If her *abuela* heard her being so rude, she'd never live it down.

"See. You like."

Izzy jerked as the voice of Tivessa spoke behind her. Darn woman was as silent as... well, a cat.

"Come. Leave plate." She gestured for Izzy to follow her. "Sleep now."

Tivessa guided her to a secluded corner of the cave. There, a bed of soft furs and handwoven blankets beckoned with a promise of a peaceful night's rest. Eyes drooping, Izzy's body lost all mobility as she lay down. How nice, the elderly female pulled a warm fur over her, enveloping her in welcome warmth. With a gentle stroke, Tivessa's soft paw wisped across the top of Izzy's head like her *abuela's* palm did so long ago.

As she drifted, an image came of a man so beautiful he took her breath away. He sported a perfect square jaw accented by a manly cleft. Full lips, a nose as straight as an arrow, high cheekbones, and a broad forehead. His hair, a rich chestnut hue with deep undertones, was thick and wavy, cascading down his back in luxurious waves. Blazing hazel eyes of ginger brown and leaf green combined with a starburst of gold flecks looked into her soul.

And good golly molly... his body was as spectacular as his face and hair. Thickly muscled, big-boned, and not an ounce of fat in sight. His copper-hued skin was smooth and flawless.

"Izzy, don't worry. I'll be there soon."

She melted at the sound of his deep baritone as it whispered in her mind. A sensation caressed her forehead as if a gentle touch came from his large, soothing hand. With a happy sigh, she surrendered to slumber.

Chapter Eight

I zzy settled deeper into her dream of the dazzling, handsome, totally irresistible man.

"Isabella."

His sensual whisper made her shiver.

A loud scream jerked Izzy awake.

"Criminy sakes!" She sat up with her hand against her chest, her heart racing. "What in the world?" Her eyes widened at the chaos in the large cave.

Pardalions of all shapes and sizes, ages and sexes, were running around like a bunch of cats in a room of rocking chairs. There was an unsettling symphony of hisses and guttural growls that echoed in the large chamber. Her groggy senses made it hard to understand why they were acting like that.

She caught sight of young Zolune running on all fours, her ability to walk on two legs long gone. Age didn't seem to cause this change.

One guard did the same, galloping on all fours with the silky fur on his back bristling.

Several of the cat-people were hiding under tables and chairs, their ears back. Some hissed, some shivered, not uttering a sound.

"Hurry, human!" The mature female cook, Tivessa, rushed to her, still on her two hind legs. "We must hide before it finds us!"

Izzy jumped out of her nest of warm furs and soft blankets. "Who? Are the zaltrixan attacking?" Another horrible thought occurred to her. "Or is it that yellow crystal lady coming to kill everyone?"

"No, worse!" The feline put her paws in the air. "It's some kind of evil demon, a *drur'az,* coming to steal our souls! *Ay-eee!* Run for your life!" She hopped and turned to run out of the cave.

"Goodness me." Izzy watched the cat-people run around howling, with no coordination.

Several of them in thick guard uniforms sprinted to the cave entrance, their weapons ready for action.

She narrowed her eyes. That's where she needed to go.

The guards lined up, their fur bristled, and their tails puffed up to twice their normal size. The primal fear in the air was thick with the electricity of their collective terror.

Keeping a respectful distance from the sentries, she reached the edge of the cave and dared to step outside. Below her, the verdant forest stretched into eternity, a canopy of colorful whispers. The crisp air smelled of pine as well as a hint of rain. Her gaze lifted skyward, caught by an unusual shadow. In the distance was a silhouette cleaving the air with unwavering purpose. Placing the edge of her hand against her forehead for shade, she narrowed her eyes, hoping to see better.

She glanced at the female guard next to her. "Is that what all the fuss is about?" She glanced at the incoming... plane?

"Don't you have some kind of flying machines here?" These folks might be living in a cave, but the technology she'd seen them use so far was beyond what they had on Earth. Air flight had to be something they'd conquered a long time ago.

"That's not a machine." The hissing words from the guard's mouth told Izzy how terrified the female was. "Our sensors tell us it's organic. And there's nothing on CeluriaVO like that. The damn thing has a wingspan that would rival any aircraft we or the zaltrixan have!"

The figure approached, gliding and rolling on a wingspan that blotted out the sun, casting a copper hue over the land below.

Now that it was closer, Izzy's eyes widened as her heart thrummed in her chest, a rapid drumbeat of excitement laced with a touch of fear. She stood rooted to the spot as the pardalion next to her hissed and growled, rushing back into the cave.

It was a dragon.

A dragon as magnificent and awe-inspiring as any fabled creature could be. Copper scales shimmered with a fiery palette of a blazing sunset in the rising sun. Each beat of its vast wings sent ripples through the air, a display of power that was as terrifying as mesmerizing.

The creature drew closer, and its massive eyes were clear to see. A sense of déjà vu struck her. Those captivating orbs of hazel carried browns and greens with shots of gold flecks that teased her memory. She couldn't look away from those deep pools of wisdom and mystery now locked on hers.

Time froze.

In one fell swoop, the dragon landed on the cliff's edge in front of Izzy. The creature's breath heated the air, bring with it the smell of smoldering embers. It landed with a grace that defied its size, the ground silent beneath it. The magnificent beast raised his head with a bellow of fire, then lowered it.

Before her astonished gaze, the dragon transformed. Scales melded into skin, wings folded into arms, and the massive beast reshaped itself into the form of a naked muscular man resting on one knee with his arm over it. Long, wavy, earth-brown hair covered his features. He slowly raised his head, his hair parting like a stage curtain.

She gasped.

He was the man she'd dreamed about.

The man's handsome features transcended mere male beauty, teasing the foundations of legends and fables steeped in human history. She couldn't tear her eyes away from his stunning face. His strong jawline, high cheekbones, and piercing gaze created an allure that held her spellbound. Each chiseled feature, as sharply defined as the ridges of the mountains surrounding them, was awe-inspiring. His hair gleamed with dark browns and copper, and his eyes...

Izzy sighed.

His eyes remained the same as the dragon's, with their depth and intensity.

Izzy couldn't move, just stared like a starstruck fangirl.

With the grace of a man in touch with his masculine bulk he stood, his skin morphing into dark-brown leather pants tucked into thick biker boots. His tan cotton shirt was covered by an open vest of soft leather that matched his pants. Around his neck hung a small leather pouch cinched on a thong of the same material.

The transformation complete, he stepped toward her. A smile played on his full lips, hinting at secrets as ancient as the stars. The air between them crackled with an unspoken understanding, a connection that transcended words.

Izzy grappled with the congruity of reality, meshing with her dreams. Just being this close to him pulled at something low and deep inside her. As he came nearer, his heat wrapped around her. A sense that her life was changing stirred within her, insistently whispering that their fates were now intertwined.

Standing on the threshold of the unknown, Izzy did something she'd never thought she'd do in a million years. Especially to someone she'd just laid eyes on.

Narrowing the small gap between their bodies, Izzy stood on her toes and wrapped her arms around his muscular neck. With an aggressive confidence she never dreamed she had in her, she put her hand on the back of his head. Threading her fingers through his silky hair, she pulled his head down and demanded a kiss.

Asmodel's gaze locked onto Izzy's as her delicate fingers stroked under his hair and cupped his head. He shivered, mesmerized by the dilation of her stunning amber-colored eyes. Her hair cascaded in a soft, dark curtain that framed her face which radiated warmth and quiet strength.

As she moved closer, she brought with her a subtle scent that enveloped him—a delicate blend of jasmine and vanilla.

A captivating essence of a serene, warm summer evening. Being near her produced a surprising surge of emotion so intense it bordered on reverence. In that moment, his heart recognized hers with an unshakable certainty. This woman belonged to him.

Asmodel's eyes lowered at the first touch of her mouth on his. Time stood still as the electric stroke of her lips made everything around him blur into an insignificant haze. Her hands moved to the sides of his face, and her thumbs caressed his cheeks with a tenderness he'd never experienced before. Drowning in a world of pure feeling, the unfamiliar sensations threatened to overwhelm him.

He had to have more... much more. With a tentative touch, he stroked the seam of her mouth with his tongue, desperate for her to let him in.

She opened. Her warm breath bathed the cavern of his mouth with unbridled passion. He took her offering and exchanged his heat with hers. She moaned and jumped into his arms, wrapping her legs around his thighs. Her dangerous tongue tangled with his in a dance of pure, erotic pleasure.

His blood burned and pounded hard, creating a booming thunder that echoed in his ears.

The kiss deepened. His cock rose and thickened, growing with a heavy ache. His mind blurred with every swipe of their tongues as the passion rose. Her mouth was unlike anything he'd ever experienced before.

Her taste was addicting.

Slipping his hand down her torso, he pushed up the edge of her shirt to claim the quivering, soft flesh of her breast under her bra. He encircled the hard pebble of her nipple between his thumb and forefinger.

She pulled back with a gasp.

He opened his eyes and gazed into her amber ones, now softened with a vulnerable glow. Her very essence beckoned him to go deeper into the bond they had just sealed. Striving to control himself, he took in a deep breath. Her heady feminine scent wrapped around him with an invisible thread, making his head swim with a sense of completeness. The powerful, overwhelming knowledge of finally finding a part of himself he never knew was missing.

"Hello, *alma gemela*." Asmodel cradled her luscious bottom with his hands. He celebrated Izzy's heritage by calling her his soul-mate in Spanish. "I am Asmodel."

He didn't need his psionic abilities to tell him she experienced the same thing happening between them. Her smile, shy yet radiant, told him everything he needed to know. She was as aware of the profound connection between them that transformed the impossibility into reality.

"I am Isabella Pilar Ramirez Torres." She tilted her head, and her soft hair framed the smooth golden porcelain skin of her face. "But I'd love it if you'd call me Izzy."

With delicate care, Asmodel released her bottom to let her stand on her own. He cupped her face, keeping his touch reverent but firm. After all, he held something sacred in his hands. His heart beat with a new rhythm, one that sang of hope, passion, and a future where every moment of his life would now intertwine with hers.

"Izzy!"

A hissing female voice interrupted the isolation he enjoyed with Izzy. Glancing up, he watched a female scikvak racing towards them, brandishing a long pole with a spiked ball at its tip.

"Back away from her." The female growled, facing Asmodel. She waved the weapon between them. "Who are you?"

Asmodel relaxed his stance and forced himself to let Izzy go. He took a step back and put Izzy behind him. "I am Asmodel from Earth." He placed his hand over his heart with a small bow of respect. "Here to take Izzy back to Earth."

"It's okay, Talira." Izzy moved to stand in front of him. "He's the one we were going to rescue from the zaltrixan."

Asmodel grinned. As if he needed her protection. He placed a hand over her shoulder, giving her a slight squeeze.

Talira glanced from him to Izzy. After a few heartbeats, the female warrior took a step back and planted the end of her weapon on the ground.

"I see." She looked behind her as the sound of rustling feet burst out of the cave opening.

A group of scikvak came through, a conglomeration of civilians and soldiers by the looks of their clothing.

"Stand down, Talira." An imposing male scikvak rushed to the female and faced her. "Izzy is right. He is the emissary from Earth."

Talira narrowed her gaze at Asmodel, her ears flattened backward. "As you say, Praetor Vorlok."

Asmodel took a chance and sent a slight psychic probe her way. What he got back didn't surprise him. An unyielding sense of right and wrong mixed with the profound need to protect her people. His eyes widened when he got a little tidbit he didn't expect. Oh, this was the female who Jaltaar, the lead guard from Panterion Prime, was deeply in love with.

"Welcome to Nekojin, man from Earth." The praetor thumped both arms across his wide chest. "Come, we have much to discuss." He gestured toward the entrance to the cave, now blocked by a crowd of pardalions watching them.

"Everyone, get back to your business! Let the praetor and our guests through!" Talira waved her arms to shoo the crowd back into the cave. Several of her fellow guards mimicked her and encouraged the group to break up. With murmurs and nervous laughs, the group headed back into the cave village.

Asmodel put his arm around Izzy's slender shoulders. The praetor couldn't have been more right. There was a lot to discuss. Glancing at the pouch hanging from the leather thong, he lifted it up to his open palm to let JR13 out.

"Contact your father and give him an update," he told his spybot. "Be sure you let them know the Krystalii here is female and has a human male she plans to take back to Lord Baelon."

JR13 shook his bulbous body, and the matte black of his torso contrasted with the shiny silver in the bright sunlight. "Already done, organic man." The bot snorted. "You'd think this was my first rodeo or something."

Asmodel had no clue what a rodeo was, but he trusted the droid did what he said.

"Oh, my gosh!" Izzy bent to get a better look at JR13 in his palm. "He's so cute!"

"My dear woman." JR13 turned to her and spoke in his snootiest tone. "I am not cute." He pranced on his six legs to shuffle closer to her. "I am the epitome of masculine handsomeness."

Asmodel snorted. With an exasperated look at Izzy, he lifted his hand to stare with narrowed eyes at JR13. "Let's concentrate on what we should do next. Agreed?"

The bot blinked as if he was running more than one program. "Sure, whatever you say. But we can't do that until you follow the cat-man back inside, now can we?" With that last shot, he scuttled to sit on his favorite perch at Asmodel's left shoulder.

Izzy chuckled. "You sure have your hands full with that one, don't you?"

Asmodel put his arm around her shoulders with a slight hug. They walked together behind the pardalions.

He chuckled. "You have no idea."

Izzy glanced at the tall, *holy gosh,* seriously swoon-worthy man walking next to her. Even his profile, as he spoke with the praetor, made butterflies dance in her tummy. She admired his sharp jawline with its cleft chin devoid of any facial hair. His deep, fascinating hazel eyes, with their striking blend of chestnut brown and leaf green interlaced with gold flecks, lit up when he smiled. And the way he moved! She yearned to lag a few steps behind, just to admire the effortless grace in his movements, the way his muscles shifted beneath those tight leather pants.

And his hands! So wide and elegant, and his copper-hued skin spoke of strength and artistry, all at the same time. She yearned to reach over and grasp his hand to cover her chilled skin with his. As he spoke with the praetor, his warm, inviting tone drew her in. It took a moment before she tuned in to what he was saying.

"I'm afraid that's right, Praetor," Asmodel said. "The female Krystalii now has a human man and is planning on taking him instead of Izzy." He stopped and faced the scikvak with crossed arms and leaned toward the pardalion elder. "The only reason she hasn't come here to destroy your village is because she had to go underground to recharge. I'm not sure how long she'll be out, so we only have a small window of opportunity to act, to get the human before she wakes up. Between her extensive psychic powers and her advanced technological abilities, she won't need the zaltrixan to help her." He stood straight. "And if she wakes up at full strength, I'm afraid she'll be unstoppable."

The elder tilted his head, and the long fur wisped around his face. "I agree. Come." He put a paw on Asmodel's arm and tugged him to the opening of the massive communal cave. "The chancellor of the Federation contacted us earlier and made us aware of your arrival, so we've begun plans to infiltrate Panterion Prime." He grunted. "But now that the Krystalii already has a human, we'd better act quicker than we thought."

He led them back into the large cave opening and into the interior conference room where Izzy had first arrived.

Asmodel smiled and a single deep dimple peeked out on the side of his luscious lips. When he reached over to cover her hand with his, Izzy caught her breath and gripped his hand back. Her grin had to be as goofy as heck. Not that she cared.

Once again, Izzy sat at the massive u-shaped rock table. But instead of being weary and starving, she was wide-awake and ready to take part. She gave the man next to her a quick glance. Just being next to him with her hand in his ramped things up to a whole different level.

Across from her, Talira took a seat next to Praetor Vorlok. The previous participants filed in and joined them.

"Esteemed colleagues," Praetor Vorlok stood and gestured to Asmodel. "It is my great pleasure to introduce the emissary Chancellor E'etu spoke of. This Earth man's name is Asmodel. As you can see, there's no need to rescue him from Panterion Prime."

Laughter and chuckles mixed with murmurs of welcome from around the table.

With a gentle squeeze, Asmodel let go of her hand and stood, with a regal nod to the room. "Thank you, Praetor Vorlok." He shifted his shoulders back and clasped his hands in front of him. "While I appreciate that you'd let me and Izzy leave CeluriaVO, we have a bigger problem than keeping her out of the Krystalii's hands."

His concerned glance at her made her warm. She beamed and nodded her encouragement with a smile.

"The Krystalii by the name of Prisma-Solara already has a human male and has threatened to come and not only eliminate you here in Nekojin, but will destroy all of CeluriaVO."

Angry growls and hissed filled the air.

"How could you possibly know that?" Madam Fexa crouched, the fur on her backside raised.

Asmodel expelled an audible breath. "I know you all witnessed how I came here. Correct?"

"You mean as that massive beast?" Calin's gold eyes narrowed. "How could we miss that?"

Asmodel sat and grabbed Izzy's hand under the table. "Just as I'm able to do that, I can get a sense of what others are thinking."

The group's angry growls grew louder.

"You can read our minds?" Calin stood, his claws extended as he leaned on the rough rock table surface.

"Believe me, I don't go around reading people's minds." Asmodel's tone was smooth. "It can be annoying and painful." He rubbed his temple and closed his eyes. "I usually have to fight to keep everyone out."

For some reason, Izzy could feel his unease. She rubbed his upper arm with her free hand.

"Calin, sit down. Let the human speak," Praetor Vorlok commanded.

With a low snarl, Calin sat, his bright eyes fixated on Asmodel.

Asmodel opened his eyes with a confident look at the Praetor. "As I was saying, the last thought I picked up from her was that as soon as she had the human man in her ship, she planned on eliminating all life here on CeluriaVO."

At once, Izzy saw what Asmodel did, in her mind. It was a violent image of the lush jungle planet under volcanic flames and massive earthquakes that no one on this planet could survive.

Izzy had a hard time getting the image of CeluriaVO being destroyed by massive earthquakes and volcanic eruptions out of her mind. She shivered and gripped Asmodel's hand tighter under the rock table. She blinked and took a moment to get her bearings. Glancing around, she took in the now-familiar scene of the council chamber of the pardalions. The first time she was here, she hadn't bothered to notice much.

It was an awesome sprawling, circular room with intricate murals depicting the lush jungle of their home planet. A soft glow from the luminescent lights gave the place a spacious feel, as if they weren't in a cave deep inside a mountain.

The heated discussion of the pardalions drew her attention. They were discussing where the human called Raxx might be at Panterion Prime. Some argued he was in their maximum-security facility. While others, including Talira, believed they put him in a stasis pod for the Krystalii to take to her ship.

"Yo, organic man."

For the first time, Izzy didn't have any trouble hearing JR13's sotto voce as he spoke to Asmodel on the man's shoulder next to her.

"Yes?"

Asmodel's absent tone told her he wasn't listening. Instead of looking at the bot, his eyes narrowed on Praetor Vorlok. Izzy tilted her head and checked out what the praetor was saying. Right now, he wasn't saying anything. Just letting Calin argue with Talira about who was going to lead the small group they'd agreed on.

"Excuse me—" JR13's impatient tone was obvious. "—I have something to say here that might ease this ridiculous guesswork you organics seem to enjoy." Now the bot's irritated voice came out high enough to grab Asmodel's attention.

Asmodel's dark eyebrows rose as he glanced at the bot. "Oh?"

JR13 wiggled his rotund hind end and tapped a foreleg as if to emphasize his importance. "Yes! I know where Raxx is."

"How can you know that?" Izzy leaned to the bot and made sure she whispered.

"Easy. I asked Echo."

"You echoed?" Izzy searched the room. How could an echo tell them where someone was?

"No, my baffled friend." JR13 huffed. "Echo is a self-aware artificial creation that can process an unlimited amount of data and perceived emotions. She is a discerning system, not a sound."

Izzy scratched the side of her head. "Huh?"

"Echo is the name of Raxx's AI system." Asmodel chuckled with a playful glimmer in his dark eyes. "And JR13 has interfaced with Echo to keep the lines of communication going between us." He shook his head. "I can't believe I'd forgotten that."

JR13 snorted. "And that's why I'm here. To pick up your slack."

"Well, golly gee JR13. That's a little harsh, don't you think?" Izzy's face flushed. Oh lordy. How arrogant of her to step in and defend Asmodel like that. It's not as if the man couldn't take care of himself.

Asmodel squeezed her hand as he leaned over and placed a light kiss on her neck. JR13 squeaked and scuttled out of the way.

The feel of his lips on her skin created a sudden flush of warmth spreading outward from deep inside her. *Oh my stars*, he was one dangerous man.

"Don't worry about him."

Asmodel's low rumble ramped up the goosebumps on her arms.

"But I appreciate you standing up for me." His gaze lingered on her before he pulled away. "Okay JR13. What did Echo tell you?"

Izzy swore the bot muttered "organics" under his breath as he moved back to his place on Asmodel's shoulder. His six legs orchestrated a complex ballet across the hilly surface of Asmodel's body, his joints flexing like tiny hydraulic pistons.

"Echo has informed me she and Raxx are fine but are in some kind of holding cell. They're waiting for you to 'hurry your happy ass up and rescue us.'"

Asmodel chuckled. "Reassure Echo we're working on it."

"Already did. I'm going to keep the line with her open so she can hear what's decided here."

Asmodel nodded. "Good idea."

He turned his attention back to the council, sitting back as his brow furrowed.

Izzy shifted in her seat and did the same. She rested her hand on his firm thigh, and his warmth eased the tension gripping her since she'd witnessed the destruction in his vision.

"The zaltrixan are notoriously secretive and well-fortified," Calin pointed out. His tail flicked in irritation. "Penetrating Panterion Prime won't be easy."

Madam Fexa raised a paw for attention. "We must consider stealth over sheer force. The zaltrixan might respect strength, but they are vulnerable to cunning."

Izzy thought of the man they were supposed to rescue. They had to get him back, not just for his sake, but to prevent the potential destruction of the entire race of scikvak. "What if we used a diversion?" Her voice cut through the murmur of the council. All eyes turned to her. She met their stares head-on, her heart pounding. "If they're stronger than us, wouldn't it be best if we create a disturbance outside the city limits—something to draw their forces out?" That type of scenario was quite popular in Earth literature throughout the ages.

Asmodel nodded in support. "Excellent idea." He brought her hand up and applied a brief kiss to her knuckles. "That way, a small team can slip into the city under the cover of the chaos. Grab Raxx before they know he's gone."

Talira sat back and put one of her paws over the other on her stomach. "I like that idea. We have enough ammunition and weapons ready to create a massive decoy just outside the city parameters that I and my team can detonate. Now who do you propose goes into the city to rescue the human?"

Before Izzy could respond, Asmodel spoke up. "That'd be Izzy and me. Since I've an open communication with Raxx, it'll be easy enough for us to get him."

Izzy suspected he had other tricks up his sleeve but wasn't willing to share it with the group. Hopefully, he'd fill her in when they were alone.

Asmodel's proposal hung heavy in the air. Every second stretched as the pardalions exchanged glances, communicating in their silent, feline way. Finally, Praetor Vorlok nodded.

"Very well." He pounded his fisted paw on the table. "And just how are we to stop the Krystalii from destroying our planet when she finds the human gone?"

"As usual, Echo and I have already come up with a viable solution to that." JR13 spoke with a raised voice so all in the chamber could hear.

Murmured growls filled the air.

"If I may?" JR13 leaped off Asmodel's shoulder and landed on the rocky table in front of him. "Since that alien contains a crystalline alloy, we can create a disruption device with a precise frequency to immobilize her. Lucky for you, we've developed a schematic of what we propose could do that."

Izzy sucked in a breath when a third eye opened on the bot's forehead and a holographic image appeared, ten times bigger than JR13.

The blueprint for building the special machine the bot mentioned lay before her. It looked like a flowchart, detailing how different parts connected and interacted. Multiple symbols, some type of hieroglyphics, covered the entire diagram.

"Can you organics do something with this?" JR13 asked.

Madam Fexa stood and leaned on the table as if to get a better look. Her fluffy tail rose into the shape of a question mark. Her eyes blinked as she took in the image.

As those around the table examined it with the elder pardalion, servers brought in food, placing platters of meats and root vegetables in front of everyone.

Izzy's stomach rumbled in appreciation. She offered Asmodel a sheepish smile, then dug into the simple yet sumptuous meal. Out of the corner of her eye, she saw him eating as well. A quiet sense of satisfaction settled over her.

Just when Izzy took the last bite of her meal, Madam Fexa jumped back and exclaimed, "Of course!"

The elder straightened with a triumphant gleam in her cat eyes. "My team and I already have something similar. We'll have it completed before morning." She nodded to the others who'd been absorbed with her in talking about the device. "Let's get this done, my friends." With a whistling whoop, she skipped out of the room, speaking excitedly with the small group that followed her.

Dang, Izzy hadn't seen anyone that excited about making something since she'd led a group of kids in the library to play with modeling clay.

"That thing reminds me of the Lumiview Prism Jaltaar had."

Talira might have spoken under her breath, but Izzy didn't have any trouble catching it.

"I wonder if it works the same way."

"All right, people." Praetor Vorlok wiped his snout with a napkin and stood. "I think it's best if we all get some rest. We'll meet up here before dawn to complete our plans."

As the meeting adjourned, Izzy glanced at the cavern entrance. Holy cow, it was dark outside! She couldn't believe how the hours had slipped away like that.

"If you'll come with me, I have a place prepared for you."

Izzy jumped when a soft feminine voice spoke next to her. It was a young female pardalion, with a shy smile and a slight bow.

"I'm Dahl. If you both will follow me, I'll take you to a private place we've prepared for you to rest." She turned and proceeded out of the chamber.

Her downy dark-blue tail with delicate orange stripes swished behind her.

Izzy looked up at Asmodel. The fluttering in her tummy made her catch her breath. Was she brave enough to be alone with this stunning man?

His warm, inviting gaze reassured her there wasn't anywhere else she'd rather be.

Chapter Nine

Asmodel's mouth dried as his imagination ran wild. He pictured holding a naked, willing Izzy in his arms along with a handy bed nearby. He stumbled. If he hadn't been holding her under his arm, he'd more than likely would have fallen face-first.

She murmured, "Are you okay?"

This forced him to pay attention to his surroundings. After all, they weren't anywhere private. Around him, it looked like the pardalions in the village gathered in the large cave to sleep. Some in family groups, some were females nestled together, while single males slept by themselves. Small cubs in several family clusters were being shushed and cradled by their parents.

Asmodel studied the groupings. Some families had more than one female cuddling around an imposing male. Praetor Vorlok appeared to have four females in his group, all with cubs or heavy with one. "Dahl, may I ask you a question?" He looked at the dainty female who was leading them to the far side of the cave.

She glanced over her shoulder at him, her tawny eyes dilated as she traversed through the dim light of the cave. "Of course."

"Why do the pardalions live in this cave while the zaltrixan live in a large city?"

She didn't answer right away. Instead, she gestured with her paw to a soft pile of furs and linens inside a recessed alcove. "Here is where you will sleep until the council comes for you in the morning."

Izzy nodded and thanked her with a soft tone, lowered herself onto the dark nest, and sat cross-legged. Her light-brown eyes were wide as she watched Dahl.

Asmodel stood with his hands behind his back and faced the young pardalion. He didn't sense the question made her uncomfortable, so he waited.

The female tilted her head and looked up at him. The long fur on her tail floated as it swayed back-and-forth on the dusty floor. "Centuries ago, we all lived in relative peace at Panterion Prime." Her whiskers fanned out as her eyes became distant. "But there was unrest among the common folk, the zaltrixan. They felt the ruling class—" She placed a padded paw over her heart. "—the pardalions were cruel and prejudiced against them."

"Wait." Izzy leaned forward. "Are you saying you're from royalty?"

Dahl nodded. "Yes." She nodded toward the praetor, nestled between two females with his eyes closed, sporting a lazy smile. "As a matter of fact, Praetor Vorlok is a direct descendant of Elio-Ferix, the last emperor of CeluriaVO."

"What happened?" Izzy laid two fingers across her mouth as she asked the question.

"I guess what happens to all dictators who overstep their authority." Dahl shrugged. "There was a revolt. And since the zaltrixan have always had the majority population, they overthrew the pardalions and exiled us, hoping the wild animals would slaughter us."

A smile creased her snout, while her ears stood upright and forward. "But we fooled them. Eilo-Ferix had made contingency plans and created this cave system in case of an emergency. This place"—she waved an extended claw from her paw— "is fortified to not only withstand any attack, but they installed a sensor shield around this mountain that repels all attempts to discover us."

Her laugh came out with a hiss. "The zaltrixan don't know where we are, and I'm sure it frustrates them to no end." Her whiskers drooped as her eyes lowered. "I believe that's why they are so determined to wipe us out." She stared with firm resolve at Asmodel. "I think they are cowards because the thought of anyone from the royal houses still existing is too much for them to bear."

"Oh, that's so sad." Izzy wiped away tears that made her beautiful eyes bright.

Asmodel cleared his throat. He'd experienced firsthand how it felt to be a slave to an unrelenting monarch, but he could sympathize with the descendants of that dictator who had nothing to do with their ancestors' actions. "Rest assured, Izzy and I will do our utmost to make sure nothing happens to you and your people."

Dahl's smile was winsome. "Thank you." She put her paws together and gave a slight bow. "May Solithar guide your path."

It was easy for Asmodel to pick up the rest of the scikvak blessing from her. "And bless you with the ability to illuminate the mysteries of life presented to you."

"Yes. For you as well." Dahl glanced at Izzy sitting on the floor. "If you need anything, please don't hesitate to ask anyone here."

With one last look at Asmodel, she turned and gracefully sauntered away.

Asmodel watched her join a small pod of females, who greeted her with laughs and playful hisses. He turned to Izzy. "May I?" No way would he presume she'd be comfortable with him sleeping next to her on the first day they met.

Her shy smile had all the warmth and welcome any man could wish for.

Izzy's heart raced, and her hands were clammy. She looked around the niche Dahl assigned them, the small alcove welcoming in its intimacy.

Most of the pardalions settled inside the cave were already asleep.

Taking a deep breath, she nestled into the plush fur and sighed. The warmth seeped into her skin and helped calm her careening emotions.

Asmodel asked if he could join her.

She smiled. "Yes, please." Scooting back, she patted a place next to her. The luxurious bedding under her hand encouraged decedent images of snuggling with the mesmerizing man standing above her.

With surprising grace, he lowered himself and sat cross-legged in front of her.

He brought his alluring scent she'd thought she only dreamed about. Catching her breath, she inhaled his musky aroma, layered with a sharp spice. Nibbling on her lower lip, she glanced at him. "Do you need anything? Would you like me to ask someone to bring you anything?" She looked over his broad shoulder to see if she could catch someone's attention.

"Bella." Asmodel cleared his throat and gently grasped her hands in his. "There isn't anything I need besides being here with you."

He brought her hands to his tempting mouth and placed a light kiss on the back of each one. She stared into his dilated eyes and watched a roll of sweat trickle down his temple. The man said and did such suave things, but his body belied his attempts to disguise his nervousness. That made her spine of steel loosen. Maybe he was as surprised about their instant attraction as she was.

"Asmodel." Izzy sighed and gripped him back. She cocked her head and took in a deep breath. "Are you as attracted to me as I am to you?" Heat flushed up her neck and blazed across her cheeks. *Oh lordy*. Where did that aggressive woman come from?

His warm smile was full of mischief. "I have to admit, I'd be more comfortable talking about anything else." He lowered their clasped hands to rest on his knees.

His unique eyes with their browns, greens, and gold held her spellbound.

"But I'd like nothing better than to explore what we have." His head tilted. "Would you?"

"Oh yes, I do!" Izzy exclaimed. "Where should we start? Oh." She snapped her fingers. "I know! I'll tell you a bit about me first..."

Asmodel's clasp on her other hand firmed. His touch was sure but gentle. "Isabella," he murmured, his voice low and enticing as he drew her closer.

His eyes locked on her with an intensity that sent a thrill through her.

"I know a deeper, more profound way we can get to know each other better." He leaned in, his gaze smoldering with silent promise. "One that would erase all doubts between us. And what that would mean to each other. Tell me, *alma gemela,* are you brave enough to take an intimate journey with me?"

Intimate? Izzy's stomach tightened low inside. She slowly blinked. An intimate what? Was he talking about sex? Right now? Here in a cave full of other people? Okay, not people, but still.

She frowned, shaking her head. "I know a lot of folks don't have any problem jumping into bed with someone they just met, but my *abuela* taught me better than that." She jerked out of his hands and scooted back. "Not that there's anything wrong with that." She cleared her throat. "Ah, for them." She gave a wobbly, self-deprecating laugh, along with a careless wave of her hand. "But that's just not me. I'm sorry I let you think..."

"Bella."

She stopped moving at the stern, exasperated tone of Asmodel's voice.

Her eyes widened at the hurt she saw there.

"I'm talking about you and me getting to know and trust each other first." He ran a hand through the silky strands of his gleaming coffee-colored hair. "I can't believe how bad I'm messing this up."

"Sheesh, I could have told you that, organic man."

For the first time, Izzy noticed JR13 sitting on Asmodel's shoulder.

The spybot waved a foreleg. "You'd think you were born a month ago and not me."

"JR13." Asmodel rubbed his eyes with his thumb and forefinger. "You're not helping."

"Well, why don't you just come out and explain to her how your psychic mojo works instead of dancing around the subject like a clueless idiot?"

Asmodel dropped his hand and gave his companion an exasperated glare. "Can't you find someone else to harass?"

"Nope." The bot folded his legs and made himself comfortable right where he was. "This is too good to pass up."

Asmodel crossed his arms. "I'd like to have this conversation with Izzy in private." He nodded to the spacious cave. "Why don't you do some reconnaissance and see what you can find that might help us tomorrow?"

JR13 stomped his front forelegs. "Fine." His iridescent wings came out. "But I'll be back." With a jump, he zoomed away from their small alcove.

Izzy watched the tiny bot fly away until she couldn't see him anymore.

Turning to her companion, she grasped his hand. "Asmodel, what does he mean by psychic mojo? Does it have to do with you being able to turn into a dragon? Can you read minds as well?" She wasn't sure about the mind-reading thing. What if he found out what a boring, bookworm homebody she was? Would he still want to get to know her?

Asmodel shrugged. "Yes, and no." As he swallowed, his Adam's apple bobbed. "What I was trying to offer you was a psyche merge." He glanced at the open cavern as if to make sure JR13 was still out exploring. "The ability for us to join our minds to experience each other on a profound level." He draped a panel of his hair behind his ear. "It's not something I've ever done before, because I've never wanted to share myself like that with anyone." His eyes softened, giving her a glimpse of the raw truth behind his gaze. "Except you."

Izzy's heart thudded at the sudden vulnerability in his eyes. She searched his face, the sound of her heart thundering in her ears. A sudden urge overcame her to grab him and never let go. She reached deep inside, and the decision was made. "I left Earth to find what you keep calling me—*alma gemela*—my soulmate. Why would I pass up the chance to explore that possibility with you?" She swallowed hard to clear her mouth before she committed herself. "I'd be honored to experience this psyche merge with you."

Asmodel's lips parted in a quiet exhale, as he visibly relaxed with a sheepish smile. "Yes, together." He gestured to the nest of furs and linens. "Let's lie down so we can get comfortable."

Izzy nodded as he wrapped her in his muscular arms. Together, they faced each other, her back against the cave wall.

"Close your eyes, my *alma gemela*."

She unwound at the sound of Asmodel's mesmerizing voice.

"And let me in."

Asmodel's back teeth clenched until Izzy closed her eyes. He expelled a throaty sigh. Having her lie with him on the cozy fur helped create the soothing ambiance he looked for that allowed him to create a Dreamwalk with her.

"That's it, Bella," he whispered. "Let yourself relax while I create what's called a Dreamwalk. It's a gentle way for my mind to touch yours. To make it more comfortable for you, I'd like to take us to one of your favorite places. There I'll share with you who I am. Would that be okay with you?"

Izzy's warm breath coated his neck as she chuckled.

"You know, my name is Izzy, not Bella."

He smiled. "Ah yes, but when we are alone, to me you are my Bella. My beauty."

Izzy giggled and scooted closer to him. Mere fractions of distance separated her body from his. If she kept that up, nothing would keep his lower half from her.

It took every ounce of strength he had to avoid touching her as it was. "Are you ready?" His whisper came out as a growl. He cleared his throat.

She nodded, and Asmodel continued. "Now, picture in your mind a favorite place where you are most comfortable.

Some place where you have no fear." He waited a moment before asking, "Are you visualizing a place like that?"

In his arms, Izzy's body softened, her sensual curves molding to his touch.

She let out a soft, melodic hum before responding. "Yes, I have it in mind."

Asmodel brushed a trail of her fine hair from her eyes. "Good. Now, stay calm as I join you."

With a quick nudge of his mind, he created a pathway between his mind and hers, opening a doorway for him to put them into a dream sequence that would feel real to them both. Satisfied everything was as it should be with her, he opened his eyes in the dream plane and took in the place Izzy had created. He might be the foundations of the dream that held it together, but she was the designer of this sanctum, complete with varied attributes.

His eyes widened at the sight of the outer heavy doors, grand and imposing. In the bright sunshine, their richly paneled dark wood boasted intricate carvings. Brass handles, polished to a shine that caught the light and reflected the grandeur of the building's surrounding architecture. The ornate doorway was framed by Byzantine stonework, adding a touch of majesty to the imposing entrance.

Asmodel had never seen a place like this. He couldn't wait to discover what was inside. He pushed through the heavy doors, and the sudden quiet swallowed the outside city clamor he hadn't paid attention to until it was gone. Looking up, he could see the vaulted ceilings of a large main hall stretched above. The air was tinged with the mild, musty scent of aged paper and polished wood, and light filtered through several tall windows that cast long, solemn shadows across rows of oak tables. Various readers hunched in silent reverence over books, tablets, and computers.

As he walked farther inside, his footsteps echoed softly on the marble floor, like a faint whisper to announce his presence. To his right, the gentle rustling of pages turning and the occasional muted cough punctuated the stillness, as patrons immersed themselves deeper into their literary worlds.

"Welcome to my world, Asmodel." Izzy greeted him with a huge grin, her hands clasped in front of her. "Isn't this great?" She whirled around with her arms flung wide and laughed. "I can't believe how real this looks!" Abruptly stopping, she rushed over to him and gripped his forearms. Her head tilted with a mischievous grin. "You even got the details of Mr. Herbert right—sleeping in the corner over there." She nodded at an elderly man nodding off in a leather chair that could have held two of his fragile figures.

He couldn't help but stare at the mesmerizing sight of a giddy Izzy. Instead of the worn-out clothing she'd been wearing since he'd met her, she now wore some kind of long fuzzy sweater that outlined her full breasts, making them appear soft and inviting. Her shapely legs, showcased by tight-fitting pants, highlighted her mouthwatering round rump and taut muscles, ending snugly at her ankles. On her dainty feet were strappy, open-toe sandals that had her pink colored toenails peeking out, inviting him to play.

Asmodel swallowed a dry throat and took in a deep breath. Damn woman was the most tempting female he'd ever laid eyes on.

"Asmodel?" Izzy put her hand on his arm. "Are you okay?" She gestured to the spacious area around them. "Don't you like it here?" Her lower lip quivered.

It was hard to understand the question. It took everything he had to keep his hands to himself and not grab the fluffy sweater at her waist and lift her up so he could kiss the living shit out of her.

When her grip tightened, he did his best to focus on her gorgeous amber eyes and not lower. "Um." He cleared his throat. "What? Is what okay?"

"You, being here in this place?" Izzy cocked her head to the building they were in. "Where I used to work—The New York Public Library. Are you okay with this place?"

"Oh." He glanced around. "Is that where we are?" Not that he noticed anything. The only thing he wanted to look at was her. "Is there anywhere we can go that's private?"

Izzy's eyes twinkled, and her grin appeared again. "Oh, don't worry. I know just the place." She grabbed his hand and led him away. "Evelyn, watch the store!" Her voice rose as she addressed a middle-aged woman behind an imposing wooden counter.

The woman laughed and shooed her with a negligent wave. "Sure, I'll mind the shop for ya. Go on now and have a bit o' fun!" The woman's laugh was infectious.

Asmodel's eyebrows rose at the thick Irish accent.

Izzy giggled and stepped up her pace until she reached a hallway with several doors on either side. When she came to the first one, she opened the solid cherry-oak door and rushed them through. The room was modest, lined with floor-to-ceiling bookshelves filled with leather-bound volumes. On one side of the room, a plush, soft, peach couch invited a moment of repose, its cushions slightly indented, suggesting Izzy used it often. A small, circular table stood nearby, bearing a solitary lamp that cast a warm, golden glow across its surface. The room had a quiet hum, insulating it from the outer world. An antique clock perched atop a bookcase, its rhythmic ticking the only sound breaking the silence.

The centerpiece of the office was the desk—a large, sturdy piece of craftsmanship made from dark, rich mahogany. Its surface was broad and polished to a soft sheen that reflected the muted light from the lamp in the ceiling above. The edges of the desk had subtle carvings—nothing ornate, but just enough to add a sense of distinction and old-world charm. On the desktop rested a slim laptop next to a vintage brass desk lamp on the corner. A few stacks of books and papers haphazardly covered the other corner.

"Is this private enough?" Izzy closed the door behind her. The sound of her twisting the lock in place made him grin.

Any restraint he held in check vanished. He captured the alluring woman in his arms where she belonged.

"This is perfect," he whispered before devouring her mouth with his.

When Asmodel's lips touched hers, all the playfulness inside Izzy evaporated. With a single touch, he took control of the kiss and owned it. As his lips slanted over hers, his wicked tongue pushed inside and created havoc. With a seamless motion, he swung her up into his arms, his mouth never missing a beat. He turned, positioning her above him, and then laid back on the couch, holding her close. Thank goodness the piece of furniture she'd purchased years ago at a charity auction was strong enough to be used for something as decadent as what they were doing.

Izzy had just enough time to catch a single breath before her senses exploded with each stroke he made inside her mouth. Forget wanting any kind of slow introductions between them. Desire, commanding and strong, seeped into every fiber of her being. And after one hot second, it dawned on her the lust between them wasn't just hers.

It was mutual.

She shared his passion. What he experienced, she did. Every sight. Every scent. Every intense touch he felt, she did, too.

No telling how she knew that.

Draping her thighs over his, he grabbed her bottom and pulled her to his groin, turning the kiss into something hungry. Her sensitive nipples rubbed against the wide contours of his chest, causing her to meet his kiss with a savagery of her own. By instinct alone, she toyed with his tongue against hers, causing a white-hot pleasure she'd never imagined.

Izzy felt his hardened cock between her thighs. Sucking in a breath, she pressed closer, grinding her sex against his. The resulting reciprocal vibration made her insane with need.

"Take what you want, Bella," he whispered, his half-lidded eyes watching her. The colors of his hazel eyes blended into something darker, something sinful. He tugged on the end of her sweater.

"This has to go," he snarled. With a flick of his hand, the sweater and her bra disappeared. He focused on her naked chest. "These are the most beautiful things I've ever seen. Look how pretty your hard little nipples are." He framed her breasts with his large hands, his thumbs stroking her puckered peaks.

With each brush he made, she garbled a strangled cry and shivered. With thumbs and fingers, he exerted just enough pressure on her tips that left her careening out of control as a pull of pressure built between her legs.

"Asmodel..." Her breathless tone cut off when he rolled his hips, making his hard length stroke her over the sensitive clit. She squeezed his outer thighs in reaction.

"Like that, *alma gemela*? Do you want more?" He stroked her hip to control her movements against his swollen hard-on. "Let's see if I can make this better." He sat up and covered one of her breasts with his lips.

All coherent thought escaped as his tongue rasped over the hard nubbin. The heat of his mouth tightened her womb with a solid hold as lightning zapped from her nipple straight to her clit. Her vagina burned as her juices spilled, dampening her panties, creating a slick surface between her delicate folds. Desperate for more, she ground herself against his masculine strength.

Izzy rode Asmodel in desperation, unable to stop moving as he went from one nipple to the next, feasting on the sensitive skin.

Steady nips, then licking over each little love bite. First, he covered the nipple, then he sucked it with a heady draw of his mouth.

Her body tightened. Soft whimpering mewls escaped her. She wanted more. She had to have more. Izzy buried her hands in his hair and held him to her as she rode him with desperate movements. The stroke of his leather-covered cock was killing her. She had to assuage the ache.

"Clothes," she whimpered. Coherent thought was beyond her. Saying one word was hard enough.

With a swiftness that left her dizzy, Izzy found herself underneath him, cocooned by his unyielding, muscular chest.

Good gosh all mighty. His spicy man scent surrounded her, ramping up the overwhelming pleasure of being held by all that glorious naked flesh. *And holy moly,* the man *was* naked. All that dazzling body warmth held against every bit of her, eased an aching chill she didn't know she carried.

Asmodel journeyed down her torso, his wide torso pushing her legs apart until he settled between her splayed thighs. His broad shoulders held them open as his head lowered.

With wide eyes, Izzy watched him kiss her exposed, hardened nub. The light kiss destroyed her. She arched her neck as the promise of total pleasure rushed through her.

Then Asmodel's tongue slid between the narrow entrance of her sex in a slow, mind-numbing stroke. The man touched her clit and circled it before sucking it into his blazing mouth. She gasped as his hands slipped beneath her rear and lifted her close, making her sensitive intimate flesh accessible to his hungry attention. She had to touch him, to feel more of him. Grabbing his thick hair at the top of his head, she kneaded the silken strands. Instinct caused her to lift her hips, even as conflicting sensations threatened to overwhelm her.

She jumped when his fingers eased inside her, filling her with their girth as his lips and tongue played with her nubbin. Arcs of elation lashed inside her, pulling a garbled cry from her lips as he steadily stroked his fingers inside and out.

Nothing should feel this good, this strong. An inner tsunami took over, all sensations refusing to relent. Each stroke of his lips, tongue, and fingers ramped up the experience, growing in intensity. She ignored anything else.

"Please," she whimpered. "I... you... Asmodel." The garbled words fell as his stroking fingers coupled with the sucking heat of his lips playing with her clit. She teetered on the edge of devastating madness.

Izzy moaned, her head twisting back and forth on the soft couch cushion. She couldn't take anymore. No way would she survive. A spontaneous, jarring rapture took hold. Unable to suck in a breath to scream, no sound came out as her body tightened before exploding in a profusion of ecstasy.

Just as the final ribbon of rapture eased, Asmodel rose between her slack thighs and pushed the broad head of his cock against the entrance where his fingers had filled her, and pushed inside.

The spasms of her slick release parted for his claim. As he burrowed in, her body stretched to accommodate his wide girth. The blazing onslaught of his occupation threw her into another rising tide of pleasure, carrying with it the last of her sanity.

Izzy gripped his shoulders as he retreated then thrust back in until he reached the end of her channel. With every move he made, her sheath stretched tighter round him, capturing him.

"Ahh... that's it." Asmodel groaned, nipping the side of her throat. "Take all of me."

She jerked her hips, clamping her inner muscles around him as he burrowed deeper.

"Yes... right. Every inch of me..." He powered inside her, driving his full length until there wasn't a place where she began and he ended.

Writhing beneath him, Izzy's inner flesh flexed and undulated repeatedly, greedy for every stroke. Her entire body sang with exhilaration. "Asmodel..."

"Holy Goddess..." His low groan fanned the sensitive skin at her neck. His body became taut, and each muscle tightened above her.

The slickness between them ramped her experience to a wanton level she never imagined existed. Her womb convulsed, driving the breath from her lungs.

"*Fruk*!" He yanked against her, then drew his hips back before pushing forward again and again, every plummet harder than the one before.

Izzy clamped onto Asmodel's broad shoulders, each nail biting into his tight skin in reaction. Lisping cries fell from her lips. Bending her knees, she lifted her hips higher, begging for more, frantic for more.

The man didn't disappoint.

Asmodel moved, each deep stroke fucking her hard and solid. Like a master, he plowed her with steady intent. He filled her, retreating then skewering her again and again. Stronger, heavy, until he drove inside her with one last thrust, pushing them both over the edge. With a cry, his body shuddered into hers, his release as high-powered as his thrusts had been.

Collapsing under him, Izzy's exhaustion took over as a gentle wave. On top of her, his stiff body trembled. With a sigh, she savored a completeness she'd never experienced before.

Home. She was finally home.

Izzy smiled. Darn, they never got around to talking. Asmodel was still as much a mystery as before. Not that she cared about that right now. After that amazing bout of lovemaking, what else did she have to know about the enigmatic man?

She yawned. Well, anything else could wait until the morning.

Asmodel groaned and rolled them over on their sides, spooning them together.

Snuggling deeper into the man's arms wrapped around her, Izzy welcomed the tranquil arms of sleep.

Chapter Ten

Asmodel swallowed a groan as he eased his semi-hard cock from the grip of Izzy's body. With barely enough sense to keep the Dreamwalk going, he tried to control his careening emotions. The last thing he wanted to face was reality. Especially when her sweet, silken flesh spasmed around his semi-hard member as he retracted.

He collapsed beside her, putting an arm over his eyes, and took in a deep, satisfying breath. The air was a heady mixture of the musk from their union. His erection twitched, as if signaling it was ready for round two.

With a grunt, Asmodel forced himself to sit up. Draping one of his arms on his upraised knee, he swept a hand through his hair with the other. He couldn't help but stare at the woman sleeping beside him. His chest clenched as he watched her.

Her luscious dark hair fanned behind her, and her lips parted as soft breaths went in and out. Her eyes twitched in REM sleep, and a sultry smile curved her full mouth. "Asmodel," she whispered.

A dreaming Izzy saying his name solidified his sense that he belonged to this woman. The instinct burrowed deep in his soul. She was a missing part of him that had finally found its way home.

The urge to share everything about him with her overrode his common sense. Here in this Dreamwalk, he had the freedom for them to get to know one another. So, why leave?

Then she took in a lungful of air. The movement caused her full breasts to wave up and down, her pert dark nipples puckering as if begging for his kiss.

He moaned. Not one to ignore such a blatant invitation, he leaned down, determined to capture the alluring nub with his watering mouth...

A painful pinch at the back of his neck jerked him awake.

Asmodel blinked until the blurry vision of JR13 hovering in front of him came into focus. The small black-and-silver spider-bot's iridescent wings kept the bot steady.

"What the hell, JR13?" Asmodel growled. The droid shouldn't have been able to yank him out of a Dreamwalk like that. "You know you're not supposed to interrupt me when I'm in a psionic mindset."

"Yeah, well, cataclysmic events make us all do things we'd rather not, organic man."

On that note, the ground shook, causing dirt and dust to rain down on them from the cave roof.

Asmodel covered Izzy with his body, wincing when several small rocks bounced off his back.

Shouts and cries from the large chamber caught his attention. Rising from Izzy's warm body, he glanced over his shoulder. Smoke billowed out of the entrance as groups of pardalions sprayed a section of the cave engulfed in flames with wands that spewed some sort of dousing agent.

"What's going on?" Izzy coughed beneath him. "Do I smell smoke?"

Asmodel scanned her to make sure she was okay.

She rubbed her eyes, then looked up at him. Her eyes were dilated, and her rounded cheeks flushed a rosy pink. She licked her lips and focused on him.

He tightened his grip.

"Hey, Asmodel!" JR13's voice raised. "We've got to get out of here before the entire mountain drops on our heads." His wings buzzed faster, as if he was ready to take off.

"What?" Asmodel tore his gaze from Izzy and scooped her up in his arms. It didn't take a genius to figure out the bot was right. Holding Izzy tight, he raced out of the alcove into the almost-deserted cave. "JR13, grab on to me, and I'll get us out of here."

"About time," the bot grumbled.

Making sure his little AI friend was secure on his shoulder, Asmodel teleported them out of the cave. He put them a few feet away from the entrance, near a thick group of pardalions gathered at the base of the towering cliff.

"You okay?" Asmodel asked Izzy.

The ground rumbled.

He planted his feet apart so he wouldn't drop his precious cargo.

Izzy shivered and clasped her arms around his neck. Her wide eyes darted around. "What's happening? Last thing I knew, we were in my office..."

"That was the Dreamwalk I told you about." Asmodel sent a quick probe into her mind, making sure she wasn't upset at what happened between them. Instead of anger or regret, her soft, feminine aura wrapped around him with no hesitation. The burning tension in his stomach eased. She was more than comfortable with what they did in the psychic realm. And, judging by the emotions crossing her face, she didn't like being interrupted, either.

"When the earthquake happened, JR13 woke me up so we could get out of the cave before it collapsed." As Asmodel uttered the last word, another hard rumble erupted. He clutched Izzy tighter as the ground beneath them heaved like the chest of a waking giant.

Around them, the jungle trembled, and feathery leaves shivered off branches in flurries of greens, reds, and blues. As the tremors intensified, the massive cave before them groaned, its ancient mouth gnashing as if in pain. With a thunderous roar, the entrance crumbled, boulders tumbling like the bones of the earth, sealing away centuries of pardalion traditions.

Dust mushroomed into the air, painting the sky a grim gray.

The pardalions' haunting cries echoed through the chaos, a sorrowful cry of loss and displacement.

Asmodel's heart hammered against his ribs, each beat a reminder of the time he and his brothers escaped a similar situation on ancient Earth. How life teetered between the thin line of survival and obliteration.

"Oh no." Izzy's amber eyes filled with tears. "I hope everyone is okay."

"JR13, analyze," Asmodel told the companion on his shoulder.

"On it."

While JR13 probed the surrounding area, Asmodel did the same with his psychic sense. He breathed a sigh of relief when he sensed all the pardalions were with him and Izzy in the clearing.

"All clear and accounted for," JR13 reported.

"That's good." Izzy sighed. She looked up at him with a grin. "You know, you can put me down now."

Asmodel couldn't resist. "But I don't want to." He nuzzled her close, breathing in the delicate scent of her hair.

"Yo, organic man."

What was with JR13 interrupting all the time? "Yes, JR13?" With a grimace, he let go of Izzy's legs to let her stand, but kept his arm around her shoulders to keep her close.

"Echo tells me she and Raxx escaped Panterion Prime."

Asmodel's eyebrows rose. "Oh? Did she tell you where they are?"

"Right here, dude!" Raxx sauntered through the thick jungle with his arms wide open. "As if I'd sit around twiddling my thumbs waiting for your sorry ass to rescue me."

Izzy's eyes widened as she locked her gaze on the man Asmodel spoke to.

So this was Raxx Jorlen. The guy who was supposed to be confined in Panterion Prime had somehow escaped not only the technologically advanced zaltrixan, but the powerful crystal lady. There he stood, chill as a polar bear's toenails, in the middle of the craziness as the jungle continued to rumble with small aftershocks.

His attractive, rugged, handsome features told the story of a hard life in every line and scar his face carried from the piercing intensity of his dark eyes, to his strong jawline. The playful smirk on his full lips radiated confidence. His weathered, dusty leather jacket was layered over a dark, formfitting shirt. The crisscrossing of scratches and gouges on the jacket had to be trophies of his many adventures.

Durable cargo pants, loaded with pockets holding a bunch of gadgets, clung to his hips as he strolled toward them over the uneven terrain. On his feet were scuffed, sturdy boots that bore the marks of countless expeditions, making him look at ease even in the wild. At his belt, a strange device that looked like an old beeper with a sleek metallic finish emitted a soft, pulsing glow. Maybe it was some kind of smart-phone doohickey that guided Raxx through the jungle. If nothing else, the guy looked right at home in the current chaos.

"Somehow, I feel like this is all your fault." Asmodel waved to the non-existent opening of the collapsed cave.

Raxx shrugged. "Maybe. Probably." He put his fists on his trim hips. "I had to get out of there before that stupid crystal chick woke up." He chuckled. "Dude, I was so totally not into her. Ya know what I mean?" He turned his dark gaze to Izzy. "Well, hello there. And who are you, besides the most sought-after woman on the planet?" He came close and extended his hand.

Izzy pressed her lips together to stop the laugh threatening to escape. "I am Isabella Torres. But you can call me Izzy." She put her hand out to shake, but he instead turned her hand over and kissed the top of her knuckles.

He rubbed his palm over the skin he'd kissed and raised his head with a mischievous grin. "I am very glad to meet you, Izzy."

"All right." Asmodel broke their connection, moving to stand between them, and crossed his arms. "That's enough."

While Izzy didn't have any trouble taking care of herself, she found Asmodel's caveman tactics quite adorable.

"Chill, my man." Raxx put his hands up and stepped back. "Just payin' my respects to this bodacious chick, is all."

Izzy giggled behind her hand. This guy sure had a strange slang, like something out of an old 80s movie. She glanced at the stern expression on Asmodel's perfect profile. Maybe now wasn't the time to delve into anything about Raxx Jorlen.

"Tell us about the Krystalii." Asmodel's no-nonsense tone and narrowed eyes focused on Raxx.

Raxx threw his shoulders back, and his own expression mirrored Asmodel's. "I'm afraid that after I left, all hell broke loose." He ran a hand over his short, thick hair, making the top ends stick up. "Echo told me that bitch used her strong psychic mojo on Panterion Prime in a blinding rage, demanding they hand me over."

Several gasps and growls filled the air from the pardalions listening to the conversation.

Talira rushed to Raxx's side and grabbed his arm, swinging him around to face her. "Were there any survivors?"

The stricken look on her face made Izzy's heart drop. Talira had to be thinking of Jaltaar.

"Maybe?" Raxx drawled out his answer, and his sharp cheeks turned a soft red. "I really don't know. I was deep into the jungle when the first tremor hit."

"We've got to go to Panterion Prime," Talira announced. A mulish scowl creased her snout. She looked at Praetor Vorlok with a hard glare. "We've got to go there, since there isn't anything left of Nekojin. If there's a chance any of the zaltrixan survived, we've got to see if we can help."

"You'd be willing to save people who wanted to commit genocide on you?"

Asmodel's question might have been harsh, but Izzy agreed, taking time to really study the destroyed entrance to the massive cave.

The mountain had torn itself apart, leaving behind a yawning chasm filled with shattered boulders and fractured rock faces. Jagged edges jutted out from the hole's mouth, the collapse having stripped away the once-majestic stalactites that adorned its entrance.

Debris scattered the jungle, feather-leaves and twisted branches were strewn around like the aftermath of a violent storm. Dust lingered in the humid air, taking its time to settle as the jungle grew eerily silent. The usual cacophony of wildlife hushed.

In the hazy light, Izzy put her hand over her aching heart at the sight of the rubble. Here was the profound history of a proud people now lost among the rubble, their legacy buried beneath the weight of nature's indifferent hand.

Talia snorted. Her whiskers fanned up. "What choice do we have? All of us have family there, and we can't leave them at the mercy of that disgusting crystal alien."

Praetor Vorlok raised his paws, his claws extended. "You are right, Talia. With Nekojin gone, we'd better find shelter before nightfall." He lowered his paws and glanced around the jungle ahead of him. "If we're left out here in the open, the skalderbeasts will be the least of our concerns."

Izzy put a hand on Asmodel. "Can you use your psychic senses to see if anyone is still alive in the city?"

Asmodel nodded and gripped her hand back. "I've been doing that." He glanced at the Praetor. "Most of the citizens of Panterion Prime survived. Only a part of the city suffered the earthquake. But many remain trapped under fallen buildings. The citizens are in a panic." He closed his eyes, as if concentrating on something eluding him. "I also get the sense their leadership is missing? Maybe just unresponsive?" His distinctive eyes opened, clear and focused. "They aren't getting any direction from the Supreme Regent, which is causing panic." With an absentminded air, he tucked her arm under his. "I also sensed that the Krystalii is spiraling out of control. And if we don't intervene, CeluriaVO will face total annihilation."

"What do you mean, out of control?" Talia demanded. "And what's this about annihilation?"

"It means if we don't stop her, she'll blow up the planet." Asmodel clarified.

Izzy clutched his firm arm. "How can we stop someone that powerful?" She glanced around and watched the scikvak talk in small groups. "Especially since I doubt Madam Fexa got her machine completed in time."

She eyed the elder pardalion speaking adamantly with a group, a hissing snarl propelling spittle from her curling lips.

Asmodel raised his head, his chin tilted, his hazel eyes bright. "That leaves you, me, and Raxx to take care of things." He blinked and focused on the praetor. "You and your people need to find whatever provisions you can and meet up with us at Panterion Prime. Hopefully, when you get there before nightfall, we'll have gotten rid of the Krystalii threat."

"And if you can't?" Praetor Vorlok growled.

"Then it won't make much of a difference, will it?"

The praetor didn't comment on Asmodel's announcement, but his calm demeanor didn't fool Izzy for one moment. As Talira and he walked off to join the circle of council members, Izzy sucked in the side of her bottom lip. No sooner did they join the group than a heated argument erupted among them. She couldn't hear what was said, not that it mattered. She snuck a quick peek at Asmodel and Raxx. She couldn't get what Asmodel proposed out of her mind. It was a pretty tall order for just him and her. Even with Raxx's help.

"So, how're we gonna do this?" Raxx spoke in a low tone, his dark eyebrows furrowed as he stared at Asmodel.

Asmodel nodded at the small spybot on his shoulder. "JR13 has been communicating with Echo to determine the best way to neutralize the Krystalii."

"That's right, organic one." JR13's bulbous head nodded. "We're still considering several options." His head cocked as if listening to something. "Yes, quite right, Echo." He once again focused on them. "But we'd have a better chance to come up with a solution if we get close enough to analyze her specific brain-wave patterns. That way, we can come up with a viable solution."

"Alright, that sounds easy enough," Asmodel said. "Since I've been through the area between here and there, I'll just teleport us to the edge of the city, and we'll go from there."

Raxx crossed his arms and cocked his head. "Sounds righteous, dude. But what do we do once we get there?"

"You're not going to make it if you don't take me with you."

Izzy jumped at the sound of Talira's voice. *Holy cow!* The female was quiet as... well, as a cat.

"Oh?" Raxx barked with laughter. "And why's that, pussycat?"

"You need someone to guide you, and I'm the best choice." Talira's firm tone accompanied her pounding the end of her weapon on the dark jungle grounds. The tips of her claws gleamed in the shadowed light under the jungle foliage.

Izzy watched the blank expression on Asmodel's face. Not sure if he agreed with the scikvak or not, but she had to make sure it was safe first. "Can you handle transporting the four of us?" She stared at Asmodel, then held her breath as he hesitated. He had to say yes. Talira quivered, probably with her need to find Jaltaar.

Asmodel's handsome face softened when he glanced at her. "Yes, that's not something you need to worry about, *alma gemela.*"

"Yeah, organic female. He's got enough psychic energy to..."

"JR13, have you finished conferring with Echo?" Asmodel interrupted his spybot.

Izzy pursed her lips. Hopefully he was hiding stuff from Raxx and Talira, not her.

I am, as your people say, an open book to you. Asmodel's voice was soothing in her mind. *And I want you to know everything about me. But you are right. Not in front of others.*

Doggone it, Izzy loved the sound of his voice. In or out of her mind. She giggled. Out of her mind. She sighed. Wouldn't it be great if she could talk to him like that? Yeah, talk about intimate.

You can, my Bella.

His masculine tone gave her shivers.

Just feel this pathway that I've created for you in our dreams. Now you can reach me anytime.

Izzy searched her mind until she was sure she found what he described. *I think I've got it.* She gave him a mischievous grin. *You know, you're not going to get away from me so easily now.*

I wouldn't have it any other way.

Her cheeks heated at the sincerity in his mental tone.

"I believe you're right, Talira. You'd better come with us." Asmodel addressed the stiff-necked scikvak. At his words, her stance loosened.

"Do you think you know where the Krystalii could be?"

Talira shook her head. "No, but I think we should go to the Regent's private chamber. He should know where she is."

"And do you know where that is?" Asmodel tilted his head.

"I do." Her midnight-blue eyes narrowed. "Here..." She kneeled on one knee. "The rooms are..."

As Talira intoned various ways and options to access the palace, Izzy watched Asmodel. He closed his eyes and his face lost all tension. She touched the part of his mind he'd shown her and got caught up in a myriad of images that were hard to follow. Endless corridors led into opulent rooms, with short-furred zaltrixan mingling back and forth. Some with a self-absorbed air, while others were obvious servants waiting on their masters. Some were long-furred pardalions, handcuffed and gagged being dragged away by guards. Their heads hung as if in defeat.

Unable to keep up without getting a severe case of vertigo, Izzy physically as well as mentally took a step back. She'd let the professional, Asmodel, do whatever he was doing.

"Do you think you can get us there?" Talira stabbed an extended claw into one of the dirt outlines she'd created.

Asmodel opened his eyes and looked where she'd indicated. With a brief nod, he replied. "I can. But, I'd rather we went somewhere in the open first. That way we can make sure we don't appear in a part of the building that collapsed."

Talira stood, leaning her weapon on her shoulder as she dusted her paws off. "I doubt the palace suffered any damage. The reinforcements in the building, as well as the shields around it, would have kept it standing. But I do know somewhere we should go first." She pointed the bottom of her spear to the side of where she indicated the royal quarters were. "It's a place only I and one other know about." She kept her eyes downcast.

It must be where she'd meet Jaltaar in secret.

"Yeah, but what are we gonna do once we get there?" Raxx asked. "I gotta tell ya, I'm not looking forward to being a guest of the zaltrixan again. They have a totally heinous way of treating a guy, ya know?" His dark gaze landed on Talira. "Any chance that's where the crystal chick will be?"

"They don't allow outsiders near the private part of the imperial palace. My guess is she'd be closer to the royal gardens, site of the richest soil on CeluriaVO. I'm sure they offered that to her to rejuvenate."

"Ah, that's right. I read somewhere that one of the best ways to revive crystals is to put them in rich soil," Izzy mused aloud. She glanced at Asmodel. "If she's rejuvenated, I wonder why you sense she's out of control now."

"Let's find out. Talira," Asmodel addressed the scikvak. "Tell Praetor Vorlok we're leaving and let him know where we're headed. Do your communication devices still work?"

She nodded.

"Good. Ask him to let you know when they're close so we can tell them it's safe to enter the city or not."

"Okay. I'll be right back." Talira strode away.

"I didn't want to say anything in front of her—" Raxx thumbed behind him, where Talira scurried off. "—but I have something that might help you with the psychic mojo the crystal bitch might throw at us."

Asmodel's eyebrows rose. "Oh? What's that?"

Raxx reached into an inner pocket of his leather jacket. He pulled out two round disks no bigger than a quarter.

Izzy leaned closer for a better look at the translucent, almost invisible objects. "What are they?"

"These, my friends, are something that just might save whatever sanity you have left." Raxx bobbed his hand up and down. "Or at least save one of us." He studied Asmodel. "Since you have the same psychic stuff she has, these little babies should protect you better than us mere mortals." He nodded to Izzy. "These are called PsyShields. I, ah, acquired them from an alien species called the Crichian. You just slap them on, and whammo... all the psychic crap around you gets blocked right out of your mind." His grin was infectious. "Cool, eh?"

"Don't you have more than one pair?" Izzy asked.

"Ah, no, chickie poo." His cheeks flushed. "I tell ya, it wasn't easy to get these when I did."

Oh, he must have taken them without the Crichian knowing.

"All you gotta do is to place one on each temple, and you're totally righteous."

Izzy frowned. "Why don't you use them?" It was awfully nice of him to offer them to Asmodel.

"I don't need to 'cause I have Echo here." He patted his belt where his doohickey hung.

"Okay, thanks. It'll be good to have a backup." Asmodel put the shields into his inner jacket pocket.

"Ready?" Talira joined them. She slung the long weapon-pole through a harness strapped to her back, making the tip of the spiked ball swing in a lazy pattern.

"As much as we'll ever be," Raxx intoned with a smirk.

"Hold hands, and I promise to get everyone there." Asmodel's expression carried a hint of mischievousness in it. "Mostly in one piece."

"Mostly?" Raxx squeaked.

Izzy couldn't hear Asmodel's answer if he gave one. She became numb, as if every cell in her body fell asleep. Unable to move or speak, the world around her became a conglomerate of light sparkles interspersed in a black unknown.

And then nothing.

It'd been a while since Asmodel teleported more than just himself. Especially with people who didn't have any psionic abilities to help. Before he began, he sent his mind on a quick astral projection to ensure the place Talira described still stood. No reason to teleport into a pile of rubble. Good thing she was right that the palace withstood the violent earthquake.

Thankfully, they reached the inner sanctum of the royal palace without a hitch. The images of the area had been quite clear in Talira's mind, even other ways to enter it. Some paths known to the public. Some... not so much. Seems like the fiery little scikvak had snuck in on more than one occasion to meet the zaltrixan male, Jaltaar. How interesting.

As he suspected, there was more to that scikvak than he let others see. He glanced at Talira. Maybe their desire for each other was the catalyst they needed to get the two scikvak races to work together.

The four of them ended up in a dark chamber large enough for fifty people. Asmodel took a psychic sweep to ensure they wouldn't get attacked by other scikvak or that yellow Krystalii. The large group of scikvak in the room didn't notice them.

"You still with me, JR13?" Asmodel whispered to the bot resting on his left shoulder. He could feel the light tips of the bot's feet scraping across the back of his neck.

"All good, organic one," the bot's tinny voice was whisper soft. "Echo and I are analyzing the surrounding structure. Looks like it'll hold for now, but if that changes, I'll give you a shout-out."

Asmodel grunted in acknowledgment. He glanced around the room.

A group of scikvak were focused on a massive bed that dominated the room. Or rather, they were focused on the prone figure laying on the angle-shaped structure.

The head of the bed was made of dark hardwood bent in a circular shape that ended in a round overhang over the top. Littered around that dome and the frame were intricate carvings.

The bedding was some kind of plush material that reminded Asmodel of sheepskin mixed with silky fur.

The tapering open front allowed plenty of room for the large male scikvak, Supreme Alpha Regent Korvex, lying motionless on it. His eyes were closed, and his large paws were tucked under his chin. His muscular frame relaxed as if in sleep, his tail slightly twitching.

Even in this position, it was easy for Asmodel to sense the power and grace of the leader's inherent strength. While there wasn't any outside evidence of a mortal wound, he didn't need his psychic ability to determine the male would soon take his last breath.

"Jaltaar!" Talira rushed to the side of the bed where the young male kneeled beside the monarch.

At the sound of her voice, Jaltaar's head jerked in her direction. Without hesitating, he stood and caught her as she threw her arms around his neck, nuzzling her head against his neck.

As if a switch was thrown, Asmodel, Izzy, and Raxx were surrounded by growling zaltrixan guards pointing various weapons at them.

"Talira." Jaltaar wrapped his arms around her waist, his eyes closed.

The grief coming off him in waves was palpable and hard to ignore.

"How did you get here?" Jaltaar's voice was muffled against the female's neck. He didn't give her a chance to answer. "Oh, Talira. He's dying and I can't do anything about it."

"What's wrong with him?" Asmodel ignored the sharp spear mere inches from his neck.

"We don't know." Painful sorrow laced Jaltaar's voice. He pulled away from Talira and glanced between Asmodel, Raxx, and Izzy. "When the Krystalii woke up, she was out of control. She screamed at him—" He nodded at the prone monarch. "—and he suddenly collapsed."

Another zaltrixan continued. "Then the alien floated in the air, and the next thing we knew, she hit us with massive earthquakes." The elder wrung his paws. "Half the population of Panterion Prime perished in the rubble while the other half are trying to save those they can."

"Everyone from Nekojin is coming to help." Talira ran a paw across Jaltaar's whiskers. "If you'll let us." She glared over her shoulder at the weapons the guards leveled on Asmodel, Raxx, and Izzy.

A different elder rushed to Talira. "We need nothing from you, you disgusting *zihu*..."

"Viscount Syrin!"

The crackling command from the intricate bed rang out loud enough for everyone to hear. Complete silence followed.

"Father!" Jaltaar rushed back to the bed and grabbed the elder zaltrixan's hand. "Are you..."

"Listen very carefully, son."

Asmodel winced at the sound of the monarch's painful rasp.

"Father, save your breath." Jaltaar placed a paw on his father's. "The healers..."

"Pay attention, boy." The firm note in the monarch's tone didn't leave any room for argument. "No one can do anything for me now. That Krystalii tore me up inside, so

I only have a few moments." He took in a rattling breath. "It's up to you to save CeluriaVO from her." His cloudy green eyes looked over Jaltaar's shoulder at Talira. "How did Nekojin fare?"

Talira stood straight, but kept her paw on Jaltaar's shoulder. "We all survived, but our village lies in ruins. Our leader, Praetor Vorlock, is bringing the pardalions here to aid in rescue as we speak."

"Good." Regent Korvex nodded. "Good." He sucked in a rasping breath. "By royal decree I lift all sanctions against the pardalions and welcome them with open arms."

"Your majesty!" Viscount Syrin's outraged roar echoed. His ears flattened as he blinked. "We can't allow..."

"Enough!" Korvex sliced a paw through the air, his thick claws extended. "I so have decreed, and my will be done."

The elder zaltrixan sputtered, but bowed and stepped back.

"Guards, stand down." Korvex's voice was weaker, but no less commanding.

Without hesitation, in unison, the guards pulled their weapons back and stepped away from Asmodel and his two companions.

"Cowabunga. 'bout time, dudes," Raxx grumbled under his breath.

"I agree." JR13 intoned.

"Jaltaar, stand before me." The next command from the dying regent.

"Father." The anguish in Jaltaar's voice matched the tears gathered in his eyes.

Asmodel often wondered what it would have been like to have a parent, but witnessing the pain Jaltaar experienced as his father lay dying changed his mind. He glanced at Izzy, noticing her pinched lips and tear-filled eyes. Her hands were clasped in front of her, knuckles white. Wrapping an arm around her shoulders, he pulled her close.

Korvex grasped Jaltaar's paws in his own. His emerald-green eyes, so like his son's, blazed as he bared his fangs. "In the presence of our ancestors and the timeless stars, I, Supreme Alpha Regent Malstyr Korvax, bestow the mantle of sovereignty on you, my son, Jaltaar Zarvix. With this edict, you inherit the wisdom of our lineage, the strength to guide our people, and the resolve to uphold our sacred laws. May your reign be just, and may our realm flourish under your leadership."

Korvex released his son's paws and flopped back onto the lavish bed. "It is done." His deep sigh rattled deep inside his chest. "I now join with the mighty Solithar in the majestic hunting grounds."

The sovereign king of CeluriaVO closed his eyes and rumbled an exhalation, signaling his final farewell.

Chapter Eleven

The room erupted in loud roars.

Izzy gasped as the scikvak declared their sorrow when the ruler of their planet died. The booming chorus from the feline scikvak were not only in the room, but echoes came from outside as well. Apparently the population shared the grief at losing their sovereign.

Jaltaar's agonizing howls broke her heart.

With his forehead on his father's still chest, he wrapped his extended claws around the deceased monarch's wrist.

Talira knelt beside him, her head on his shoulder as she rubbed her whiskers against him, a rumbling sound vibrating from her in a comforting melody.

Putting her hand over her throat, Izzy swallowed a piercing ache. Poor Jaltaar. Who would've thought he was the king's son? He was the one who'd saved her by taking her to an outlaw faction for safekeeping. With a frown, she watched him as he muttered in a low tone only Talira could understand. Guilt was a terrible burden for anyone to bear.

A hard shake from the ground broke the spell.

Izzy grabbed Asmodel's arm to steady herself.

He swept her into his arms and braced his legs to keep them upright.

The scikvak growled, some resorting to all fours while others fell onto their backsides.

Jaltaar grabbed Talira into a tight hug as they rode out the rolling earth.

When it subsided, Viscount Syrin rushed to Jaltaar and bowed. "Sire, we need you to address the populace." He glanced around the room, wringing his paws. "Before things get out of hand."

Most of the scikvak in the room ran around like crazy cats. Hissing and snarling at each other as if they'd devolved into a primal species.

"Oh dear. I'm afraid he's too late." Izzy observed from her comfortable position in Asmodel's embrace.

One of the older adult females howled as she raced by them on four paws, her back arched with puffed-up fur.

Asmodel tightened his grip around her. "I agree." His rumbling reply vibrated against her.

Izzy tightened her hold around his neck and tugged him to look at her. "I'm fine now. You can put me down."

He put his forehead on hers. "But I don't want to." With his eyes half closed, he sighed. "But I will if you insist."

Izzy giggled. "This is becoming a bad habit of yours." She kissed the tip of his perfect nose. "I insist, Mister Macho Man."

Before she squirmed out of his hold, he captured her lips with his in a scorching kiss before setting her on her feet. She pulled away and wobbled, putting her hand at the side of her head to get her bearings. When she steadied, she narrowed her eyes at him. In retaliation, she licked her lips, enjoying his flavor.

His eyes mirrored hers as he repeated the gesture.

Darn man was lethal.

"We have to go, Jaltaar." Talira's soft tone caught Izzy's attention.

The powerful female kept her paw steady on Jaltaar's shaking shoulder. "Your people are dying, and they need you."

Sucking in a hiss, Jaltaar raised his bloodshot eyes to her. "I can't. I..."

"Jaltaar." Talira stepped back. "It is time for you to do as your father decreed and take your rightful place as Supreme Alpha Regent." Her tone left no room for argument.

Jaltaar closed his eyes and sucked in a deep breath. With paws clenched, he hissed and opened his eyes. "You are so right, my *tsuki*." Throwing his shoulders back, he rose, leaving behind the frightened boy and stood as a mature male of worth. His sturdy stance and firm expression told everyone in the room a new monarch was born.

"Oh wow," Izzy said under her breath. She'd never witnessed anything so profoundly moving in her entire life. Watching someone grasp the reins of leadership in one quick motion was a beautiful thing to witness.

"Indeed."

JR13's agreement from Asmodel's shoulder made Izzy grin. Little bot was growing on her.

"Enough!" Jaltaar's command was loud and clear.

As though a switch flipped, all the scikvak in the room stopped, eyes wide as they focused on Jaltaar standing tall by his dead father's bedside.

"Chief Jenara." Jaltaar pointed to a female zaltrixan standing against the wall with her arms crossed.

One of the few scikvak in the room who hadn't run around like the others.

"You and your guards need to assess what is happening within Panterion Prime. I want a detailed report on where the critical areas are within the hour. Talira will be your commander, so synchronize your Lumiview Prisms with hers."

Some guards started to rumble and hiss.

Izzy caught the curse *zihui* from more than one in the room.

"As regent, it is my right to decree who does what." The pupils in Jaltaar's bright-emerald eyes expanded. "As of this moment, the scikvak race is one." He waved his paw with the claws extended. The thick tips shone in the low light. "No more pardalion or zaltrixan. *We are one*."

Izzy held Asmodel's hand while gripping his forearm with her other hand. She'd always wanted to be part of some historical act. And here it was, a new day dawning. Darn if she was lucky enough to be here for it. Even if it was on an alien planet.

Jaltaar approached Talira and cupped the sides of her snout between his paws with his claws retracted. "Talira Cyndor of Nekojin. Will you do me the greatest honor of becoming my ever-mate? My Queen Regina? To aid in ushering in a new age for the scikvak on all CeluriaVO?"

Talira's fathomless dark blue eyes were clear as she responded. She covered his paws with hers. "I'm honored to claim you as my ever-mate, Jaltaar, my love."

"Long live the Supreme Regent Jaltaar Zarvix and his Queen Regina Talira Cyndor!" Viscount Syrin announced, flinging his arms wide.

Most in the room growled, roared, and shouted their approval.

Others were noticeably quiet.

Asmodel chuckled. "At least one male is smart enough to know how to keep himself in power."

Izzy grinned. "Oh, hush. Let's not politicize this beautiful moment."

"Why not?" JR13 asked. "The ramifications of what Jaltaar is proposing are more political than romantic." The small bot snorted. "No need to claim it as anything else."

"Oh pooh." Izzy dismissed JR13's cold assessment. "There's nothing like romance."

"And on that note—" Asmodel waved at Raxx to come close. "—you ready to take down the villain of this plot?"

Raxx batted his eyes with a palm over his heart. "Oh, you smooth talker, you. I can't think of anything I'd rather do than be part of a blooming romantic tragedy."

Asmodel jerked when a psychic wave of malevolence rushed through him. He waved for Raxx and Izzy to step closer. Keeping their heads together, he whispered, his tone urgent. "We'd better hurry." He glanced over Izzy's shoulder and watched a small group of scikvak congratulating Jaltaar through light scratches from their claws on his back. Around them, other felines rubbed the sides of their snouts together as happy purrs filled the air. So the danger wasn't from them.

"I can sense the Krystalii is gathering her strength to release another strong psychic blast. If we don't stop her, she'll destroy the entire planet," he stated.

The pinched look on Izzy's face made it clear she understood what he was saying. Damn it, he couldn't let her go into this unprotected. There had to be something he could... wait. *Oh, for the love of a motherless goat.* He should've done this when Raxx first told him about the PsyShields. He could hold his own against the Krystalii, but Izzy couldn't.

Asmodel reached into his jacket pocket and pull the small disks out. "Quick, Izzy. Put these on." He looked over at Raxx. "She just puts one on each temple, right?"

Raxx nodded. "Yeah, they'll work right off the bat."

Asmodel placed them on her palm.

She brought them close and studied them. Her teeth worried the lips on the side of her mouth.

At her concerned expression, Raxx chuckled. "Don't worry, chica. They don't hurt." He snorted. "In fact, you won't feel a thing." He winked at her. "Trust me."

Izzy's dubious look made Asmodel grin. He put a comforting hand on her shoulder. "While I haven't used them myself—" He nodded to Raxx, who rocked back and forth on his heels with his thumbs hooked through the loops on his belt. "—I do trust what he says about the PsyShields."

"But what about you?" Izzy tucked a panel of her baby-fine hair behind her ear. "Won't you need these to fight her since you've got psychic abilities and I don't?" Her bright-amber brown eyes carried a mix of worry and excitement.

Ah, his little human loved to try out new things just like he did.

A condescending snort from JR13. "He doesn't need help from some alien tech. He's got some serious abilities to protect himself with."

"JR13's right. I'll be fine." He reassured her. "I've had a lot of practice guarding my psychic senses from others." Namely, his brothers. Especially when they were in a mischievous mood to play tricks on one another. If he could protect himself from their pranks, handling the crystal entity should be easy enough. "Go ahead. Put them on, and I'll teleport us to where the Krystalii is."

"You'll find her at the city center." Jaltaar came to them with Talira's paw looped through his elbow.

Her dark-blue eyes assessed the area as if to keep her mate safe.

"Our security forces are scattered, trying to save as many citizens as they can. I'm afraid they won't be much help."

Asmodel nodded. "Actually, that'd be a good thing. The fewer people around, the easier it'll be for us to handle her." The last thing they needed was to cause more scikvak deaths. "If you and your people will coordinate the rescue operations, the three of us will handle the Krystalii."

Talira's whiskers drooped as her eyes narrowed. "You think you can handle her?" She leaned close. "We won't be able to help, even with my people arriving soon. We'll have our hands full trying to keep the two races from killing each other as it is."

"Don't worry, we've got this." Raxx jumped into the conversation. He patted the Echo device on his belt. "With me and Echo here, the Krystalii bitch is history. Nothing can stand in our way."

Asmodel hoped Raxx's arrogance was justified. He sighed. They'd find out soon enough. "Izzy, please put the PsyShields on." He rubbed her back. "I'll be here to make sure nothing happens when you do." He sent out a small tendril of energy to her, ready to act if necessary.

With a grimace, she placed the first disk on one temple and waited.

Asmodel didn't feel or sense anything unusual, so he nodded encouragement at her.

With a steady hand, she put the other one on.

At once, Asmodel lost all sensation of Izzy's mind. Wait, not just her mind, but her entire body became a blank slate. As if she wasn't there.

"Are you okay?" He gripped her shoulder. Losing the ability to sense her psychically felt like losing one of his physical senses. He might not like it, but he wouldn't admit it out loud.

Izzy's bright-brown eyes met his. "I guess so." She shrugged. "I don't feel any different."

"See?" Raxx crowed. "Told ya so."

Izzy glanced at the other man. "How do I know if they're working or not?"

"Tell us, big guy." Raxx pointed at Asmodel. "They working?"

Keeping his focus on Izzy, he gave a brief nod. "I can't psychically sense you at all."

Izzy beamed. "That's good!" She frowned as she studied his face. "Isn't it?"

Asmodel forced the tense muscles in his face to relax. The last thing she needed to worry about was him. "Yes, *alma gemela*. Now you'll be invisible to the Krystalii."

The ground violently shook.

"We'd better get going, dude." Raxx said after the tremor softened. "Like Mr. Miyagi says, if we don't go now, we'll get squished like a grape."

Asmodel didn't know who Mr. Miyagi was or why he talked about grapes, but the jest was sound. He tilted his head at Jaltaar and Talira. "Please stand back." He glanced at his bot companion on his shoulder. "You know what to do."

For once, the bot didn't spout any snark as he scurried to the nape of Asmodel's neck, his pointy feet making the skin prickle. Once the spybot was secure, Asmodel held out his hands to his two companions and instructed, "Hold on and don't let go."

"Alright, folks, buckle up, secure your luggage, and make sure your table trays are in the upright position. This ride's gonna be bumpier than a bull on a trampoline!"

Of course Raxx had to have the last word.

Izzy materialized between Asmodel and Raxx in the heart of Panterion Prime. Her eyes widened. The formerly awe-inspiring sight of the once-grand skyscrapers now had jagged edges, their glass facades occasionally shattered like a frozen, glittering waterfall. The ground beneath her hummed with the aftershocks of the earthquake, a low, continuous vibration she felt through the soles of her shoes. A cloud of dust hung in the air, filtering the light into a dull, ghostly gray haze. The scent of ozone and concrete teased her nose. The sharp, metallic tang mingled with the earthy smell of uneven rubble.

She turned to Asmodel and gripped his forearm. "Where is everyone? Do you think Jaltaar and Talira can get them out safely?" Her voice was no louder than a whisper over the city's eerie silence.

Asmodel narrowed his hazel eyes, his lips pressed in a firm line.

Raxx pulled Echo off his belt and scanned the horizon. He responded with a grim nod. "Shit! This sucks. A lot of them are vaporized." He nodded to the piles of dust and clumpy dirt littered across the square.

"Vaporized?" Izzy gasped. "Is that true?"

"I'm afraid so," Asmodel replied. "There isn't a living soul within a mile of here."

"But what caused..."

"Hide!" JR13's voice rose. "She's coming back!"

Izzy didn't have time to do anything but run since Asmodel gripped her upper arm and shoved her behind a wide column pillar now broken in half. He planted his body around her, his chest pressed against her back. Raxx next to her, clutched Echo with white knuckles.

Appearing from nowhere, Prisma-Solara materialized. Her brilliant, shimmering figure was planted in the square's center. Facets of her crystalline form caught the hazy light from the semi-destroyed buildings. Despite her striking beauty, she carried an unmistakable air of chaos. The yellow crystals on her body crackled with unstable energy, the color fading and coated with clumps of dirt. As her figure flickered, her sharp edges cast chaotic shadows across the broken pavement.

Once again, the ground heaved beneath Izzy and her companions. *Oh, my stars.* The crystal female's psychic energies not only manifested as visual distortions, but she was altering the environment as each tremor grew in intensity.

Around the Krystalii, the air was thick, charged with a pulsating power that sent waves of dissonance through the atmosphere.

The hairs on Izzy's arms stood on end.

The look of agony etched on Prisma-Solara's face was hard to watch.

"Oh, my goodness!" Izzy shouted. "She's in pain and losing control!" The roar of another quake drowned out her words.

Asmodel pressed her close to the column, his solid body shielding her. Without him, she'd get tossed around like a kite in a high wind.

When the tremor subsided, Asmodel moved to her side, giving her some space. Fortunately, his comforting warmth remained close. Out of the corner of her eye, she saw Raxx give Asmodel a grim look.

His eyes were wide, his tone urgent. "If she keeps this up, she'll bring the entire city down on us."

Asmodel's brief nod told Izzy he was assessing the alien's deteriorating state.

"I'm trying to probe her mind without her knowing. So far I haven't..."

"I must... I will... my duty... Lord Baelon!" The Krystalii screamed with her arms wide and her hands clenched in fists, causing wads of packed earth to fling free. Her words came out fractured and garbled by the spasms shaking her body. Prisma-Solara, caught in her psychotic storm, continued to thrash. Her yells and shouts created a haunting echo that resonated through the ruins.

As Izzy watched the alien suffer, she couldn't help but wish there was something she could do to help her. The spectacle of the alien's madness—a radiant being torn apart by her own powers—made Izzy both terrified and sad for the tormented female.

Asmodel, his jaws set, turned to Izzy and Raxx next to her. "I have an idea." His grim declaration came through his steady voice. "If I can make her believe I'm Lord Baelon, maybe she'll calm down enough so I can put her in a stabilizing hold."

"Dude, that's the dumbest thing I've ever heard," Raxx intoned. "So lame it just might work."

Izzy blinked. Things were happening too fast. "I..."

"Here, hold him while I do this." Asmodel held out his hand with JR13 on his palm.

With a quick toss, the small spybot landed on her arm. She didn't feel his pointy toes touch her through her shirt as he scrambled to rest on her shoulder. "I..."

Before Izzy had a chance to say anything, Asmodel's figure morphed. His stature grew, his features shifting to adopt the imposing presence of Lord Baelon, a crystal male figure twice the size of Prisma-Solara in height and width. His body was a mixture of crystals, mirrors, and glass with sharp protrusions jutting in all directions in various lengths of brilliant blues.

Izzy clutched her hand over her heart. The only thing she heard was the sound of her thundering heartbeat as she watched Asmodel's imposing figure. Her throat closed in terror.

"I'll be right back." Asmodel's attention turned to the out-of-control yellow Krystalii.

"But..." Izzy reached for him.

He was already gone.

"Do not concern yourself."

JR13's matter-of-fact tone took her by surprise. She'd forgotten he was there.

"Organic man will be just fine."

"Okay, if you say so." Izzy couldn't help the doubt creeping into her voice. Watching the man she loved put himself in danger like that was beyond... wait. In love? Really? When did that happen?

"Hey, look." Raxx chuckled. "She's buying it."

As Asmodel approached Prisma-Solara, his steps emanated a false sense of sovereignty.

Izzy caught her breath as he extended a hand in a gesture of peace.

"Prisma-Solara." Asmodel commanded with the authoritative cadence of the false Krystalii. "I will not tolerate this primitive display. Cease this destruction at once and attend to me."

Prisma-Solara's glowing, multifaceted eyes fixated on the figure approaching her. She still radiated chaotic energy as a cruel laugh escaped her cracked lips. Her voice came out grating and otherworldly. "You insignificant flesh born." She sneered. "You think you can deceive me, Asmodel?" She spat shards of glass at the ground that trembled beneath her fury. "I see through your paltry mind tricks!"

With a swift, sweeping motion, she extended her arms, making more dirt to fly free.

Izzy gasped as Asmodel lifted off the ground, his body stiff.

His face was contorted in pain, as if an invisible, crushing grip seized him.

Izzy cried out, "Asmodel!" and jumped up, her instinct to help her man.

"Damn it, Izzy!" Raxx grabbed her arm and pulled her down. He hissed. "What do you think you're doing?" He waved at the alien, who tossed Asmodel's prone body, now reverted to his normal self, to the other side of the square. "We can't risk getting closer to her. We've got to think of something else."

Izzy sniffed away unwanted tears. "JR13?" She glanced at the spybot on her shoulder.

His black-and-silver bulbous head focused on Asmodel.

When she spoke, his luminous eyes swung her way. "Can you check to see if Asmodel is okay?" She had to know if he somehow survived the brutal flight the Krystalii sent him on.

"From here I can tell organic man still lives, just unconscious. However," JR13's back panels opened and iridescent wings appeared. "I'll monitor his vitals and report back to you."

Without another word, the droid flew close to the ground, blending into the disheveled scene with debris and other insects buzzing around.

Putting her hand over her mouth, she watched JR13 make it straight to Asmodel who was lying on his back, his arms wide. After making sure the bot was as safe as he could be, she turned to Raxx. "You got any ideas?"

If Asmodel, with his strong psionic abilities, couldn't stop the Krystalii, what chance did she and Raxx have?

The crystalline alien let loose a bloodcurdling scream.

Izzy jumped.

"Son of a bitch!" Raxx flopped to the ground, thrashing as he held his ears. "Make it stop! I can't stand...!" His body shook, and his arms and legs whipped violently before he became unnaturally still.

"Raxx!" Izzy rushed to kneel by his side. She put a hand over his chest and sat back on her heels with a sigh when his heartbeat was strong and steady. What in the heck just happened? Why did he do that?

"Looks like the Krystalii hit a nerve."

JR13's voice near her ear made her jump. "Darn it, JR13. Warn a person next time, will you?"

"Echo asked me to come back when she lost control of Raxx after the Krystalii screeched like that. The psychic energy she let loose was off the charts. So much so even Echo couldn't filter it for him." JR13 informed her. "He'll be okay. Eventually. I think."

Well, wasn't that just great? Izzy considered the prone Raxx, then looked across the way to scrutinize the vulnerable Asmodel. "Why wasn't I affected like Raxx?"

"Because of the PsyShields you've got on."

JR13's matter-of-fact tone made Izzy roll her eyes. Well, duh. She'd forgotten she had them on. She peeked around the column to see what the crystal lady was doing. Poor thing looked like she was in pain. Bowing on her knees with her arms around her waist, she moaned and muttered. Clumps of mud and dirt dulled the glassy sheen of her body.

"No... I must... have to... Lord Baelon," Prisma-Solara's voice broke into a pained whisper. One of her fists pounded the side of her head. Crystalline dust, dirt and shards of clear-cut panels fell off her body.

"Oh, that poor thing." Izzy bit her bottom lip. "How can we help her?" And everyone else, for that matter.

"Well, see..." JR13 began. "Echo and I have an idea."

A hopeful jolt raced through Izzy. "Really?" She glanced at the Krystalii rocking back and forth, her eerie eyes closed. "What do you have in mind?"

"Between the two of us, we can generate a counter frequency tuned to disrupt the Krystalii's psychic brainwaves. It should create enough dissonance to bind her powers, at least temporarily." JR13's voice carried a blend of synthetic tones, as if he joined with Echo to answer.

Izzy's eyes widened. "Wow, do you think it'll work?" Another wail from the Prisma-Solara made her wince. "What do we do if it doesn't?"

"There is a 99.85% probability it will succeed." JR13's snooty tone was all him.

A minor tremor rumbled under her. Well, couldn't ask for anything better than that at this point. "Okay, JR13. Let's do it." The ground gave another grumbling roll under her knees. "Quickly please!"

The little droid's eyes blinked. "Initiating now." He paused, likely communicating with Echo.

A faint hum filled the air, starting quietly but growing in intensity.

Prisma-Solara's moans cut off as the frequency took effect. She stiffened, and her chaotic energy flickered as if in confusion.

The air vibrated with the force of the counter frequency, making Izzy's ears ring.

"What... what's happening?" Prisma-Solara's voice faltered. She clutched at her head, the crystals covering her face and body dimming from a vibrant yellow to a dull, throbbing amber. "My... my powers are weakening."

Izzy clapped. "It's working! JR13, keep it up!" she shouted over the rising whine of the counter frequency.

"Of course. Maintaining frequency." JR13's body vibrated in tune with the sounds he generated.

"What's going on?"

Asmodel's deep voice next to Izzy made her jump. *Holy cow!* What was with everyone sneaking up on her lately? "Oh my gosh! Asmodel!" She flung herself into his arms. The feel of his powerful embrace lightened the tension making it hard to breathe. Grasping his firm upper arms, she pulled back to check him out. "Are you okay?"

His hazel eyes twinkled as he brushed a wayward strand of her hair from her eyes. "It'd take more than a powerful crystal alien from another dimension to keep me down." He glanced around before cocking his head as he watched the moaning alien. "Is that sound coming from JR13?"

Izzy nodded. "Yes, with a little help from Echo." She motioned to Raxx, who now sat up and rubbed his eyes. "The bots have devised a way to create a disruptive counter frequency to hold her psychic powers. Neat, huh?"

Asmodel's expressive eyes met hers, filled with a mixture of gratitude and concern. "We'd better take advantage of it while she's disoriented." He cleared his throat. "I think I can hold her steady now. JR13, slowly diminish the sound you're making."

"Affirmative."

The ringing noise turned into a soft whisper.

"Wait, before you do anything, let me see if I can talk to her." Izzy placed a hand on Asmodel's chest. "You know, woman to woman." She glanced at the Krystalii, who now appeared fragile. Her once-formidable presence had been shattered by the dissonance caused by the AI duo. "I'd like to help her."

Raxx joined them, his lips white and pinched. "I'm not sure that's a good idea, chica." He shrugged one shoulder as if to loosen a knot. "Ya gotta admit that bitch is one Looney Toon. If it weren't for these bots, we'd be toast." He patted Echo strapped to his belt. "Good job, baby. Daddy's proud of you."

Asmodel's intense focus on her made Izzy swallow hard in a dry throat. She threw her shoulders back. It was easy to understand his unspoken concern. Yet, something deep inside urged her to talk to the Krystalii. This had the feeling of one of those pivotal moments when destiny offered a unique opportunity to make a difference. A moment meant only for her.

"I promise I'll be okay." Izzy placed her hand on his strong, clean jawline. "If not, have JR13 start the signal up again. Okay?"

Asmodel closed his eyes, holding the back of her hand in his. "If anything happened to you..."

"You'll be there to save me, won't you?"

Izzy had never spoken a truer word in her life. Putting her trust in Asmodel set her free in ways she never imagined, setting her free to take chances she once dreamed impossible.

Chapter Twelve

"**I**f only we had some more of these PsyShields." Izzy tapped her temple and glanced at the moaning Krystalii still on her knees with her arms wrapped around her waist. "I bet if she had those on, it'd help her."

JR13 snorted. "He's got more." He pointed a thin metallic leg in Raxx's direction. "He just didn't want to admit it."

"Way to rat me out, terminator." Raxx growled with crossed arms.

Izzy chuckled at the puzzled expression on Asmodel's face. Looked like her man wasn't familiar with some old movies. Something to look forward to when they went back to Earth. Once they cleaned up this Krystalii mess, of course.

"I can't tell you how great these work! Maybe they'll help her out too." Okay, that might be a bit of an exaggeration. But if Izzy hadn't been wearing the shields, she was sure she'd have suffered more than either Raxx or Asmodel.

"Could you possibly spare them?" she implored.

Raxx dropped his arms and rolled his dark eyes. "Of course I can." He reached into his jacket pocket and pulled his fist out. Stepping closer to her, he opened his hand and exposed the two round disks on his palm. He pointed to the mumbling Krystalii. "So, how are you going to get her to wear them?"

Izzy held out her hand for him to drop the disks on her open palm. "Easy. I'll just ask her."

"Izzy..." Asmodel put an arm around her shoulders.

His dark baritone combined with his body warmth made her shiver in pleasure.

"All right, I'll go with you. I can hold her for now, but I don't want to take a chance she'll break free and attack you." He glanced at the spider bot who jumped back to his shoulder. "JR13, you and Echo stand by with the disruptive blast if needed. Confirm?"

"No need to state the obvious, organic man," The bot's large eyes rolled. "We've got you covered."

"And just what am I supposed to do?" Raxx put his fists on his trim hips, his stance wide. "Stand here and look pretty?"

"I'm sure with practice, someday you just might pull it off."

Asmodel's voice was steady, but the twinkle in his eyes made Izzy giggle.

"Instead, why don't you make sure none of the scikvak gets close enough to interfere?"

Raxx's arms dropped. "Whatever." He glanced around. "That's me. I'll just narc around the hood and flush out any hostiles who are hiding." He ran a thumb across Echo's smooth surface. "Come on, baby. Let's check things out."

"Don't go far." Asmodel warned.

Raxx snorted with a hand wave. "As if." He headed in the opposite direction, but remained visible.

Izzy might enjoy the banter between the two, but she had a job to do. Without another word, she approached the rocking form of the Krystalii.

"Prisma-Solara, we don't mean you any harm." Izzy approached the moaning Krystalii with an open palm and spoke in a soft voice, making sure she kept her words gentle. "We only want to help you." Ever since she could remember, people had been telling her she was too nice and someday she'd regret it. Hopefully, today wasn't that day.

Prisma-Solara looked up, her blank gaze full of confusion and pain.

The minor tremors rolling around them faded. For a moment, the ruined city seemed to hold its breath, waiting to see what happened next.

The counter frequency JR13 hummed stayed quietly in the background.

Izzy approached Prisma-Solara with cautious steps. She frowned at the dullness of the alien's once-vibrant crystalline form. The muck covering her somehow made her appear smaller, less imposing.

Kneeling beside her, Izzy made sure she came across kind and non-threatening. "Prisma-Solara"—she kept her voice soft but clear—"can you tell me what happened to you?"

Prisma-Solara turned toward her, the facets of her crystals catching the light with a subdued shimmer. "I do not understand it myself." The alien admitted, her voice hollow, lacking its usual resonance. "My kind are not used to what is happening to me here. We exist in a state of order and logic. But here, on this planet... I felt a flood of something overwhelming. And I couldn't stop..." She choked out a whisper.

Izzy reached out and placed her hand over the Krystalii's and squeezed. She gasped at the warmth in the hand she held. Oh, this wasn't some automaton. This was an actual living creature in pain. "It sounds like you experienced emotions for the first time. This planet, CeluriaVO, might have triggered something deep inside you that's unfamiliar to you." She brushed off a clump of dirt on Prisma-Solara's arm. "Especially when you immersed yourself in the ground."

Prisma-Solara's crystals flickered weakly, as if attempting to process this information. "Emotions? Is that what these disturbances within me are called? When I woke up from my restorative sleep, chaos filled me instead of strength. It was uncontrollable and fierce."

"Yes, emotions can feel very intense, especially if you're not used to them," Izzy explained. "Most organic beings experience them all the time—they can be beautiful, but also very destructive if not managed."

"Why would your kind tolerate such disturbances?" Prisma-Solara demanded. Her tone was tinged with anger.

"I'll answer your questions if you'll let me give you something to help you manage these new feelings you're experiencing." Izzy released Prisma-Solara's hand and opened her other one where she'd held the disks. "These are called PsyShields." She tapped her own temple. "See, I'm wearing them to protect me from unwanted psychic stuff. I believe it will help regulate the powerful emotions you're experiencing so you can analyze what is happening inside you without foreign interference from this planet."

Prisma-Solara's crystalline citrine-yellow eyes focused on the round orbs in Izzy's palm before her intense gaze studied her. With her head tilted, her eyes widened. "You are correct!" she gasped. "I cannot read or control you. How amazing." She took the disks from Izzy's hand. "How do I apply them?"

"Place one on each temple," Asmodel supplied, standing a few feet behind Izzy. "You will feel disoriented at first, but that will fade. However, be prepared for your psychic sense to be muted as well."

The dull crystal of Prisma-Solara's mouth frowned. "For now, that will be acceptable." She scanned the surrounding destruction. "I did not intend to do this." Her gaze came back to Izzy. "At least not at this time." Now her lips creased into a small grin.

Izzy breathed a sigh of relief. Oh, lookie here, the crazy, evil alien made a funny.

Keeping her gazed focused on Izzy, Prisma-Solara put the disks on. The effect was immediate. Her eyes rolled back in her head before she flopped onto her back, legs and arms spread wide.

"Oh, my gosh!" Izzy rushed to her side, putting her hand on the female's hard crystal cheek. It was warm, so she still had to be alive. She turned to Asmodel. "Do you think she's okay?"

Asmodel kneeled next to her, hovering an open palm over Prisma-Solara's chest. "Yes, she'll be fine," he declared.

"Holy cow, chica!" Raxx exclaimed, leaning with his hands on his thick thighs. "Dang, knocked her out with one punch."

"I did no such thing," Izzy retorted. "She's just getting used to the PsyShields, that's all. But she'll wake up soon, won't she?" She glanced at Asmodel.

He placed his comforting hand on her shoulder. "I believe so. When she wakes up, we'll find out what her intentions are."

"Yeah." Raxx straightened. "Just so you know, if she reverts into her bad ol' self, Echo gave me a way to stop her once and for all."

A residual tremor rolled beneath Asmodel's feet. Looked like the chaos Prisma-Solara unleashed earlier still echoed in the earth and the air. He held still as his psychic senses hummed with the aftershocks of her power, a heady mix of fear and awe he associated with the Krystalii.

"That's good to know." Asmodel stood next to Raxx. "But I think the PsyShields are going their job. Look at her." He gestured to the unconscious alien.

Prisma-Solara's crystalline form shimmered in the hazy sunlight. Instead of her usual vibrant glow, her body had a fine film of silky crystal dust covering most of her protruding crystals. Other sections had broken off, leaving jagged edges.

"Do you think she looks like this because of the PsyShields?" Izzy gasped, touching her mouth with her fingertips. "Did I do this?" She turned to Asmodel, her face ashen.

Asmodel wrapped an arm around her shoulders. His heart slowed to a rhythm to mirror hers. The urge to hold his empathic woman was a strong one. One he had no intention of ignoring. His woman was a treasure. He gripped the tip of her shoulder when that thought hit him. His woman.

"You are not the cause of any harm to her, *alma gemela*." He pulled her close. "She was already disintegrating when we arrived."

"Yeah, could be why she turned into a total nutcase." Raxx nodded in agreement. "Hang on. I think she's waking up. Remember, Echo and I got this if she goes sideways."

Asmodel opened his mouth, then snapped it shut. Not worth asking what sideways meant.

Izzy reached out a hand towards Prisma-Solara, but stopped before touching the crystalline female again.

The Krystalii's eyes, usually blazing with an inner fire, were now dim. She looked fragile, a stark contrast to the devastating force she'd been moments ago.

"How are you, Prisma-Solara?" Izzy pulled her hand back into a fist. "Do you want any help?"

The crystal female sat up, clutching the side of her head. "I'm empty. Like something inside me has been ripped away." She looked at them. A clear, rolling orb trailed from the edge of one of her eyes and traveled in slow motion down the side of her face.

"How can we help you?" Izzy kneeled beside her, keeping her hands laced together on her thighs. "What do you need?"

Prisma-Solara frowned, causing several crystal panels around her mouth to loosen and fall off. For the first time, Asmodel watched as the cascade of light shining through her crystal body was now lighter. As if the brilliant yellow color had turned clear.

"I need to be cleansed." Prisma-Solara's voice was a melodic echo. "It's possible a natural waterfall will eliminate the poisonous dirt and energy of this planet on me while recharging my essence."

"I saw one in the jungle when Jaltaar took me to meet Talira." Izzy glanced up at Asmodel.

"What are your intentions after we take you there?" Asmodel frowned. He couldn't connect a psionic thread to the alien. Not that he expected he could with her wearing the psychic shields. But he had to try.

Prisma-Solara blinked, her face tight. She shut her eyes before opening them with a cry. "Lord Baelon!" She wailed, holding her head between her hands. "My lord is gone."

"Prisma-Solara!" Asmodel barked. If he let her wallow in her fears, they'd never get a handle on her. "You will answer me."

The female stopped and her eyes blazed.

At first, the look confused him. Then, as he watched her jaw set, he relaxed. It was a look he recognized. He'd seen it on his brothers when they first realized their servitude to the Akurns was over. This female wasn't afraid because she lost something. It was something altogether different.

Prisma-Solar kept her eyes on his as she stood.

Izzy got off her knees and joined him.

"For the first time in my life, I'm free." As she straightened, crystal dust and clumps of CeluriaVO dirt dropped off her. "I'm no longer a slave to a brutal-and-cruel master." Throwing her head back, she flung her arms wide, causing a maelstrom of broken glass and crystals mixed with silt and dirt to fly. "My fate is my own." She brought her head back and stared at him and the others, the color of her eyes dull but the determination clear. "Take me to a waterfall so I may get rid of the last of my captivity."

Her words sent a rush of conflicting emotions through Asmodel. The chains, the endless experiments, the sheer helplessness of the servitude he'd endured as a slave washed over him. The Krystalii's declaration stirred within him a deep, fierce sense of kinship with her. Something he'd never imagined would happen.

With a surge of determination, Asmodel knew what had to be done. He closed his eyes to get a feel of the jungle and the animals within it. There, a fearsome-looking beast that looked like a cross between a wolf, a panther, and a porcupine was lapping water near a waterfall. The harsh quills lining its spine quivered with each movement.

"I have a visual on a nearby waterfall. Make a circle and hold hands." He reached out with both hands.

Izzy took his hand without hesitation.

Prisma-Solara hesitated for a moment before she placed her warm, crystal hand in his.

Raxx joined them between Izzy and Prisma-Solara.

Asmodel glanced down at his shoulder to make sure JR13 was secure before letting his eyes drift close. Good thing he was holding on to Izzy and the Krystalii since he couldn't connect with them psychically. Convinced he had a handle on all four of them, he reached out with his mind, connecting with the essence of the waterfall and the area around it. That image, surrounded by lush greenery, was solid. "Got it." He opened his eyes. "Alright, hold tight."

The world around them shimmered and dissolved as Asmodel concentrated, and teleported them through the in-between space. The sensation was familiar to him, but he sensed the others' discomfort as they moved. Good thing the trip was instantaneous.

Reaching their destination, he ended the flight at the edge of a waterfall in a flash of light.

The roar of the water was deafening, and the ensuing mist created a refreshing coolness in the air.

He glanced at his companions, making sure they'd all arrived safe and sound.

The three of them wobbled a bit, but were soon steady.

Looking around, he opened his senses and studied his surroundings. The place was serene, untouched by the destruction they'd left behind. The jungle, usually alive with the sounds of exotic creatures, was eerily silent.

"Freakin' A, dude." Raxx grumbled, dropping his hold on Izzy and Prisma-Solara. "I hate doing that."

Prisma-Solara stepped away from them, her eyes fixed on the cascading water. Her expression was almost reverent. "This will do," she said in a soft whisper. Her voice was barely audible over the roar of the waterfall.

Izzy squeezed Asmodel's hand. "I'm so glad," she said with a smooth smile. When she looked up at him, her smile widened. "We did it!"

Asmodel nodded, his eyes on Prisma-Solara as she glided in the waterfall. He could see the energy beginning to flow back into her, the glow of her crystals brightening with each passing moment. "Yeah," he replied with a mixture of satisfaction and exhaustion. Teleporting others always took a lot out of him. "We did."

"We're not out of the woods yet, dudes." Raxx came over to them, his eyes on the Krystalii. "Echo, JR13, and I are ready if she wigs out again." He pulled Echo off his belt and aimed it at the crystal woman.

Asmodel's eyebrows rose. He'd have to remember to ask Raxx later what the guy and his Echo planned if things hadn't worked out.

Silently, Prisma-Solara waded into the shallow pool, now waist deep, before stepping under the waterfall. The effect was immediate. Her crystals pulsed with light, the water washing away not only the physical dirt, dust, and loose crystals, but also removing the aura of darkness clouding her. She closed her eyes, a look of peace settling over her sharp features.

As Asmodel watched, a sense of accomplishment made him smile. Her calm demeanor was a welcome contrast. She'd was back from the brink of destruction. Not only for the planet, but for herself as well. It wasn't over, not by a long shot. But at least it was a step in the right direction.

"Let's give her some space." Izzy pulled Asmodel back from his thoughts as she tugged on his hands.

With one last look, he nodded and turned away from the waterfall. The three of them walked a little distance away, but Asmodel kept half an eye on Prisma-Solara. Even though she was under a tight leash with those PsyShields, he'd never assume she wasn't still dangerous.

"All we can do is hope it helps," he said to Izzy. "For all our sakes."

"So, whaddya think, dude?" Raxx nodded at Izzy. "Time to book, eh? We got the babe, and the villain is chilled. Let's get out while the gettin' is good. Yeah?"

Asmodel rubbed the side of his head. Why did he get the feeling he was missing something?

Izzy shook her head. "Oh my gosh, we can't leave yet! Who knows what Prisma-Solara will do with the scikvak once we leave?" She leaned close to Asmodel. "And I think we're the only ones who can control her if she gets out of hand, right?"

Asmodel glanced over her shoulder toward the waterfall.

The Krystalii female stood beneath the cascading water, her form blurred under the shimmering spray.

He reached out with his psionic abilities, but the PsyShield did an admirable job of keeping him from reading her. If whatever Raxx had in mind didn't work, he could manipulate the surrounding environment. Either have the water hold her down or create a sinkhole big enough to swallow her. If worse came to worst, he'd turn the water into muriatic acid to dissolve her crystalline form.

The roar of the waterfall faded into a gentle background mummer as he considered Izzy's imploring look. He answered the best he could, mindful of her tender heart. "I believe you're right." He reassured her.

A movement out of the corner of his eye made him look at the waterfall.

Prisma-Solara emerged from the frothing spilling water, her crystalline body shimmering in the dappled sunlight.

Asmodel watched her, satisfied she remained calm. The residual tension cramping him loosened. Taking a deep breath, he enjoyed the humid jungle air that clung to his skin, as well as the earthy scent of damp foliage.

Izzy watched the alien as well, her gaze steady on the bright-yellow crystal form. "You've got to admit, she looks different," Izzy murmured, her voice carrying a hint of awe.

Asmodel nodded, unable to stop studying the Krystalii.

She moved with a grace that belied the chaos she'd caused, her eyes now a clear and focused lemon-yellow.

"Yeah, I guess she does." He glanced at the bot on his shoulders. "JR13, what's your assessment?"

"Of the Krystalii or just everything?" The spider-bot wiggled his bulbous silver bottom. "Because if that's what you want, we'd be here all day."

With a humph, Asmodel resisted the urge to roll his eyes. "On the Krystalii."

"Well, that's easy." The bot turned his little head towards the crystal female walking toward them. "She may not be an organic, but she might as well be." He snorted. "I can't analyze something that chaotic. So, the formal answer to your question is, I don't know." He shrugged with his abdomen, making his upper legs wiggle. "But if you're asking my opinion, I'd have a hard time trusting her. I find you non-mechanicals cannot change your overall nature."

"I think you're wrong." Izzy chimed in. "People change all the time." Her dark eyes softened watching Prisma-Solara approach them. "That is, if they want to."

"I think the crystal Betty found her chill." Thank the goddess Raxx interrupted with his own opinion. Even with his ever-present smirk in place. "Yo, so what's the plan, boss?" He turned to Asmodel. "We's outta here or what?" With Echo in his hand, he kept it aimed at Prisma-Solara when she stopped in front of them.

"I want to help the scikvak." Prisma-Solara's voice was firm, her posture confident. "Now that I'm free of Lord Baelon's influence, I can make it right with them. Since I'm the one

who caused so much harm, it's up to me to fix things." She threw her shoulders back with a steady glare. "Take me back to Panterion Prime, where I can at least make the offer to them."

Asmodel stilled, watching Izzy studying Prisma-Solara with a narrowed focus. "What makes you think they'll listen to you?" He glanced at her as he kept his tone cautious.

"If I wasn't sincere, all I'd have to do is to remove these PsyShields." Prisma-Solar tapped one of her fingers to her temple. "But I won't. I want to keep them on to show I'm not their enemy." She grinned. "Plus, they keep Lord Baelon from finding me."

Raxx chuckled, crossing his arms, keeping a grip on Echo. "Well, ain't that fine and dandy? So, what do ya think, Ace?" He aimed his twinkling eyes filled with mischief at Asmodel. "Think those cat people will be down for a friendly chat with our sparkly friend here?"

He didn't know if he'd describe their return as "friendly" after what Prisma-Solara did to the cave city of Nekojin, as well as the city of Panterion Prime. Asmodel sucked in a deep breath as he considered. While he couldn't psychically connect with the Krystalii, the residual hum of

Prisma-Solara's subdued power was easy to sense. What wasn't there before was a sincerity that now came off her in waves. "How do you propose to help them?"

A corner of Prisma-Solara's lips curved as a playful light danced in her clear yellow eyes. "The PsyShields don't bind everything."

Raxx's dark eyebrows furrowed. "Oh shit. That can't be good." He dropped his arms, holding Echo so tight his knuckles turned white.

"No!" Prisma-Solara raised her hand, palm outward. "No, no. I don't mean that in a bad way. It's a gift I can use for good." She glanced at each one of them, her smile quivering. "I can help them by moving heavy objects and sense those trapped where no one hears them." She clasped her hands together. "In a limited way, I can transform materials from one form to another."

Asmodel had no trouble visualizing what she said. He too could transform matter. Like when he shapeshifted or teleported. "I think we should take her back to Panterion Prime." He decided with a shrug. "If she wants to help, we should let her try. I agree, if she wasn't sincere, all she has to do is remove the PsyShields."

Izzy nodded in agreement. "Maybe if we vouch for her, the scikvak will listen. I'd like to at least give Jaltaar and Talira the chance to listen to her. They must be overwhelmed by now."

"Raxx?" Asmodel nodded to the other man. "What do you think?"

"Dude, what choice do we have at this point but to trust her?" He put Echo back into the halter on his belt. "But nothing's gonna stop me from keeping an eye on her."

"I second that," JR13 intoned. "Hey, organic man, hang on. Let me get situated before you teleport us." He scurried to the back of Asmodel's head and clasped onto the neck of his shirt.

No matter how many times JR13 did that, the feel of the bot's spindly feet made chill bumps zip down his spine.

Prisma-Solara's gaze lingered on each of them. "Thank you." Her voice bore a soft quiver. "I promise I won't let you down."

Raxx clapped his hands together. "Well, cool beans, then. Time to roll. Maybe they'll let us chat first and shoot later."

Asmodel grinned at Raxx's irreverence. He turned to Prisma-Solara. "When we get there, stay close. We'll do everything we can to make sure they understand we're there to help."

The Krystalii nodded.

The weight of what they planned lay heavy on Asmodel. If it was true Prisma-Solara was no longer a force of destruction, she'd be a formidable ally. Not only here on CeluriaVO, but against her people invading this dimension.

With a quick command for the four of them to join hands, he teleported them back to the city square of Panterion Prime.

Izzy stood at the edge of the devastated city center of Panterion Prime. Her chin trembled at the sight of the destruction around her. The once-bustling metropolis now lay in ruins, buildings reduced to crumbling structures, their sleek metallic facades twisted and broken. The air was thick with the acrid scent of smoke and the faint, metallic tang of blood.

Everywhere, the sounds of the city's slow collapse echoed—the groan of strained metal, the crack of shattering glass, and the distant rumble of debris falling.

Beside her, Asmodel surveyed the wreckage, his expression closed and guarded. Even with the PsyShields on, it was easy to feel his psychic touch as a steady pulse in the back of her mind. It was a comforting reminder of their connection.

Raxx, with his ever-present smirk, leaned against a toppled hover-bike, his eyes darting around as he took in the scene.

Prisma-Solara, her body of shimmering yellow crystals, stood close.

It was easy for Izzy to see the faint tremor coming off her, as if the destruction affected the Krystalii as much as it did her. "Remember, we're here to help them," Izzy quietly said to the Krystalii. "But don't worry. If anything happens, Asmodel will teleport us out." She glanced at the handsome profile of the man next to her. He took her hand with a brief nod.

"Look, Jaltaar is heading this way." Izzy pointed to a scikvak walking toward them with Talira at his side.

Both had snarls curling their snouts, their ears flattened sideways. Following close behind was a group of growling guards brandishing various weapons, all pointed at Izzy and her companions.

Raxx stood straight with his arms crossed. His smirk turned into a blank expression.

Jaltaar stopped in front of them, his nostrils flaring, his emerald eyes narrowed. His fur, normally sleek and his orange stripes vibrant, was now marred with soot and grime. "You have a lot of nerve bringing her back here." He snarled, exposing his fangs. "She killed my father and over a thousand of our people!" He pointed an exposed claw in Prisma-Solara's direction. "I thought you said you'd take care of it."

Talira, standing in a battle-hardened stance, exuded a fierce strength. Her midnight-blue eyes, sharp and clear, held a mixture of anger and sorrow.

"We have." Asmodel's stance was open, his arms hanging at his side. "Prisma-Solara had an adverse reaction to CeluriaVO soil that made her uncontrollable. In addition to her cleansing herself in the waterfall, she has agreed to wear PsyShields to confine most of her psychic power."

Talira cocked her head, her thin black lips around her snout rippled with a snarl. "What is a PsyShield?"

"They're disks that filter psychic abilities," Raxx supplied. "I got them from a Crichian."

Jaltaar's whiskered eyebrows rose. "I find it hard to believe a Crichian gave those to you willingly. They're notoriously stingy with their technology."

Raxx's only answer was a grin.

"Prisma-Solara is in complete control of herself, aren't you?" Izzy made sure her words were soft but clear. "She was a psychic prisoner held hostage by her leader. With all ties to her people cut, she has the freedom to make her own choices. Now she only wants to help with the rebuilding and caring for the injured."

Jaltaar's eyes narrowed, his gaze shifting to Prisma-Solara. "Is this so?" he asked in a bitter tone. "Are you claiming you created the devastation on CeluriaVO because someone forced you to do so?" He snorted.

"Yeah." Raxx chuckled under his breath. "The devil made her do it."

Izzy pressed her lips together. Darn man came up with the funniest things at the worst time.

Prisma-Solara stepped forward, her voice a melodic hum. "Yes, it's true. I lost control when I tried to replenish myself in your soil. When I did that, it brought out unfamiliar emotions within me. They were so strong I couldn't control my reaction to it." She looked over her shoulder at Izzy, Asmodel, and Raxx behind her. "Without their intervention, I would have destroyed your planet." She faced him again with her hands behind her back. "I am deeply sorry for the ruination I caused. I wish to atone for my actions and help your people heal any way I can."

Talira crossed her arms, her expression hard. "Why should we trust you? Your actions caused the death of many and destroyed my home. How do we know this isn't a trick? It sounds like there's nothing to stop you from taking the PsyShields off."

Raxx snorted, leaning on a hover-bike lying in two pieces. "Chill, warrior princess. Prisma-Solara didn't even have to put those shields on. It's true she can take them off whenever she wants, but she hasn't." He shrugged. "And I don't think she will. Besides, we wouldn't be risking our necks if we didn't believe her."

"And why don't you want to take them off?" Talira insisted, ignoring Raxx's statement.

Prisma-Solara fixed a stare at Talira. "I won't risk the chance of Lord Baelon gaining control of me again. With these on, I am my own person. If I remove them, I'll once again be under his control. I'd rather live here with you and have limited psionic abilities than go back to being a mindless slave to that cruel dictator."

Asmodel nodded, his eyes meeting Jaltaar's. "We understand your hesitation, but think of this. Prisma-Solara's powers can be a great asset in rebuilding Panterion Prime faster and better with her than without her."

Izzy stepped closer to Jaltaar, keeping her gaze earnest. "Just as you resisted the unfair practices of your leader, she can finally do the same to hers."

"If I may interject," JR13 piped up from his place on Asmodel's shoulder. "Echo and I have a way to program your Lumiview Prism to contain a distinctive sound that renders her immobile, whether she has the shields on or not. Would that not be acceptable?"

Jaltaar exchanged a glance with Talira, then sighed. "Yes, if we had a way to protect ourselves, that is very acceptable. But know this—if there is any sign of betrayal, we won't hesitate to act."

"Prisma-Solara, do these terms work for you?" Asmodel asked the Krystalii, his voice calm.

The yellow citrine of Prisma-Solara's cheeks darkened to a vibrant orange tourmaline. Her eyes darted from Jaltaar to Talira and then to the soldiers. "Only if you can assure me they won't abuse it."

"Faith and trust are the foundation for any civilization." JR13, perched on Asmodel's shoulder, chimed in. "The organic species here possess the intelligence and moral fortitude to work together. Your combined resources have a greater chance to lead efficient and successful rebuilding efforts. Without it, you'd probably spiral into a pre-evolution existence."

Talira raised a whiskered eyebrow as her snout wrinkled at the small spider-like droid. She said nothing, but tilted her head in Prisma-Solaria's direction.

Jaltaar lifted his snout. "I am a scikvak of his word." His tone was firm. "You will have the same rights and privileges as any other citizen on this planet. No harm shall come to you from us unless you provoke us first." He kept his bright eyes on her as he crossed a paw over his heart with a slight bow. "You have my vow as the Supreme Alpha Regent of CeluriaVO."

A deafening crash erupted as a large part of a nearby building collapsed, billowing dust into the air.

Izzy coughed. Her ears rang with the sound of shattering glass and twisted metal, the roar of the chaos momentarily overloud. Her heart leaped into her throat as she waved dirt floating around her away. The ground beneath her feet trembled, making her steady herself against Asmodel.

"Aaaand, the sooner we wrap this up, peeps, the better," Raxx quipped once the silence resumed.

Prisma-Solara nodded, her eyes shimmering with determination. She faced Jaltaar, back straight. "I agree with your terms. We will build this planet together and make it greater than before." She turned to Asmodel. "But first, I'd like to give you some details about Lord Baelon's invasion plans that might help you defeat him."

Chapter Thirteen

After excusing themselves from the scikvak, Asmodel led Raxx, Prisma-Solara, and Izzy aside for privacy.

"Now, what can you tell us about Lord Baelon?" Asmodel asked the Krystalii. He eyed the yellow crystals of Prisma-Solara that appeared to be softening. If he wasn't mistaken, the sharp edges of her protruding stalks were smooth instead of sharp and hard. Without taking his eyes off her, he spoke to his droid companion. "JR13, please record."

"Affirmative, organic one."

Prisma-Solara's explanation was brief and to the point.

When she wound the narrative down, Raxx whistled and Izzy gasped.

Asmodel rubbed his chin between his forefinger and thumb. He had to admit her proposal wasn't something any of them would have imagined was possible, but it was at least it was something in their favor.

With a final wish for their success, Prisma-Solara headed back to Jaltaar and Talira, who had watched their brief conversation.

As Asmodel observed her walking away, it took some time before the acrid scent of smoke mixing with the metallic tang of the burning city caught his notice. In the distance, the rumble of collapsing structures and the occasional crack of shattering glass filled the uneasy silence. He glanced at Izzy, her eyes narrowed on the departing Krystalii. "I guess we'd better figure out what to do next," he said, his voice heavy with the weight of urgency.

Izzy nodded.

Raxx shrugged. "Echo, babe, start up the *Shadow Drifter,* pretty please." He glanced at Asmodel. "So, are we headed to the chancellor's palace or what?"

"Yeah, I guess we'd should head back to the Federation Consortium headquarters," Asmodel stopped stroking his chin, his tone serious. "Time to share with them what Prisma-Solara stated would help defeat Lord Baelon and the rest of the Krystalii."

Izzy's eyes widened. "But what about the scikvak? Shouldn't we stay here and help them?"

"We can't help them if we're all dead," Asmodel replied in a tight voice. "Prisma-Solara said she believes Lord Baelon has not only upped his timeline for coming to this dimension, but the havoc his interdimensional armada would create the minute they get here may be unsurmountable." He looked off in the distant, lost in the memories of being held a slave under a violent dictatorship.

A deafening crash in the distance jerked him out of his musings. Another large section of a nearby building collapsed, sending more dust into the air.

Izzy flinched, coughing as she waved the dirt away. The ground trembled beneath their feet, and the sound of twisted metal and shattering glass filled the air.

Asmodel wrapped his arms around her, feeling her heart pound in her chest against his.

"We can't just abandon them." Her voice cracked. "They've suffered so much already."

Asmodel wanted more than ever to send comfort to her through his psychic sense. While he agreed with her, he wouldn't let his emotions cloud his judgment by asking her to remove the PsyShields. "Izzy, I wish we could stay, but we don't have a choice. While I can communicate with the governing body, it's best to be there in person to coordinate with my family what we need to do." He hugged her. "Besides, with Prisma-Solara staying, she'll give them the extra protection they'll need to survive the Krystalii invasion if we fail."

"Shit," Raxx crossed his arms. "When you put it that way, I'm tempted to stay here. Besides"—his dark eyes flicked around them—"I doubt the chancellor's palatial palace is ready to roll out the red carpet for me anytime soon."

Asmodel grinned at him. "I promise that won't be a problem. Will it, JR13?"

"What?" The droid glanced at him. "You expect me to do miracles now?" A harsh huff. "The man's wanted in five systems."

"JR13."

"Fantastic. Just what I always wanted to do. Commit a cover-up crime."

Asmodel nodded. "Thank you, JR13. I knew you could do it."

"Of course I can, you insufferable organic creature. Already done." The bot trotted with harder steps to his place at the back of Asmodel's neck. "But it's temporary. The only way to expunge it must come from the chancellor himself."

The droid's exasperation made Asmodel grin wider. He loved pushing the AI's buttons.

"Hey, that's awesome!" Raxx rubbed his hands together. "Hear that, Echo? We'll be free to go anywhere we want in the galaxy!"

The galaxy. Asmodel glanced at Izzy watching the scikvak walk away. He had to make sure she was safe before they went anywhere. The thought of putting her in danger as he and his family fought the Krystalii was unacceptable. "But first you have to take us to Earth."

"Why Earth?" Izzy cocked her head, an eyebrow arched. "If time is so urgent, shouldn't we head straight for the palace?"

"Normally, yes. But we've got to take you to safety first. Putting you in the middle of this upcoming conflict isn't going to happen." He turned to Raxx. "Now, tell me what you need…"

"What does that mean, take me to safety?" Her gruff tone matched the twitch in her left eye. "You talk like I'm some kind of nuisance you have to get rid of."

"What? Izzy, no!" He shot a look at Raxx, who shook his head and took a step back with his palms up.

"Nope, no can do, dude. You're on your own." Raxx pointed to the group of scikvak talking to Prisma-Solara getting farther away. "Oh, wait. They're calling me. Gotta split."

The coward sprinted off as if the hounds of Gilgamesh were after him.

"I thought we were in this together."

The slight quiver in her voice made Asmodel frown. "Izzy, it'd be better for you if we take you back to Earth," He searched her face for understanding.

Her reaction was immediate. Her jaw dropped and her eyes filled with tears. That expression of shock pierced him more than any physical wound. "I mean so little to you that you'd do that? Leave me behind?" Her voice was barely a whisper.

Asmodel's heart clenched. "Oh, my goddess, no... no! It's not like that. The only thing I want is for you to be safe, that's all. With Lord Baelon coming, things are going to be unpredictable and dangerous. I can't protect you if—"

"So, instead of a partner, you view me as a burden?" she interrupted, stepping closer. Those damn tears spilled over. "You think I'm a liability? If it wasn't for me, Prisma-Solara would still be destroying this planet!"

He pulled her into a firm embrace, his heart aching for the warmth and comfort of her having her in his arms.

She was stiff and unresponsive.

"You're right. You couldn't possibility be a liability to anyone," he reassured her. "No, Izzy, it's because I care too much about you to take a chance. Just because you did that here, doesn't mean it would work with this formidable threat." He swallowed hard, his mouth dry. "I couldn't stand the thought of anything happening to you." He was desperate to make her understand. "You mean far too much to me."

Her shoulders trembled as she pushed away, her nose in the air. "So you think getting rid of me will keep me safe? Is that right?"

Asmodel's chest tightened. How did this turn into such a chaotic, emotional mess? All he wanted to do was protect her. Shield her from the impending danger ahead. But every time he opened his stupid mouth, he ended up pushing her away.

"The last thing I want, Izzy, is to put you in more danger. Can't you see? I'm afraid if you go with me, I won't be strong enough to protect you." His words came out scratchy, his mouth and tongue were so dry. "And I couldn't live with that." Now she'd know what a frail coward he was when it came to her. It was a weakness hard to admit out loud.

Izzy leaned toward him, close enough for Asmodel to bathe in her alluring, honeyed scent laced with a sting of acidic anger. "I thought we were partners, Asmodel. I believe, no, I know, we're stronger together. Why don't you?"

The urge to tear the PsyShields from her hit Asmodel hard. That way, he'd take the easy way out and enter her mind to manipulate her emotions. To force her to see things his way. His mind raced, confusion clouding his thoughts until one thing became crystal clear. His shoulders slumped. Since when did he turn into someone who'd force others to his will? If he did that, he'd be no better than the Akurns who enslaved him.

Reaching out with his trembling hand, he touched her arm. "*Alma gemela*. Never doubt I believe in us. In what we have. That's why I want to do this. Because I love you too much to lose you."

She yanked out of his hold, her shimmering tears held at bay with a narrow stare. "Then don't push me away. Let me fight by your side. I'm stronger than you think."

Asmodel's heart ached at the sight of the grimace of disgust on her pretty face. Where did his soft, agreeable female go? He closed his eyes and took a deep breath. Now that she wasn't in his arms, the stench of smoke and ruin of the city filled his lungs. He opened his eyes, and her unwavering stare held him hostage. Her determined, blatant intent seared into his soul. He only wished he was strong enough to deny what she demanded. But he was man enough to admit he wasn't. The bleak thought of separating from her made the decision for him.

"Alright." He hung his head. May the goddess of the underworld, Ereshkigal, grant him mercy in the afterlife. "We'll face this together. But please, understand why I wanted to take you to Earth in the first place. It's not because I don't need you. It's because I can't bear the thought of anything happening to you. If you got hurt, it'd be all my fault."

Izzy ran into his arms.

He tightened his hold on her and rested his head on hers before she pulled back, loosening the hug for her to look up at him. The pain in his stomach went away when her disarming smile replaced the pinched expression thinning her lips.

"Oh gosh, Asmodel. This isn't just about you. Don't you see I feel the same way about you? I can't stand the thought of you being away from me when all this is happening." She wiped a lone tear from her eye. "I can't imagine being anywhere but at your side as we fight for our lives. Without you, I'd be lost, my love." She sniffled.

He didn't have the words to refute that statement. No, wait. There was only one word that mattered. She'd called him "my love". No one ever said that to him... just *him*. While he and his brothers had a deep and abiding love for each other, they never went around saying it. His only response was to pull her back into his arms, where she belonged.

As they held each other in the ruins of Panterion Prime, Asmodel allowed a flicker of hope to spread. Maybe she was right. The only way to defeat evil was together.

Izzy relaxed in Asmodel's secure embrace. She grinned at the conflicting expressions crossing his handsome face. Typical man. It must be hard for him to verbalize his feelings, so he relied on the physical. Not that she cared. She hugged him tighter. Physical was good. There'd be plenty of time to guide him on the freedom of expressing his feeling verbally later. Once things calmed down and the threat to their way of life was gone, then she'd take off the PsyShields and encourage him to use his psychic mojo and merge his consciousness with hers.

She shivered. What would that be like? Making love in real life instead of inside what he called a Dreamwalk. She licked her lips and snuggled her face against the hard hills and valleys of his wide chest. That would be a fantasy come to life. She'd read many a paranormal romance where the two lovers enjoyed such a thing and longed to experience something like that herself.

"What are you thinking of, Bella, to make my body react like this?" Asmodel captured both of her buttocks in his large hands and pulled her close enough to feel his hardness pressed against her stomach.

Izzy buried her nose, her face heated. "Oh, my stars. Are you reading my mind?" His firm pecs muffled her mortified voice.

He leaned back and put his finger under her chin.

Her eyes widened at his sensual smile that made her womb clench.

"I don't have to read your mind when your luscious scent tells me everything I need to know." Still keeping her in his arms, he whispered into her ear, "I know of a perfect place on Raxx's ship where we can explore each other to our hearts' content." He nipped the lobe of her ear. "If you're willing, that is."

"Willing?" Izzy took a deep breath for courage. "Oh no, I insist." Her internal shivers intensified. Lordy, she wasn't normally a demanding person. What if she drove him away?

"Oh, my *alma gemela*. You take my breath away." Asmodel's voice was rough. Then he kissed her. His lips drifted over hers in a sensual exploration.

Without hesitation, she peeked her tongue out to run over his lower lip, tasting his masculine musk.

Asmodel's tongue slid against hers in an erotic dance.

Izzy groaned at his demanding kiss and rubbed her aching breasts against his ironclad chest. Her core spasmed harder, dampening her panties.

"Damn, people. Wait 'til we get to the ship, will ya?"

Izzy gasped and pulled back at Raxx's laugh. She put her fingers over her wet and swollen lips. She'd forgotten where they were. Her face burned as she regarded Asmodel. His sharp, almost flawless features were relaxed, his eyes glowing with adoration.

"We'll take you up on your offer, Raxx." Asmodel answered the man standing behind him without taking his dilated hazel eyes from hers. He brought the back of her hand up to his mouth for a light kiss. "Isn't that right, my Bella?"

Mute, the only response Izzy could give was a nod.

He placed her hand into the crook of his arm and turned to face Raxx.

"Raxx—" He walked them over to the smuggler and followed him back to the scikvak. "How fast can you get us to the chancellor's palace? We've got to tell them what Prisma-Solara told us that would turn the tide against Lord Baelon."

Raxx nodded, for once his expression serious, as he scratched the five o'clock shadow on his chiseled jaw. "Well, that all depends. The QLR is low on Etherium. Don't suppose you got some around here, do ya?" They reached the other group, but he directed the question to no one in particular.

"We have a very limited supply," Jaltaar supplied. "What do you need it for?"

Raxx's expression turned blank. "My ship. Can't leave home without it."

"He needs it for the QLR installed on his ship." Prisma-Solara studied the smuggler with a knowing look in her eyes. "To show my good intentions, I can create as much Etherium as you need." She glanced at Jaltaar. "That is, if you don't mind showing me where you house the mineral."

"Hey! How did you know that?" Raxx's jaw clenched.

"Although the PsyShields constrain most of my powers, I can still read what's uppermost in your mind," she said.

Raxx's cheeks darkened.

Oh dear. Izzy glanced at Asmodel, noticing his bemused smile. Seemed like Prisma-Solara's announcement didn't catch him by surprise.

"We aren't showing you anything until we know what a QLR is and what it's used for." Talira was firm as she glared at the Krystalii.

"That, my friend, is something unique. Not only in this galaxy, but I assure you, Lord Baelon would do anything to get his hands on one." The crystals in Prisma-Solara's body caught the low light and gave her an ethereal glow. "Once a theoretical device, it's comprised of synthetic Quantum Crystals grown in the micro-gravity of deep space. Each crystal aligns at the quantum level, creating a lattice capable of resonating with the very fabric of space-time. It needs rare elements like Etherium to provide the stability for a ship to fold space. Without it, the unforgiving forces of space would obliterate the vessel it was in." She eyed Raxx. "Are you telling us you have such a thing?"

Raxx pressed his lips together and glared.

Asmodel turned to Prisma-Solara. "If you know so much about the QLR, I'm surprised your people haven't already created it."

"You heard me say they were made of synthetic crystals, didn't you?" When Asmodel nodded, she continued. "Lord Baelon decreed all production of synthetic crystals was an abomination and outlawed. The QLR never got past the theory stage in our dimension."

"Yet, he'd take one and use it if he could," Izzy mused. Any dictator she'd studied in Earth's history wouldn't have any qualms about using something they'd outlawed for others.

"That is correct." Prisma-Solara answered with a short nod. "It would accelerate his timeline in advancing his forces to this dimension."

"I may have, ah, borrowed a QLR from the Vargrux. But, believe you me, whoever they stole it from probably has more." Raxx made this warning with a steady stare at Jaltaar and Talira.

"Then it's imperative we get to the Federation Consortium as soon as possible," Asmodel stated. "Once your ship is ready, how long will it take for us to get there?"

"Once I install the Etherium, all I gotta do is input the coordinates and let my baby do her thing. Then, *whammo*!" He snapped his fingers. "We're there. Easy-peasy. Trust me, it got us here in the first place that quick, eh?"

"Trust me, the organic buffoon says." JR13 spoke up from Asmodel's shoulder in a whisper.

Izzy strayed nearer to Asmodel so she could hear what else he said.

"I wouldn't trust him to point out the exit in a one-room cabin," the bot continued. "But rest assured, I'll work with Echo to make sure everything in the QLR is working properly."

Asmodel nodded, then glanced at Raxx. "If I can help, just let me know."

Raxx "pshawed" and waved the offer away. "No worries. We've got it."

"So, just to make sure, you're okay with providing the Etherium?" Asmodel asked the scikvak.

Izzy glanced at Jaltaar and Talira, whose faces bore a mix of distrust and reluctant hope. After a moment, both nodded.

"Well, good." Asmodel folded his hands behind his back. "Here's how we'll compensate you for the mineral. If at any time you have trouble, use this with your communication system to contact us." He opened his palm and a swirl of light morphed into a square disk. "It's a direct line to our friend's ship." He patted Raxx's shoulder. "And he'll come running as if the hounds of Gilgamesh are after him to aid you with whatever you need," he assured them with a grin.

"Hey!" Raxx exclaimed with a step back.

Asmodel's hand dropped away.

"I never..."

"As for you, think of this as a goodwill gesture to the chancellor, along with the QLR, when we bring your case before him to have your, ah, past indiscretions wiped clean. Sound good, dude?"

Izzy chuckled when Asmodel said, *dude.*

Raxx's eyebrows furrowed as his dark eyes turned black and he glared. Crossing his arms, he spoke through pinched lips. "I suppose so." He pointed his finger at Asmodel. "Next time, ask before you go pimping me out like that. At least buy me a drink first. I have some standards, ya know. Not much, but some."

Izzy's grin widened. The mischievous twinkle in Raxx's eyes reassured her he wasn't too stressed about it. She doubted he'd agree if he didn't mean it.

Jaltaar's eyes narrowed as he gazed between Asmodel and Raxx before his black lips curled into a cheeky grin. "In exchange for the Etherium, how would you like having exclusive trading rights with CeluriaVO?"

Raxx's jaw dropped. "For reals, dude?"

"We'll need lots of supplies to rebuild." Talira hooked her arm through Jaltaar's. "I bet it'll take years to set everything right again. Let's go somewhere to discuss our next steps as well as figure out how to get the Etherium for you."

Raxx rubbed his hands together. "You hear that, Echo? That'd like set us up for life!"

With a sigh, Izzy mirrored Talira and slipped her arm around Asmodel. Well, wasn't this nice? She always loved a happy ending.

Now, all she and Asmodel needed to figure out was how to stop a maniac from another dimension from ruining their own happily ever after.

Asmodel, holding Izzy's hand, followed Jaltaar and Talira through the debris-littered plaza with Raxx by his side. They ended up in one of the surrounding buildings deemed sturdy by a team of inspectors. As dusk settled, most civilians found refuge in any sturdy shelter they could.

Fortunately, there was a nice roomy conference room available, complete with chairs and an intact table.

As Asmodel took a seat next to Izzy, it occurred to him their little group was increased by several more scikvak. Short-furred zaltrixan as well as a smattering of pardalions with their silky long fur.

Before long, the air buzzed with loud conversations as plans were made, itineraries created, and personnel assigned.

Asmodel couldn't care less.

The only thing he wanted to do was spend some overdue time with the gentle woman next to him. He longed to indulge in Izzy's unique fragrance, preferably up-close and naked. Unable to resist, he rubbed a section of her lustrous hair, twiddling the strands resting on her shoulder between his thumb and forefinger.

"I'm sure that's okay with organic man. Right?"

JR13's voice jerked Asmodel out of his slumbering sensual haze. He was too busy imagining wrapping her hair around his closed fist to pull her steady as he pressed her naked body under his. He frowned. What did the bot say?

"Not surprised you lost your ability to speak. Expected it a long time ago." Sarcasm laced JR13's voice. "But could you at least nod in agreement?"

Asmodel's eyes lingered on Izzy leaning toward an elder pardalion female, her head tilted as if to catch every word the scikvak said.

"Asmodel!"

JR13 shouting his name yanked Asmodel back to the conversation at hand. "What?" How could anything get done if everybody just sat around and yapped all day?

"Is... it... okay... with... you... if... I... go... with... Echo... and... Raxx?" JR13 huffed, his black-and-silver body wiggling. "That clear enough for you?"

The room got quiet. Even Izzy turned to him with a contemplative frown.

Asmodel clenched his teeth. Ever since the bot met Echo, he'd turned into a real pain in the ass. Or maybe it was all Raxx's fault. Either way, they were welcome to him. At least for now. It sure wouldn't take much to disown the annoying little thing. He sighed. But facing JR13's "parents" without the little guy was a definite no-go. "If you think you can contribute more than a constant stream of criticism, go ahead."

"I only give advice when warranted." The iridescent wings on JR13's back slid out and fluttered. The bot lifted off Asmodel's right shoulder and buzzed over to land on Raxx's.

Raxx smiled at his new passenger. He sent Asmodel a grin and a wave. "No worries, dude. He'll be a big help with me and Echo. We'll meet you back on the *Shadow Drifter* in a few." He waved a palm up.

And there was the exit line Asmodel had been waiting for. "Ready?" His lids went half-mast when he addressed Izzy. His heart raced and his palms were slick. *For the love of a motherless goat.* He couldn't remember the last time he was this nervous.

Izzy's brows raised. "What?" Her pretty brown eyes dilated as she studied him. "Oh my, yes." She nipped the side of her bottom lip.

Asmodel put his arm around Izzy's shoulder and stood with her, facing the others in the room. "If you folks will excuse us, we're going to head back to the *Shadow Drifter*."

Not waiting for anyone's response, he teleported himself and his woman to his cabin aboard the spaceship for some much-needed privacy.

Alone at last.

Now that the moment had arrived, Izzy shivered, a tangle of nerves wracking her body. She stood next to Asmodel in his cabin aboard the *Shadow Drifter*, too anxious to take in her surroundings. It was only as an afterthought that she noted the cabin's compact, yet comfortable, layout. There was a bed in one corner with crumpled blankets and plump pillow, while a single chair beside a small round table caught her eye on the other side. The material of the table was puzzling—wood, steel, glass? Its composition seemed to shift depending on whether she looked at it directly or from an angle.

Asmodel moved behind her, his warm body enveloping her back, covering her in his musky, spicy scent. She agreed to this, didn't she? Here she was, getting ready to... do what she... hoped? Dreaded? All with a man she'd just met a day ago.

But, after going through several life-threatening situations, she knew some things about him already. General things, like he had four brothers whom he was close to. He was a caring man, ready to come and rescue a woman he'd never met before. He treated the alien scikvak community with dignity and chose to help the murderous Krystalii rather than figuring out how to kill her.

Then there was his constant companion, JR13. He never lost his temper with the bot, even when the droid was sarcastic to him. That showed patience.

Let's not forget his extraordinary psionic abilities, like changing into a dragon. Holy guacamole, that had to be the sexiest thing she'd ever seen. Again, he could have used all that power to destroy the pardalions' village in one swoop. Instead, he transformed back into his normal self. For a split-second, standing unabashedly, gloriously naked. Talk about making a good first impression...

More importantly, he could have used his psychic powers at any time to invade her mind. Izzy suspected if he'd done that, he could also have taken her will away. She might not have any type of psionic abilities, but she was pretty sure she'd have known the moment he touched his mind to hers.

"Would you like something to eat or drink?"

Izzy jerked when his hands rested on her shoulders. Leaning into his warmth, she shook her head. "No, I'm good." She cleared her throat when her words came out garbled. "Thank you."

Asmodel's warm breath caressed the side of her neck.

"Are you sure this is what you want, Bella? I won't presume you are ready to take what we have to a more physical level."

His low baritone made her shiver, and his brief kiss on the side of her neck made her entire body break out in chill bumps.

"If you prefer, we can go to the main galley and wait for Raxx there."

In self-conscious move, Izzy threw her shoulders back. "If that's what you want." She made a move to step away. Maybe if she wasn't so close to him, it'd be easier for him to back off if she was rushing things.

"No, that's not what I want." The disbelief in his tone came through loud and clear. "I'd give anything for us to be closer." His rumbled chuckle was deep. "I've never wanted anything more in my life." He closed the minuscule distance between them. Turing her to face him, he grasped her hand and pressed her palm against the firm muscle of his thigh.

Izzy stared at her captured hand, noticing how much larger his was, holding her against his firm leg. She half expected to see sparks spring from where she touched him. An electric slide of arousal built inside her, making it hard to breathe.

"I haven't been close to anyone for a long time." Her self-deprecating laugh was short. "I may have forgotten how." To stop from making a fool of herself, she bit the side of her mouth at the confession. Would she even remember how to please a man? She glanced up at his near-perfect features. Could she somehow satisfy this outstanding man? Could she, a plump librarian more comfortable surrounded by books, satisfy someone as magnificent as him?

Asmodel pressed a finger to her lips as if to stop her from confessing her shortcomings. "Neither one of us has experienced what is happening between us." He breathed out the words.

She couldn't pull her eyes away from their hands.

"What's between us is unique to us alone. I want you to know whatever we do is because you want it and are comfortable with it." He lifted her hand and placed a gentle kiss on her knuckles. "Whatever you wish is yours. If I do anything you don't want, all you have to do is say so and I'll stop. Agreed?"

Izzy swiped her tongue over her dry lips and lifted her gaze to him. His plump lips captured her attention. His lower lip was a tad fuller than the upper, giving him a sensual aura. It was all she could think of, having those lips on hers.

"Will you kiss me?" The words came out on their own. That's it, Izzy. Beg the man when you just offered him a way out. Brilliant.

"I dream of nothing else," he whispered.

She blinked and watched as his lips lowered, the whisper of his breath a prelude to the heated, velvet command of his lips caressing hers. She closed her eyes to savor his masculine flavor.

Izzy's breath caught as an intense communion surged through her from his mere touch. She'd never experienced this kind of hunger before. It took over, dominating her every thought.

He tilted his head, wrapping one of his hands around her neck in a tender hold.

Waves of unexpected pleasure washed through her as his tongue licked her lips, then slid inside. Parting her mouth just a bit more, she reached out to twirl her tongue with his. Immersed in their intimate dance, she trembled.

He pulled back, his eyes turning a golden brown. "So soft, my Bella."

Izzy's hands slid up the clothed hardness of Asmodel's chest before wrapping around his thick neck. Offering herself to him, she moaned when he met her invitation, meshing his lips with hers. Molten fire consumed her. Her sex throbbed in reaction—her swollen clit straining from the hood it normally hid behind. She pressed against him, whimpering when she couldn't connect with his steel-hard erection where she wanted it.

Mewling cries of need escaped her and drowned in the heavenly cavern of his possessive mouth. She'd raised onto her toes, still trying to connect her sex with his. The careening mass of sexual tension tightening her low inside made everything hard to handle.

Even the instinctive act of breathing was beyond her. Not that she cared. All she wanted was to grind her hard-as-nails nipples and swollen clit against his solid masculinity. Even the dream love she had with him didn't dare to come close to the reality. She burned out of control like she'd never burned before. "Asmodel."

Tearing her lips from his, she dropped from standing on her toes, moaning when her sex slid over his. All the while, his large, commanding hand still held the back of her neck, keeping her from moving away.

"Easy, *alma gemela*." His voice was smooth, but his body remained tense.

His heartbeat thundered so hard she felt it through their pressed-together bodies.

"I wish to savor this first time together and do not wish to hurry."

His words were clear, but laced with a thickened accent.

Izzy sucked on her lower lip, craving to have him cover hers again. No, she wanted something more. Much, much more. Whoever said patience was a virtue was an ignoramus.

Her only coherent thought came out as a demand. "Shirt."

Grimacing at her lack of verbal skills, she reached underneath his loose garment while his lips moved along her shoulder. When had her shoulder become bare? The question flew away when he nuzzled the sensitive line of her neck and shoulder.

Izzy sighed with pleasure. The scrape of his nimble teeth sent tremors racing down her back, straight to her convulsing womb. She cried out in surprise.

Grasping the front of his shirt in a tight grip, she tried again to get her naked skin against his. "Off."

"Whatever you wish," came his rumbled response.

She blinked. Not only was his shirt gone, so was everything else he wore. Her knees weakened as she took a step back to survey the bounty before her. *Oh my stars.* She'd never been anyone as spectacular as he was. Dark-copper skin covered a bevy of solid muscles from his broad shoulders to his tight calves. A smattering of black curls covered the hills and valleys of his chest, just enough for her sensitized nipples to stand at attention and beg, "Yes, please".

Izzy lowered her gaze to his magnificent erection, straight and thick. She sucked in a breath. The circumference had to be as wide as her wrist. She swallowed, not sure if she was excited or terrified, imagining all of that fitting inside her.

Asmodel reached down and engulfed his uncircumcised self with a firm hand, rolling the deceptive looking pliant flesh in a rounding motion. With lazy, half-lidded eyes, he gazed at her as a panties-melting smile creased his full lips. "Izzy," he growled, his eyes narrow.

Her womb clenched tighter and her vagina tightened, causing a trickle of her cream to coat the outside of her sex.

Oh my.

"I have to touch you." He closed the distance between them. "I cannot think straight for the desire to feel your soft skin. To immerse myself in all the ways a man does with a woman." He gripped her upper arms and stared down at her heaving breasts.

Noodles. Her legs were nothing but wet noodles. How could they possibly work when he talked like that? Izzy swore the room spun. Good thing her hero was there to save her from fainting like some Victorian maid. Oh yes, him sweeping her up in his massive arms was worth everything that had happened to her since she left Earth. She wrapped her arms around his neck, pulling him down for a kiss. Her heartfelt moan slipped inside their kiss as he lowered her to the bed.

He eased over her, covering her with his heated body. "Izzy—" He pulled back. "—I'm going to taste every luscious ounce of you and your precious body."

She was beyond words. Quivering, she arched her back as an offering.

Asmodel didn't disappoint. His hands encased each breast, plumping her nipples into sharp points. Keeping his dark gaze on her, he covered one mound with his mouth, while the other hand continued to play mercilessly with the other. He sucked the peak hard enough his cheeks hollowed.

She cried out when a turbulent surge of lust tore through her womb. "Asmodel!" She shook her head. Not that she wanted him to stop. He had to keep going. Every movement of his fingers created minute explosions that shot straight to her clit, making her empty womb spasm.

"Easy, Bella." Asmodel's breath was harsh as he lifted his head. His face and neck were flushed. His hand left her breast and traveled down her side, while he fervently suckled the neglected crest. "Don't worry, *alma gemela*. I won't leave you behind." His words came out mumbled as he spoke around her captured flesh.

His other hand wandered over her hip before his mouth let go of her breast with a loud pop. Now his traitorous fingers found the super-slick, swollen folds of her sex. With lazy intent, he circled a finger around the hardened nub of her clit.

Straining to make him reach her clamoring prize by shifting her hips, he finally found purchase and tweaked it with a mild pinch. Just enough pressure to bring her closer to the release she sought. "Oh my, yes!" Izzy exclaimed with her head thrown back. When his mouth settled on her over-sensitized flesh, she gasped. She couldn't breathe. She couldn't think. He hurled her into a wild roller coaster, its overwhelming force threatening to rip her apart.

"Yes, that's it, my love," he whispered. "Let's get there together."

Asmodel had never encountered such an intense, unprecedented situation before. Lying with Izzy, with nothing guiding them but their passion, left him unsure of what to do.

When he and his brothers ended up in the modern world, sex opened a whole new chapter in his life. One he never knew was missing before. But it didn't take long before the experience ended up hollow, leaving him unfulfilled. Like eating a favorite food over and over. It might be enjoyable, but after a while it ended up mundane and hardly worth the effort.

But being with Izzy was the difference between eating at a fast-food place and dining at an exclusive gourmet restaurant. She alone showed him the depth of what two people with a profound connection could share. He took in a deep breath. Case in point, the air infused with Izzy's sweet, arousing perfume was intoxicating, like nothing else. Especially when he'd brought her to the brink of orgasm.

"Open your legs wider for me, Bella." Asmodel stroked the softest skin of her inner thigh, eager to explore her there with the tips of his fingers. Her glistening, swollen sex was captivating. He licked his lips, longing to lap and savor her sweet essence. "You are so beautiful in your passion." The words came out in a guttural rasp.

With her face a nice, rosy glow, Izzy threw her hands above her head and spread her legs, giving him a clear view of what she offered. The open expression on her face humbled him while at the same time brought out the uncivilized man ready to mate with his woman.

It took what little control he had, but he stifled the urge to mount her like a savage when all he wanted was to push his straining cock inside her slick, hot pussy. *Damn Gilgamesh's balls*. He was better than that. Yes, he *had* to be better than that. Especially joining with this astounding woman for the first time.

Lowering his head, he shouldered between her splayed legs and inhaled her scent before letting his tongue stroke the tantalizing treat. He inserted first one finger, then another, to stroke inside her burning channel. Keeping his gaze locked on hers, he pressed in deeper and brushed the bundle of sensitive nerves just under her straining clit. Her strangled cry gave him immense satisfaction. Lowering his eyes, he concentrated on suckling her tender bud.

"Asmodel... please... I can't... don't want... to come without you inside me."

Asmodel lifted his head to look at her. His wicked grin was to let Izzy know her plea fell on deaf ears. Once again focusing on her womanhood, he ramped up his efforts, determined to have her explode under his tongue. His fingers thrust, a back-and-forth movement, fucking inside her as his lips resumed their suckling on her hard nubbin.

His tongue stroked over it, rasping it until she stiffened and froze.

Then Izzy's back bowed. With her eyes wide, she screamed his name, slamming her thighs tight against his head.

Ah, music to his ears.

"That's it, my *alma gemela*," he crooned. "Fall apart for me." Watching her come was the most satisfying thing he'd ever witnessed. He rose to his knees, letting her legs fall loosely to the bed.

Her quivering body made her breasts jiggle as the hard tips of her berry-brown nipples pointed up.

Her shuddering breath unlocked something deep inside him.

He snapped.

With a savage grunt, he stretched on top of her and plowed inside her slick channel. Yes, finally, he was inside. It was too much. Damn, it wasn't enough. Ah, shit. Her rippling channel grabbed him. Any coherent thought was beyond him. Of their own accord, his hips moved, shifting and working inside Izzy as a violent claw of lust tore him up inside.

He groaned. Izzy's name became a song of worship. Leaning down, he captured one of her nipples in his mouth before reaching up to take her mouth with his. His kiss was demanding, claiming her as his cock claimed her pussy. Pulling away, he shifted onto his knees and grasped her legs and draped them over his arms. All the while, he kept a steady beat between them, ramming deep inside her. Her eyes widened as she gripped his forearms, her fingers digging into his skin with a surprising strength.

"Izzy, sweet," he moaned, his hips jerking and driving, plowing deeper inside her. Her woman's channel strangled every hard inch of him. The stroking of her feminine sex held him as a willing captive.

Her groan created a vibration that stroked around his flesh. He clenched his teeth. So close. So close... almost there. He hissed in agonizing pleasure as he watched her expression turn sharp, hungrier, while her eyes gleamed with excitement.

Asmodel's hips tightened, arched. His cock throbbed hard, a violent flex of flesh as the first spurt of semen shot inside her.

Izzy screamed, her body spasming around his. Milking him for everything he had.

And just like that, his control shattered.

At the height of his release, the psychic barrier between them blew apart. Somehow, with her forceful release, the PsyShields she wore tore away. Now, nothing prevented his consciousness from flooding into hers. He merged their minds together. They both cried out as an unbreakable bond that transcended time and space carried their combined pleasure to a never-imagined height of shared ecstasy. Together, they soared to an unprecedented pinnacle of higher awareness neither dared experienced before.

It made them into something more.

It made them whole.

Epilogue

"**D**amn, *ahu*. You were supposed to rescue the human woman, not have sex with her."

A deep masculine voice snatched Asmodel awake from a deep slumber.

"Who do you think you are? Arakiba?" The annoying voice continued.

Asmodel, his eyes bleary, glanced at Izzy, who slept on her side facing him.

Adapa stood beside the bed, his fists planted firmly on his hips, casting a judicious stare in his direction.

Groaning, Asmodel rolled onto his back with his arm across his closed eyes. "Go away. I'm sleeping." He'd like nothing better than to throw the bastard out, but unfortunately, his brother wasn't there in person. He'd somehow put Asmodel into a Dreamwalk as he slept.

"I haven't heard from you in a while, and I was worried about you." Adapa snorted. "I should have known better."

Asmodel let his arm fall as he sat up. With a humph, he rolled off the bed on the opposite side from his brother. Even though he was on the psychic plane, he was careful not to wake Izzy. She might not be a psychic, but she was an intuitive lady.

He took a moment to watch her sleep. Her arresting face was slack in slumber with her upper body partly exposed. Asmodel frowned and pulled the sheet over her naked torso.

She murmured and nestled into her pillow with a sultry smile.

Asmodel's cock twitched as if he hadn't indulged in the fine art of lovemaking with her for hours.

Turning to Adapa, he crossed his arms, uncaring of his nudity. He and his brothers spent most of their young lives without clothes around each other, so it wasn't worth the effort to conjure clothes for his older brother's so-called sensibilities.

"Yes, you should have. I'm fine." Asmodel jaw tightened at Adapa's teasing grin. "I assumed JR13 kept everyone posted on what I was doing, so I didn't bother."

Adapa nodded. "Your JR unit has been quite useful that way." He chuckled. "He went out of his way to... ah, what is the modern term?" He tapped his forefinger against his scruffy jaw. "Oh yes." He snapped his fingers. "Tattle. Every chance he got, that droid tattled on you. With more information on what you were doing than any of us wanted to hear. Maybe we should have JR10 look at his creation when we get back. Must be malfunctioning."

The gleam in Adapa's eyes gave Asmodel a slight headache. He rubbed his temple and grimaced. "Don't you have something better to do than harass me? I'm sure you know we'll be back at the chancellor's palace by tomorrow."

"Yes, we are very interested in the QLR on this ship. Do you think we can replicate it?"

Asmodel shrugged. "That's a question for a quantum mechanic, not me. At least we'll have access to it. But there's one condition."

Adapa's eyebrows rose. "Oh? What's that?"

"Have the chancellor pardon Raxx Jorlen from all warrants and bounties out on him." Asmodel made sure his voice carried his non-negotiable intent.

"That's already done." Adapa waved an expressive hand. "We did that when you first hired the smuggler. Can't have you galloping around the galaxy where any mercenary would stop or kill you because you were with him."

"What about the Vargrux he stole it from?"

"They've been monetarily compensated." Adapa shook his head. "I still have a hard time understanding this business about money. Or what the Federation Consortium calls the credits they use." He grinned. "Hard to believe it all started with the gold the Akurns needed for the shield to protect their rogue planet."

Asmodel eyed Adapa. Why was he wasting time making small talk? The personal power he expanded using his psionic abilities over this vast distance had to be draining him at a rapid rate. He'd never seen his brother so unsure before. "What's the real reason you're here?"

Adapa grimaced. "I don't know why I try to hide anything from any of you." With his head down, he paced in the small space. "It's Arakiba. We haven't heard from him since he left FiPan."

"What about his JR unit? Surely he's been in communication."

Adapa shook his head with an impatient snort. "Unlike your JR unit, his has been silent too."

Asmodel considered what Adapa was saying. There had to be something... "Oh, wait! Wasn't he using the chancellor's spaceship run by a sentient AI?" He couldn't remember the ship's designation. Not that it mattered.

Adapa scratched his jaw. "See, that's the other part of the puzzle that bothers me. If something happened to that ship, she wouldn't hesitate to send out a distress signal even if her systems were down." He shrugged. "And I doubt anyone could have snuck aboard her and stopped her from communicating with Chancellor D'zia."

"I assume you've tried to mentally touch him?"

"Of course I have!" Adapa growled. "I'm not an idiot."

Asmodel's blood ran cold. They'd always been able to connect with each other. Unless... He looked in horror at Adapa. "You don't think he's dead, do you?"

Adapa crossed his arms, his face losing most of the tension. "No, that's the only thing I am sure of. Why don't you try to connect with him and see what you find?"

Asmodel didn't need any encouragement. He closed his eyes and connected with the shared mental path reserved for him and his brothers. In the blackness, he saw four expanding lanes, each leading to a different brother. Sky blue for the serene Azazel, violet for the introspective Abalim, green for the calm balance Adapa had. Last, there was a brilliant yellow ribbon for the vibrant energy of Arakiba. Asmodel breathed in a sigh of relief. While the yellow ribbon was still there, it was now tinged with slices of red, turning the yellow to a soft orange.

"He's still alive." Asmodel confirmed. He stared at Adapa. "But something has happened to him. I sense he's changing into something different. What do you think that means?"

Adapa's face turned gray. "I'm not sure. But I have a feeling we've got to find him before it's too late."

Discover Arakiba's fate in Alien Legacy Brotherhood Book 3

A Small Ask...

Now that you've finished reading *Asmodel*, it'd mean the world to me if you left an honest review wherever you bought it. This type of feedback is an authors lifeblood and helps others find their work.

The adventures can't continue without you!

Books in Reading Order

An Alien Exchange Universe:
An Alien Exchange[1]
D'zia's Dilemma[2]
Ki's Redemption[3]
Chloe's Turn[4]

Ancient Alien Descendants
Alien Legacy: The Empath[5]
Alien Legacy: The Shapeshifter[6]
Alien Legacy: The Psychic[7]
Alien Legacy: The Vampire [8]
Alien Legacy: The Mage [9]

1.   https://books2read.com/Exchange

2.   https://books2read.com/u/ba0PZa

3.   https://books2read.com/Kis-Redemption

4.   https://books2read.com/chloes-turn

5.   https://books2read.com/Empath

6.   https://books2read.com/the-shapeshifter

7.   https://books2read.com/The-Psychic

8.   https://books2read.com/u/bQAjAE

<u>Novellas</u>
<u>Qhasheik's Pod</u>[10]
<u>Claude & Amata</u>[11]
<u>Lok's Love</u> [12]
<u>_Alien Legacy Brotherhood_</u>
<u>Abalim</u>[13]
Asmodel

About The Author

Keri Kruspe, award-winning *"Author of Otherworldly Romantic Adventures"* loves nothing better than writing about romances that feature "feisty heroines who aren't afraid to take a chance on life... or love". Her writing career started when she became determined to indulge in something different in the SciFi romance genre, turning "the alien kidnapping trope upside down" (Vine Voice) in her ***ALIEN EXCHANGE*** trilogy.

After the ***ALIEN EXCHANGE*** universe was born, she created another SciFi Romance series, ***ANCIENT ALIEN DESCENDANTS***, then carried on the adventures in the *ALIEN LEGACY BROTHERHOOD* that continues to mix sensual, romantic themes to otherworldly adventures.

A native Nevadan, Keri is a lifelong avid reader who lives in northwestern Michigan with her hubby and ruling member of the family, a Jack Russell Terrier (aka the *Terrorist*) named Hestia. When not immersed in her made-up worlds, she enjoys discovering the fascinating landscape of her home and pairing red wine with healthy ways to cook. Most of all, she loves finding her next favorite author.

If you want to know when Keri's next book will come out, please visit her at her website[1] where you can sign up for her mailing list. You'll get a ***FREE*** copy of the novella, *The Day Behind Tomorrow* that is a prologue to the **ANCIENT ALIEN DESCENDANT SERIES**. Not to mention being kept updated on the life of a dedicated, obsessed author.

Social Media Links:

Facebook[2]

Pinterest[3]

Instagram[4]

---

1.   https://www.kerikruspe.com/

2.   https://www.facebook.com/klkruspe15

3.   https://www.pinterest.com/kerikruspe/

4.   https://www.instagram.com/kerikruspe/?hl=en

Did you love *Asmodel*? Then you should read *Abalim*[5] by Keri Kruspe!

[6]

With enemies closing in, can their newfound love survive the life-threatening trial ahead?

In a future where Earth narrowly escaped alien domination, Abalim, a human-alien hybrid from our ancient past, wields extraordinary psychic abilities. Haunted by a world he barely recognizes; he plunges into a perilous quest across the cosmos. His mission? To rescue a human woman named Lisa, a spirited science fiction romance author, was snatched by ruthless space pirates from an interstellar

5. https://books2read.com/u/mVnW06

6. https://books2read.com/u/mVnW06

exchange program and sold to an advanced species called the Xeltrians. In the depths of space, as Abalim nears her location, he's seduced by vivid, psychic dreams of Lisa, igniting an uncontrollable passion between them.

Lisa, awakening in an alien world, confronts a harrowing reality far from the romanticized extraterrestrial cultures she once wrote about. Her fate hinges on how she survives the Quandary of Existence, a high-stakes trial the Xeltrians forced her and Abalim to face together. The fate of the galaxy rests on the life and death choices they make.

Now, with their journey fraught with danger, a new, sinister force emerges. Beings from another dimension are hell-bent on capturing Lisa for their dark experiments. Abalim and Lisa find themselves thrust into a desperate fight against time as their formidable foes grow stronger by the minute. Even in this desperate chance of survival, they discover an escalating need for each other. As adversaries advance to tear them apart, their burgeoning bond becomes their greatest strength.

This epic science fiction romance weaves a tapestry of vivid worlds, heart-stopping action, and a love that defies the vastness of space. Join Abalim and Lisa as they navigate a universe brimming with peril and desire. Will their love triumph against cosmic odds, or will it crumble before it begins? Embark on this enthralling odyssey of love, resilience, and the human spirit's indomitable will to exist against all odds.

Read more at https://www.kerikruspe.com/.